keeping
minds.

a seductively sexy story about the
human brain.

by Vinal Lang

As you read this book, keep in mind that some things may not make sense at first. Please just keep reading, and they will all fall into place. The story is based on fictional locations, events and characters.

This book contains mature, adult content.
Please read with the expectation of unedited human behavior.

v.2
Copyright © 2022 Vinal Lang

ISBN-13: 9781658800624
ISBN-10: 1658800624

the chapters.

Vinal Lang

****

"A mountain is composed of tiny grains of earth. The ocean is made up of tiny drops of water. Even so, life is but an endless series of little details, actions, speeches, and thoughts. And the consequences, whether good or bad, of even the least of them are far-reaching."

- Sivananda

****

Vinal Lang

Chapter 1 – Anna.

"Anna, don't go in there," her father said softly. Anna looked through the crack between the door and the frame. Her small face almost fit all the way through it and into the bedroom.

She could see her mother, still sleeping in bed, and hoped that she felt better.

"I want to give her something," Anna said.

"Go ahead then," her father replied with a nod.

Anna quietly walked into the room. Her footsteps were soft and almost inaudible once she reached the area rug on which the bed sat.

The bedroom was softly lit, with just a little sunlight coming through the small cracks in the blinds. Anna could see little specks of dust as they floated through the beams of yellow light. They lightly swirled around her as she disturbed them with her gentle passing.

The air felt sleepy and old with a heaviness that made Anna feel tired. She took a deep breath and then exhaled slowly.

Even with the air somewhat stale, it still held the hint of a slightly familiar fragrance. The smell was almost like the spring blossoms on the fruit trees in the yard, but more subtle and dull. It was odd that she smelled them at this time of year, she thought. The trees outside had already lost half of their red-and-yellow leaves, so there were definitely no flowers.

Still, the crisp feel of autumn outside seemed to make the room feel more golden.

"Hello," her mother whispered.

"Hi, Mommy," Anna whispered back.

She handed her mother a white piece of paper with a colorful picture drawn on it.

"I made this for you," Anna said with a smile that seemed to make the room glow even more.

The picture, drawn with crayons, was of a Halloween costume. Anna wanted to be a horse, so the Van Gogh-esque picture was of an elaborate pink horse costume. She had carefully included all the details she needed, like a saddle and reins. She must have drawn it earlier in the day, but she didn't really remember.

It was Saturday morning, and not much was going on. She just wanted to see her mom, and that was all she could think about.

Her mother smiled at her, her face glowing a soft, radiant orange. Anna just stood there and smiled back, absorbing every moment.

This was it.

This was one of the memories that Anna could feel. It was a memory that was made up of all the little details—all the tiny pieces that are normally forgotten. It was the kind of memory that could put someone back in that place and make them feel like they were right there reliving it again.

Anna's mother had been sick and in bed for a couple of days. The memory itself was not even that significant.

Her mother was not terminally ill. She did not die that day. There was no pivotal event that made this memory stand out.

The reason this memory stood out was because of the way Anna could still feel her mother's smile and see the love in her eyes…the way she could still smell the fruit blossoms and feel the crisp autumn air of that day. It was because of the way she could close her eyes and relive it again anytime she wanted.

Anna stared at the water and thought of her childhood, now twenty plus years behind her. She didn't have many of those kinds of memories. Most of her memories were stories that played like movies. She could watch them over and over again but could never actually feel them or truly relive them.

Her mother lived well beyond that vivid memory and didn't pass away until Anna was in her late twenties. This was when her mother eventually succumbed to cancer.

Anna sat thinking about her parents. She thought about all the times her family went camping and the times her mother took her into the city from their upper-class home in the suburbs. Anna had a good childhood.

Anna's father, John, had always lovingly been there for his wife. In the final years he accompanied her to every doctor's appointment and every treatment session during her long battle with cancer. Anna knew that he was never really the same after her mother died. Her father had lost half of who he was and never really seemed to move on after that. Throughout her entire life, Anna had watched her parents love each other more than anything else in the world. She almost felt as if her father had died the same day her mother had.

Anna had always been a person who tried to remember every little detail about everything she saw, touched, and felt. She made a point to try to never take anything for granted.

From her mother's bedside in the softly lit orange room, the youthful Anna looked back at the younger version of her father still standing in the doorway. He was gently silhouetted by the sunlight beaming behind him through the big picture window. The leaves on the trees outside were a brilliant combination of yellow, gold, and red.

Anna could still see her father standing there, smiling; it was as if she were six years old again.

Suddenly, the sound of the alarm on Anna's cell phone broke through her thoughts. It was time to go back to work. She brushed the crumbs—all that was left of her sandwich—off her long, brown skirt, as she stood up.

Sometimes, Anna walked to the city park behind her office when she brought her lunch from home. She loved spending time in the natural oasis tucked away in the city. When it was warm, she would listen to the birds, sit in the grass, and read books. When it got cold, she would bring a blanket and a cup of coffee, and then curl up on the bench and read.

Anna loved her job at the research lab. She worked with a team that conducted brain studies. She had always been interested in the human brain and science in general. Even as a young girl, she was more interested in science experiments than dolls.

Anna followed in her father's footsteps; he had been a pioneer and one of the top scientists in brain and mind research and general neurology.

She had always found talk about his work interesting and listened intently to his stories.

He was always working on some project that Anna found intriguing.

She used to lie on the couch, listening to her father talk for hours about the hippocampus, dopamine, and the argument of dualism versus materialism.

Anna now worked for the same company where her father had been a pioneering scientist for almost 30 years.

Unfortunately, her father had died in a car accident; the one-year anniversary had been last month.

Growing up, Anna had excelled in school. As a young adult, she had spent years getting multiple degrees in the field of neuroscience. The subject had come easy to her. For Anna, college had been fairly uneventful. Even though she had been able to graduate early and with honors, she had continued to take classes related to neurology and the human brain.

She was currently heading up a study to help reverse deteriorated motor skill symptoms of patients with Parkinson's disease. Over the years, doctors like her had found that movement-related symptoms, such as shaking, were related to the death of cells in the substantia nigra.

Anna's team was working to find a way to recover, regenerate, or replace those cells.

Her work was her life and her passion.

Anna herself was very plain and understated, wearing mostly neutral earth tones that matched the rest of her bookish appearance.

She always wore her glasses when she read, because she couldn't stand contact lenses. Anna never really did anything with her slightly wavy, brown hair, other than put it in a loose ponytail. Her long bangs sometimes fell into her eyes, brushing against her naturally long lashes.

Anna was in her mid-thirties now and lived in a modest apartment downtown with her cat, Ruff. She didn't really keep many acquaintances, and she kept even fewer friends. Her work kept her challenged, busy, and away from social settings, and that was how she liked it.

Anna had previously been engaged for a few years, but it had ended abruptly after they had finally agreed that they just weren't right for each other.

He was a successful scientist and an Ivy League graduate from the same school as her. Unfortunately, their lives continued to take them down different paths, causing them to grow apart. It was something that had been slowly happening since just after they had met.

Anna's parents loved her ex-fiancé because they didn't see the side of him that she did. He was always controlling and manipulative. Toward the end of their relationship, he became very shallow and materialistic. This was the change that pushed Anna over the edge.

After that breakup, she changed somewhat. She became very self-conscious and thought the idea of a true long-term relationship was hopeless. She fought the usual breakup-related depression and self-doubt monsters daily. These were feelings that an insecure, unconfident Anna had trouble shaking.

She walked through the grass and up the walkway, following the winding sidewalk between the two tall buildings to the entrance at the front of the office. She walked up to the big glass entrance door and opened it, feeling a sudden rush of cold air from inside. An air-conditioned chill that steals your breath for a split second.

"Hello Stan," Anna said with a smile and a wave, as she walked past the security officer.

Stan was an African American man in his early fifties. He stood stiffly in the lobby in a black SWAT-style uniform. He was in excellent physical shape and, if it weren't for tiny hints of gray hair coming in, he would have looked like he was in his early forties.

He had worked at the lab ever since Anna could remember. Over the years, he had become a good friend to her father and someone whom they considered part of their family. After her father died, Stan had always been there anytime Anna needed him. He was one of the nicest people she had ever met.

Stan, the security guard.

"Good afternoon, Doctor Smith," he replied with a nod.

Anna got to the elevator door, pressed the 'up' arrow,

and waited. She stared at the glowing green button with the black arrow. She was thinking about her father and how much he loved this place. Her mind wandered to an old memory.

Anna was about six years old. Her father pushed open the same large glass office door, that she had just walked through, and held it for her.

She walked past him, feeling a sudden rush of cold air from inside. An air conditioned chill that steals your breath for a split second.

Anna turned and waited for her father, holding her hand out. He let the door close and took Anna's small hand in his.

"This is Mr. Row," Anna's father said, as he led her over to a man she had never seen before.

The closer they got to Mr. Row, the taller and more intimidating he appeared to Anna.

"Hello, Mr. Row," little Anna said with a shy smile.

"Hello, it's a pleasure to meet you, my dear. You can call me Stan. I have heard so much about you—all good things, I promise!" he replied with a chuckle.

DING!

The chime of the arriving elevator echoed loudly through the marble-tiled lobby and snapped Anna out of her memory. Another rare memory that she could relive and actually feel—the day she met Stan, the security guard.

Anna got on the elevator, swiped her security key card, and then pushed the brushed-aluminum button that had a one and a zero punched out of it. The number ten lit up brilliantly, and the elevator started its ascent to the floor where Anna's office was.

The elevator chimed its arrival at the tenth floor and the doors opened. Anna walked up the hallway, almost to the end and swiped her key card on the security pad outside her office door.

There was a loud click from the lock and Anna opened the door. She walked into her office and took a seat in the large, black leather executive chair. Anna sat behind a dark mahogany desk with her laptop on it.

She didn't like being at her desk; she tried to spend as much time in the lab as possible. Today though, she had to finish writing up some reports.

'The patient has been exhibiting a difference in general mood since the last brain activity test. The results show better sleep patterns with less stressful events during REM sleep. This indicates he should be experiencing less frequent and less intense nightmares,' Dr. Smith typed.

The patient she was writing about had been in a coma for about a month. After coming out of the coma, he had lost all previous memories—complete amnesia.

Dr. Smith had been working with the patient for about two years, but nothing was really changing, and it was frustrating her. She was ready for some kind of progress...anything!

Anna wrote and did research for almost five hours, taking a quick break only to read the latest science and technology news. Time flew by. She finished her day and started organizing her desk. She put things away where they belonged and straightened the bookshelf, which hadn't been touched that day, yet somehow still seemed to need the attention.

It was starting to drizzle outside. Anna looked down at the people on the sidewalks below. She could see three kinds of people: the ones who were running because they were unprepared; the ones who were prepared with umbrellas and raincoats, seeming to go about their day as usual; and finally, the people who didn't care either way and were just walking exactly the way they always did, as if nothing was different.

Anna thought about how, in life, she felt like all three versions of those people at different times.

There were three different kinds of happiness. The first was the happiness to get out of the rain; the second, a content happiness because you were in the rain but knew you were protected; and the last was a genuine happiness to be alive—to have gotten caught in the rain and just decided to enjoy the moment.

Today, she wasn't prepared, and she didn't want to get

caught in a downpour, so she rushed through the rest of her end-of-day tasks.

Anna grabbed some folders from her desk and threw her laptop bag over her shoulder. She had already put her laptop in it before she had started needlessly straightening the bookshelf.

She walked down the hall to the elevator, swiped her key card, and pressed a button. The 'L' on the button glowed, and the elevator doors closed. Anna looked at the button with the three and the zero on it and smiled.

Her father's office had been on the thirtieth floor. Anna had gone up there almost every day until her father passed away.

When the doors opened again, Anna walked out into the main lobby.

"Have a good night, Stan," she said with a smile.

"You do the same, Doctor Smith," Stan replied with a nod.

"I'm going to try and beat this rain. Wish me luck," Anna said, waving to the security guard.

"Good luck! It looks like it's going to start storming really bad soon," Stan replied with a grin.

"I'm not going to melt," Anna said, looking back at him while she pushed the door open.

She walked out through the front glass doors and to the edge of the curb. Normally, Anna would walk behind the building and down through the city park, but not with the kind of storm that appeared to be brewing.

She raised her hand to hail one of the oncoming cabs. The closest cab went past, but the next one stopped right where she was standing.

"Fifth and Belmont please," Anna said, as she got into the cab and put her seatbelt on. The cab driver started on his way.

"This looks like it's going to be a really big storm," the driver said.

"Yeah, the weather has been crazy this year," Anna responded. She watched the rain bead on the windows and trail along as they drove.

The rest of the ride was silent, except for the sound of the windshield wipers and the normal city noises that became easy to tune out over time.

The cab approached the intersection that Anna had told him, and it slowed to a stop.

"Thank you. Have a great night," Anna said, as she handed the driver money for the fare.

"You too," the driver said with a nod.

She walked to her building, took the elevator up to her

floor and walked to the front door of her city home—a modest but decent-sized two-bedroom condo. Anna had turned the second bedroom into an office, which had been quickly claimed by Ruff, the cat.

Once Anna got inside her condo, she immediately walked to her bedroom so she could get out of her work clothes. On the way home, they had gotten damp enough to become cold and uncomfortable.

Raindrops had collected on the lenses of her glasses, and they had started to fog from the temperature change inside her humble dwelling. Grabbing a tissue, Anna dried her glasses off and set them down on the dresser. She looked at her reflection in the mirror. She had always thought that she looked completely different without her glasses.

She pulled on the brown ribbon that was holding her usual loose ponytail together. Her hair fell down, leaving the ribbon in her hand. She ran her fingers through her hair, feeling the cool dampness from the rain.

Anna watched herself in the mirror as she started undressing.

She slowly finished unbuttoning her shirt while she looked at her body in the reflection. Anna let the shirt and the ribbon from her hair fall to the floor.

She was tall and thin but still curvy. She hardly thought of herself as sexy anymore, but right now seemed different.

Maybe it was the way the storm outside was causing the room to be oddly lit with a darkish blue glow.

The unusual light made Anna's body look bright and defined against the black bra she was wearing—all that was left on her exposed upper body.

Gazing in the large mirror was almost like looking at a black-and-white film negative. Her bedroom, which was normally colorful, bright, and comforting, was instead dark, drab, and almost menacing.

The reflection Anna saw in the mirror was of a sexy, enticing brunette, replacing the average, boring-yet-charming woman who was usually staring back at her.

Anna watched the woman in the mirror as she took her hands and slid her dress down her thighs. She stopped mid-thigh and turned her back toward the mirror, looking over her shoulder slightly. Her sheer black underwear hugged her body as she bent down, sliding her dress the rest of the way to the floor.

Anna reached back and unclasped her bra, sending an instant chill across her entire body. The bra fell to the floor in a tangle of rain-dampened black lace landing on top of the discarded dress.

"Who are you?" she quietly whispered to the mysterious woman.

CRAAAAAASH!

There was a sudden, bright white flash of lightning accompanying an extremely loud crash of thunder, which made the room seem to shake with a deep rumble. Anna jumped and let out a soft, subdued scream. She grabbed her chest in relief as she laughed at herself.

"I can be sexy," she said out loud, as if to reassure herself.

Anna felt something soft brush against her bare leg.

"Ruffles..." she said with a sigh. "You aren't afraid of storms, are you buddy? Huh?"

Ruff purred loudly and continued to rub against Anna's legs.

"Hold on," she said, as she grabbed a sleep shirt from her closet and pulled it over her head.

"Okay, let's go."

She walked out of the bedroom with Ruff following right behind her.

Anna walked to the kitchen and poured a glass of water. She grabbed a book, which she had just started reading, from the counter. She walked to the living room, set the glass of water and the book on the table, and collapsed on the couch.

Ruff was right there in a flash, climbing up on Anna and rolling over for a long stretch.

Puurrrrrrrrrrrrr!

Anna rubbed his belly while he seemed to almost fall asleep instantly.

"Let's see what's on," she said out loud, as she grabbed the TV remote.

Anna loved documentaries and educational shows. She would be content to watch almost anything having to do with science, nature, or history.

She was browsing through all the streaming movies available, looking for any new documentary she wanted to see. Nothing really jumped out at her, so she decided to read the book instead.

Anna looked to see if any baseball games were on. As odd as it sounded, sometimes she liked to put a baseball game on in the background while she read.

She wasn't a sports fan, but her dad used to listen to baseball games on the radio all the time when she was little. The sound of a baseball game in the background was always relaxing to her.

She didn't find any baseball games, so she decided to read in silence. She grabbed her book, lay back on the couch, stretched her legs to the other end, and started to read. She had only gotten a few chapters in when she started to get sleepy. She could hardly keep her eyes open.

"You got to get up, Ruff," Anna said, as she picked him

up and put him on the floor. He quickly went running off to the office—or his bedroom, depending on who you asked.

Anna got up and walked to the kitchen. She warmed up a bowl of soup, leftover from some she had made earlier in the week.

Anna loved to cook and bake. She had spent about as much time learning from her mother in the kitchen as she had learning from her father about science.

Anna walked back to the couch with her steaming hot soup and sat down.

Looking back through the TV guide, she found a show on PBS about stress and its effects on the human body and brain. She put the show on and quickly became immersed.

It was a multipart series, and Anna had fortunately caught the first part. She learned a few things she didn't know about how stress affects the brain. As the final show ended, Anna looked at the time.

"Wow, it's 10 o'clock already?! Time for bed," she said out loud to Ruff, who had returned.

She walked to the bathroom to start getting ready for sleep. Anna looked at herself in the mirror. The mysterious woman from earlier was gone; instead, she saw the plain, ordinary, shy woman she always did.

Anna pulled her nightshirt off over her head. She

looked again at her naked body; there was definitely nothing sexy about her reflection now.

Anna stood looking at herself, wishing she always felt sexy like that other woman; but that was not who she was, and she was okay with that.

She brushed her teeth, washed her face, and climbed into her queen-sized bed, which was covered with pillows.

At any one time, Anna used about four pillows while she slept, and she always had four or five more surrounding her, plus one cuddly cat named Ruff.

Exhausted, Anna curled up in her sea of pillows and fell fast asleep.

Chapter 2 – Bern.

Bern awoke suddenly, startled by the sound of a passing freight train. There weren't many that took the tracks by his house anymore, and the rare sound of one still surprised him sometimes.

He looked at the clock—10:22 a.m. He must have fallen asleep watching TV again. He stumbled off the couch to his feet and made his way to the bathroom.

Bern didn't have a schedule that day—or any other day for that matter. He had just planned to write a few pages and finish up a painting he had been working on.

Bern walked to the wooden blinds over by the couch and cracked them to let a little light in—just enough to make the entire warehouse studio glow softly.

The steel beams spanning the twenty five-foot-high ceiling had collected dust and cobwebs over the years, and they helped illuminate the sun's stray rays.

Bern peered outside; everything looked crisp and alive. He walked to the kitchen and started the one-cup coffee machine.

He leaned against the cool, bare brick wall, waiting for

the machine to do its magic.

Finally, after what seemed like forever to the groggy-headed artist, he heard the melodic tone that meant the morning had officially started.

He grabbed an orange prescription bottle from the counter—some new drugs that his doctor had given him to try. He put one of the pills in his mouth and walked to the sink. He turned the faucet on, leaned forward, and put his mouth under the running water. He swallowed the pill and the mouthful of water as he straightened himself back up and wiped his mouth.

Bern grabbed the steaming hot cup of coffee from under the dispenser. It smelled like roasted hazelnuts with a hint of vanilla. Bern put the cup to his lips and gently blew, sending a swirl of steam into the air.

He was thinking about the dream from which he had just awakened. Bern had already started to forget it, so he struggled to remember anything he could. He thought he was a little kid on some kind of vacation. He was fishing, he thought...maybe. Right when he woke up, it seemed like he remembered every detail and now...almost nothing.

Bern walked outside onto the back patio, where he had a wrought iron breakfast table and two chairs. It was a cool and breezy morning. He sat in one of the chairs, enjoying the golden sun, until he finished both his coffee and the newspaper he had started reading.

Of course, when Bern bought his beloved warehouse, he insisted a modest pool be built out back, now one of his favorite places to spend time.

He took his shirt off and dove into the sparkling water with just his boxers on. He swam underwater, surfaced at the shallow end, and then doubled back and swam a series of laps back and forth across the length of the pool.

Bern was in great physical shape, and his body showed it.

He had broad shoulders, strong arm muscles, and a well-defined chest. He didn't appear overly muscular and still kept an overall slender, lazy appearance. He had a sleeve of mostly tasteful tattoos covering one of his arms and part of his right leg.

The water dripped off his inked skin as he climbed out of the pool and wrapped a dry towel around him.

Bern headed inside to the bathroom to take a shower and get ready for the day. He looked in the mirror as he ran his hand down his face to his chin, feeling his stubble.

Bern always had stubble, if not a short but full beard. He actually couldn't even remember the last time he was clean-shaven. To him, his face looked too square and defined without facial hair.

Bern's dark hair made his blue eyes seem more

brilliant. He ran his fingers through his hair and watched it fall, examining the length. It was almost time to get it cut, he thought.

After his shower, he threw on his favorite jeans, a soft, heather green tee shirt, and some old Converse.

Bern had a look that made women lustful and men envious. He was very modest but confident. He didn't make an effort to impress people; he let his personality and art do that for him. He didn't really care what anyone thought of him; he was just himself...and that made him sexy.

Bern decided to take a trip downtown for a few things he needed. He called a taxi because he didn't feel like driving. Since his place was an old warehouse building in a mostly industrial part of the city, there were rarely taxis around.

"Nickels!" Bern called as an adorable, long-haired, black and white, Australian shepherd came running from the bedroom.

Bern kneeled down and his loyal companion ran into his arms.

"Hey buddy! Let's go outside."

He took Nickels out front and walked with him as he waited for the taxi to arrive. He got out his phone to text a friend who worked in the area where he was headed.

'Lunch today? I'll be over there getting a few things done.'

He sent the message and put his phone in his pocket.

He walked Nickels back to the front door, opening it just long enough to let him in and hit the 'arm' button on the alarm panel. Bern made sure the doorknob was locked as he pulled the door shut.

There were three steps leading up to the front door of the old warehouse. Bern turned and sat down on the middle step.

It was a beautiful morning. He watched the birds on the power line as they hopped around and chirped at each other.

Bern got a pack of cigarettes out of his pocket and pulled the last one out of the box. He put it between his lips and lit it with the vintage Zippo lighter he always carried with him.

Bern closed his eyes and listened to the birds continue their chirping and whistling. He could still hear the city noise in the background, but the day seemed more peaceful than usual.

With his eyes closed, the bright sun made him see red as it tried to shine through his eyelids. Peeking out from behind clouds, one last time, until ultimately being blanketed for good. Bern brought the cigarette up to his lips again and breathed deeply, inhaling the white smoke.

The cigarette was about half gone when Bern heard the cab pull up. He opened his eyes and threw the cigarette into an old coffee can that was sitting next to the steps for just that reason.

There weren't many butts in the can because he didn't really smoke out front that often.

Bern got in the cab and greeted the driver.

"Can you take me to the Metro building?"

"Sure thing!" the driver said, as he pulled away from the warehouse.

Bern felt his phone vibrate. He got it out to read the response from his friend.

'I'm really busy today, so I can't do lunch. Maybe later this week?'

-'Sure, just let me know.'

The cab arrived at his destination about fifteen minutes later. Bern paid the driver and got out of the cab.

"Where to first?" Bern asked himself out loud.

He needed to go to the art store to get more paint and some canvas that he could stretch onto frames himself. He decided to make that his last stop so he wouldn't have to carry all the supplies around. After a minute of thinking, he decided to go to the bookstore first.

Bern headed up the street amongst the crowd of people. It was busier than usual because it was lunchtime. Everyone was in a hurry on their lunch breaks; to and from their jobs they went.

He got to the bookstore and started browsing. He wasn't there for anything specific. Bern picked up two interesting-sounding titles and read the back cover of each. He put one back and kept one titled *Sustainable Artist*.

It sounded interesting, so Bern decided to buy it. He didn't read books as often as he wanted to, but he always liked to have a few new books around for when he did want to read.

Bern paid for the book and headed up the street.

He grabbed a new pack of overpriced cigarettes from one of the newspaper and magazine stands. He tapped the cigarettes against his palm, two times on each side, like he always did, and then he put them in his back pocket.

Bern ran into a downtown department store and grabbed a couple of pairs of dark denim jeans; his others had faded in the wash, and this was a legitimate errand in his mind.

The next stop was the art supply store. He got the paint he wanted but decided to wait to get the canvas once he realized that the size of the roll he needed would be an issue for the cab ride home. He would have to drive back down sometime later that week for it. He finished up at the art store pretty quickly and was on his way again.

After a few blocks, Bern walked up to the front door of a corner grocery store. He remembered that he needed to pick up a loaf of bread; he was completely out at home.

He walked in, grabbed a loaf of bread from the rack, and squeezed it to make sure it was soft and fresh.

"Bern!" a tall blonde woman exclaimed from across the store.

Bern looked across the small grocery store and saw a beautiful, sexy blonde woman walking toward him. She was wearing a tight black skirt and a white button-down dress shirt. She looked very professional but with an undeniably sexy twist.

Bern absolutely appreciated her subtle lean toward the naughty secretary look.

"Hey, Alice!" Bern said, with a surprised hint of recognition, as he watched the bombshell coming toward him. He set the loaf of bread back down on the rack.

The temptress's curvy body swayed as she walked in her tall, red high heels.

"I didn't get your number the other night," the woman said in a disappointed tone, as she reached the spot where Bern was standing.

"I'm sorry; I was in a hurry to get out of there. There was an emergency, and I couldn't find you on my way out," he said, referring to the party a few nights ago where they had met for the first time.

They had spent almost the entire night at that party, drinking and flirting in the pool. Bern was mesmerized that night by the light glistening off Alice's amazing, nearly naked body. She had been wearing an extra-revealing, risqué bikini that Bern admired, maybe a little too much. Alice had sexy tattoos covering parts of her nearly perfect body. She was exactly Bern's type. He imagined his mouth all over her beautifully inked skin.

Unfortunately, Bern had to leave the party suddenly that night while Alice had gone inside to use the bathroom. He couldn't find her before his rushed departure and had to leave without getting her number or even saying goodbye.

"Oh, is everything okay?" she asked, as she gave the handsome, alluring artist a big hug.

"Yeah, it was just that a good friend that had some car trouble and needed my help. Got stuck in a bad part of town, so I went right away." Bern had a hard time focusing on anything other than her amazing cleavage and hard nipples, which were now showing through the blouse.

He remembered how irresistible she had looked that night—almost naked in her small red bikini. Seductive.

"You look good!" she said with a wink. "Let me give you my number."

Alice had finished writing on a playing card using a marker from her purse. She handed the card to Bern as her other hand brushed sensually down his chest.

Bern looked at the playing card, the queen of hearts, with the flirtatious woman's handwriting now on it. A fantasy, just a phone call away.

"Queen of hearts. Very nice." he said.

"Sorry, it was all I could find in my purse to write on."

"No, It's great. I like it."

"You want to get dinner Thursday night?" Alice asked, followed almost immediately by, "We can go back to your place afterwards."

She slowly slid her hand down his tattooed arm.

"Sure! Thursday it is," Bern said with a barely noticeable nervous quiver. He was still holding the queen of hearts in his hand.

"Text me and we can make some plans," the woman said with a mischievously sexy grin.

She kissed Bern on his cheek, whispered "Bye," and then turned and slowly walked away.

Bern couldn't help but watch her incredibly perfect thighs moving under the tight black fabric. He followed her tanned legs all the way down to the red high heels and then back up again. Amazing. This woman nailed every fantasy Bern could ever remember having. He could think of many bad things that he wanted to do to this woman.

She seductively drifted back to where she had apparently been shopping for cereal when Bern had walked in.

Bern slid the playing card into the pocket of his jeans, and then walked outside and hailed a taxi.

"Over by the old train depot, on the north side. First and National," he said, ducking his head into the cab.

The car pulled away to join the stop-and-go traffic, which was usual for a downtown afternoon.

It was a dreary, overcast day. Bern watched the people walking on the sidewalk as the cab drove past them. Most people had their umbrellas out, even though it was only lightly drizzling off and on. Bern never owned an umbrella. He was one of the people who enjoyed getting caught in the rain.

Bern had planned on spending the rest of the day painting and writing. He got out his phone along with the queen of hearts: 'Alice – 555-3467.' The numbers were written in black ink over a hand-drawn outline of a heart—a beautiful, cursive work of art.

"Stick heart..." Bern said softly, as he laughed to himself.

Anytime Bern saw a hand-drawn heart like that one, he thought of his friend who called them 'stick hearts.' "You know, because they're drawn like stick people...stick people's hearts..." she would say if Bern had anyone ask her about it, which was every time he got the chance to bring it up. He thought the idea was hysterical and laughed every time she tried to explain 'stick hearts.'

Bern finished putting Alice's number in his phone and sent her a text message *'Pick you up at 8:30. Send me your address sometime ;)* '

The cab pulled up to a large brick warehouse building. Bern gave the cab driver the fare and then got out of the cab.

He was still lustfully daydreaming about Alice. He wanted her very badly... so badly that he forgot to buy the loaf of bread, leaving it behind at the store.

"Damn it!" Bern mumbled, as he realized this.

He walked up to the front door of the warehouse building and reached in his pocket for his keys.

"Fuck!" he mumbled to himself when he realized he didn't even have his keys. He went around to the side of the building and through the gate in the metal fence.

He unlatched the fire escape ladder, pulled it down to

the ground, and quickly started climbing. When he got to the top, he could see the taxi pulling away below.

He walked to the roof access door, where he could hear a chiming sound coming from the other side. He grabbed the key from on top of the ledge above the door and unlocked the doorknob.

He walked down the short set of stairs, which landed on an open loft suspended above the large, warehouse living space. He was greeted by Nickels.

"Hi, Nickels!" he said, gently patting his best friend on the head.

Bern walked to the keypad on the wall, which was the source of the chiming, and entered his pass code.

"System disarmed," the robotic female voice said.

The loft was small but had enough room for a couch and a small desk. It was softly lit from a white skylight above.

This is where Bern spent a lot of time alone, writing stories. He walked to the railing and looked down over the edge. Below, he saw the large painting he had been working on. It didn't really look like anything...yet.

He turned and walked over to the brown leather couch. As he sat down, the soft, overstuffed couch pulled him in.

Bern grabbed a notebook and pen from the small table

next to the couch. He was going to at least try to get some writing done.

Bern liked pens that bled easily. He liked the way the ink flowed and how the wet parts pooled and smudged. To him, it was the most relaxing feeling in the world—next to painting, of course.

"Bern," a soft voice called from the living area below.

"Bern...wake up!" the woman called again.

"I'm not asleep. I just got home," Bern said.

"Bern, the house is on fire," she said in an increasingly panicked voice.

"Bern, the house is on fire!" she screamed loudly.

Bern immediately took the focus off his writing. Looking up, he saw nothing but a veil of thick, white smoke. He could barely see; the smoke stung his eyes. The panicked man grabbed a glass of water from the side table and splashed it on his face. He rubbed his eyes in a failed attempt to end the irritation.

Bern started toward the stairs that went down to the living area below. He leaned forward to stay as low as possible.

Through the thick smoke, he could see flames coming through the far wall.

Bern missed the first step, his foot only finding air

where he expected the step to be. He started to tumble violently down the long flight of stairs.

Everything around him slowed to a crawl; the flames even seemed to burn more slowly. Every time Bern saw the flickering orange-and-blue flames upside down, he knew that he was still falling. He hit the wall at the bottom of the stairs with a brutal thud. The dazed man could barely open his eyes, and he felt confused.

Bern could feel the water that he had splashed on his face starting to heat up. He was so sleepy, but he knew he had to try to get up or this would be the end. He wiped what was left of the water off his face and opened his eyes.

Bern gasped loudly as he woke up wiping his wet face. Nickels was standing right above him, wagging his tail. He nudged his favorite toy and licked Bern's face one more time.

"Holy shit!" Bern said, as he turned his head and looked up the stairs. The sleepwalking nightmare had abruptly come to a painful end almost as quickly as it had started.

He sat up, patted Nickels on his head, and then threw the dog's toy into the living room. Bern grabbed his ankle and rubbed it for a few minutes while he sat at the bottom of the stairs.

"Ouch. I'm going to feel that tomorrow," he mumbled.

Finally, he got up and limped to his bedroom, grabbing a joint that he had laid on the side table next to his bed.

Bern hobbled out the sliding glass door to the patio, where he sat in a chair and lit the joint.

He saw his ankle already starting to bruise and swell— definitely a sprain. He deeply inhaled the thick, white smoke. It looked eerily like the smoke that had engulfed him in his dream. He closed his eyes and relaxed. The pain disappeared, and Bern started to fall asleep.

He woke up only a few minutes later, remembering that he hadn't yet brought inside the stuff that he had bought. It was all still sitting in the back, behind the building, under the fire escape ladder.

Bern brought all the shopping bags in, limping along the way. He then poured himself a Scotch and relit the extinguished joint.

He opened his new paints and quickly started adding the vibrant colors to the large canvas—his creation. The paints smeared, splattered, mixed, and blended. Intoxicating.

Bern spent the rest of the evening drinking, smoking, and painting. He played his favorite albums along the way, through the night and early into the morning.

Bern was in heaven.

He loved his job.

Chapter 3 – The Doctors.

Along with heading up the Parkinson's research project, Anna also had a few volunteer patients assigned to her. These were all special cases. Each one of them had some kind of trauma that resulted in long-term changes in their brains and the way their minds worked. All the patients had volunteered for research and testing with the hope of recovering their lost memories. Anna hoped that working with them would at least help advance the science of neurology.

Anna would bring the patients in a couple of times per month to run tests and scans, and then she would do research on the results. Her father's name and how he impacted the brain science community made Anna feel like she had to live up to his achievements. She knew that, with his passing, she had big shoes to fill.

One of her patients was a woman who was around the same age as Anna. She and her fiancé had been in a severe car accident that left him unharmed and her in a coma for over six months. When she awoke from the coma, she had no memory. Her former lover was now a stranger who oddly existed only in her pictures and videos. Hers was a case of severe retrograde amnesia; the woman had no loss of self-identity, as in most amnesia cases.

The second patient was a boy aged around ten who had been hit by a falling tree limb during a storm. He suffered head trauma and now had savant traits. He had actually retained his previous memories but had a hard time creating new ones unless they were related to music. Despite having had little musical instruction before the accident, he could now hear a classical piece and reproduce it on numerous instruments. His parents had volunteered him with hopes of a partial recovery and a chance at a normal life.

Her final patient was the one scheduled to arrive in just a few minutes. A couple of years ago, he had been in an accident that had caused a lack of oxygen to his brain. The damage caused long-term amnesia-like symptoms, but he had a few abnormalities that were inconsistent with a traditional diagnosis of amnesia. The man could only remember small pieces of memories older than a few years.

"Good morning," Anna said, as the patient walked into her office.

"Good morning, Doctor," he said with a smile, taking a seat in the large chair opposite her desk.

The nameplate on her desk read 'Dr. Smith.' Her desk was very neat and organized; everything was in its place.

Behind her was a floor-to-ceiling bookshelf full of

hundreds of books all related to neurology and the human brain. Anna had read them all—some of them twice.

Her degrees hung on the wall to her left, and on the right was a large picture window overlooking a bustling downtown morning.

"What happened? You're limping," Dr. Smith asked.

"I sprained my ankle. I have it wrapped now; it'll be fine," Bern replied.

"How have you been sleeping?" Dr. Smith inquired, as she focused on Bern's facial expressions.

"It's been better with the new medication" Bern said, staring out the window at the city below.

"How much better?" she asked, as she typed notes on her computer.

"I am having fewer nightmares, or at least ones that I can remember," Bern responded while rubbing his eyes as if he had a headache.

"Tell me about some of the nightmares," Dr. Smith said softly.

"They aren't as bad as they used to be, but more...I don't know...confusing maybe?!" Bern continued to stare out the window.

"I am having dreams about myself as a little kid. I am

starting to think they are pieces of the memories that I'm missing. I don't really recall much detail to tell you about." Bern didn't want to say anything about the sleepwalking, house fire nightmare; the real reason he was limping.

"How do you feel overall? Are you noticing any side effects?" Dr. Smith asked, as she skimmed over the list of side effects sent by the drug manufacturer.

"I think I'm having more migraines, but that could just be my head fucking with me," Bern said, as he laughed a little.

"When was the last time you smoked marijuana?" Dr. Smith asked, looking up at him.

"Yesterday." He smirked.

"Can you please try not smoking marijuana, at least for the next couple of weeks? It will give us a chance to see if the new drug is really making a difference by itself. Let's keep you on this new drug for another month, and then we will see how you're doing. I also want you to get another brain scan."

"Okay; you're the doctor," Bern said with a nod.

"Can you do the scan now if I have a technician available?" the doctor asked.

"Of course I can."

"You know it will only take about fifteen minutes." She

handed him the paperwork for the scan.

"Let's plan on a follow-up on the third of next month. I'm pretty sure the scan will be fine, but I will let you know the results when I get them," Dr. Smith said, looking at the calendar on her phone.

"I've got a question for you," Bern said inquisitively. "Why can people who lose their memories still remember things like language, writing, and math? Why do I remember how to drive a car, and why can I name every color? I didn't have to relearn them because I didn't forget those things. I can remember a spoon is a spoon and a fork is a fork, but I can't even remember my own mother's or father's name. Why is that?"

"Well, procedural memory is what those types of memories that you didn't forget are called. Procedural memory represents memory for objects or tasks. That type of memory depends on cortical processors, and they aren't usually damaged in amnesia scenarios," the doctor explained.

"Well, that makes sense in a very boring, textbook kind of way," Bern said with a grin.

"In normal memory-loss cases, people rarely forget how to do things or what objects are called and how to use them. Your condition is similar to retrograde amnesia, which is caused by an issue with the hippocampus. Procedural memory doesn't use the hippocampus," the doctor further explained very factually. This was all basic information that she had learned many years ago.

"Brains are crazy! So complex it's amazing!" Bern said, picking up a spongy model of one from the doctor's desk. He inspected the different colors and sections of the normally dull-colored gray matter.

"I agree," Dr. Smith said with a smile, as she went back to adding items to her calendar.

"Alright, well I'm out of here, if that's it," Bern said, as he stood up.

"Yes, we're done. What are you doing later tonight?" Anna asked, without looking up from her phone.

"I'm just going to be painting or watching some random documentary. You should stop by," Bern offered.

"Maybe I will. You know I never have any plans...and sorry about lunch yesterday; I just had too much work to get done." Anna apologized with a smile, as she looked up at Bern.

"Oh it's no big deal; I was just in the area. Text me sometime," Bern said, as he gently tossed the spongy brain back to Anna, and then turned and walked out of her office.

Dr. Smith set the brain back down on her desk, making sure it went back exactly where it should go. She finished up the rest of her notes and started to review the next report on her list. She still had a full day of work ahead of her.

Bern headed down the hall to the technician's room on the same floor. He walked into the small waiting room and sat down since there was no one at the desk. He picked up an old magazine and started flipping through the pages.

After a few minutes of reading old news, the technician walked in. She was a young, attractive blonde woman, wearing a white coat.

"Hey, Bern. How've you been?" she asked.

"Hi, I'm good. Doctor Smith sent me down. She wants me to have another brain scan today," he said, as he handed her the paperwork.

"Okay, let me get everything ready. It will just be a few minutes," the beautiful technician said.

Bern grabbed another one of the old magazines and patiently flipped through the dated pages.

"Alright, we're ready," the tech finally said. Bern got up and walked into the next room, which contained a large machine.

Bern was used to the scans, so he knew what to do.

He climbed up on the table-like bed and lay down.

He stared up at the ceiling as the technician leaned

over him, placing a couple of electrodes on his chest and head before strapping him down so he didn't move.

Her touch gave Bern chills all over his body. This technician was his favorite. She was very sexy and was always flirtatious, even though she was married.

Bern loved the way she smelled today. As she leaned over him and her shirt fell away from her chest, he could see all the way down to her smooth stomach. He could see her pink nipples through the lace of her black bra. The view was amazing.

The tempting woman slowly climbed on top of Bern, who was still strapped to the table, completely restrained. The seductive woman slowly unbuttoned and then unzipped his jeans.

"Shhhh..." she said quietly, as she gently put her soft index finger on his lips.

She pulled her shirt over her head, exposing her plump breasts, still sitting in the sexy black lace bra, which Bern had already caught a secret glimpse of.

He was already aroused from her touch, and the weight of her body on top of his turned him on even more.

She leaned down slowly and whispered in his ear, "Are you ready for this?" as she kissed along the side of his neck.

Before Bern could answer, a loud beep from the machine interrupted, ending his sensual daydream.

The technician, now on the other side of the room, finished checking some machines and exited the room, shutting the door behind her.

"Are you ready for this? She asked again.

The main machine had a big arm with what looked like a series of cameras at the end of it.

Bern closed his eyes and listened while the arm circled his head about twenty-five times. It started at his neck and progressively moved up to the top of his head. It then reset itself and started a series of scans up and down his head, while slowly going around it. It beeped a few times and then was finished.

"Alright, you're all done," the technician said, as she walked back into the room to reset the machine and free Bern from the straps that restrained him.

Bern got up from the table and walked out after thanking the gorgeous technician. He walked down the hall and into the elevator. He scanned his guest security card and pressed the 'L' button.

The 'L' glowed and the elevator doors closed. When they opened again, Bern walked across the lobby to the security desk, where Stan, the security guard, was standing.

"Have a good afternoon, Stan," Bern said, as he

handed him the guest security card.

"You too, sir," the security guard replied with a nod.

Bern walked out onto the busy street and hailed a cab to take him home. He had been up until early in the morning painting, and he planned to go back to sleep.

The cab pulled up in front of the warehouse building that Bern called home. Bern thanked the driver and gave him his fare plus ten dollars extra.

Thankfully, today he had remembered his keys. Bern opened the front door, and Nickels was right there to greet him. He had his favorite toy—a squeaky rubber hamburger.

"Hey, buddy!" Bern said, patting Nickels on the head.

He walked inside and entered his pass code in the alarm panel. "System disarmed," the voice said.

Bern headed to his bedroom and flopped over on the soft down duvet on his bed. He was exhausted. It took only a few minutes for him to fall asleep.

Bern opened his eyes to find himself in a hospital room. He looked around, trying to get his blurry vision to focus. He could hear a series of beeps and talking from outside in the hallway. Looking around, he saw an ordinary hospital room, just like ones he had been in many times before. The door on the other side of the room opened, and a doctor walked in.

"Hello, Bern. Do you remember what happened to you?" the doctor asked.

Bern was confused. He shook his head and asked, "What happened?"

"You were in an accident. Do you know what year it is?" the doctor asked, looking at Bern's chart.

"Ummmmmm...1995?" Bern said in an unsure tone, scrunching his face.

"Tell me the last thing you remember." The doctor's stare seemed to pierce right through Bern.

"I can't remember anything," Bern said, shaking his head with a puzzled expression.

"What about your parents...what can you tell me about them?" the doctor pressed on with more simple questions.

"I don't know."

"What about where you grew up? Where are you from?" the doctor continued his inquiry.

"I'm not sure." Bern drew nothing but blank memory after blank memory.

"How old are you?"

"I don't know!" Bern became more and more agitated by not knowing any of the answers to simple questions with which he should have had no problems answering

"You just get some more rest. We'll be doing some tests in the morning," the doctor said, closing his chart.

Bern went to scratch his nose and realized that he was strapped down to the hospital bed. His arms and legs were bound to the rails, and his head has strapped down across the top.

Bern struggled to break free, but he remained confused and trapped.

"What the fuck!" he growled, as he tried to get a hand free.

Bern's body twitched and shook him awake. He saw that he was in his bedroom with Nickels by his side. There were no doctors...no hospital.

"Oh fuck that, Nickels! What a nightmare! That was a horrible feeling." Bern got up and went to the kitchen for a glass of ice water.

He then decided to smoke a joint and take a nap. So, that's what he did. He smoked.

Chapter 4 – David.

It had been a long day of work, and Anna was finishing up at the office. She took her focus off her responsibilities for a minute to check her phone.

"Want to do something tonight?" a message from Bern read.

"I would, but I'm having dinner with David," Anna replied and set her phone down on her desk as she stared out the window.

David had been her father's good friend since before Anna was even born. Her father, John, had been a mentor to him, and they had worked very closely together on many projects over the years.

After her father died, David was always there for Anna if she needed him. He had almost become a father figure to her.

Anna still made sure that she saw or talked to David a few times a week. David was retired now and spent a lot of time fishing and traveling.

He loved experiencing new things and now had

nothing to hold him back.

Anna heard her phone vibrate on her desk.

"How about tomorrow night?" the message from Bern read.

"Sure," she replied.

Anna finished up with her normal end-of-day routine after straightening the books on her wall. She headed out of her office and took the elevator down to the underground parking garage.

She had driven today since she was going to pick up David. The plan was to head to their favorite Thai restaurant—the same place where David and John used to eat lunch at least once a week.

Anna fought the downtown rush-hour traffic for the few miles that it took to get to David's house, where he lived alone in a very modest apartment right on the riverfront.

Anna parked in an available spot out front and headed into the boring-looking lobby. It was a very dreary building, and she always wondered why he still lived there, especially after retiring.

Anna got on the abused-looking elevator. Most of the numbers didn't light up anymore. She pressed a button and waited for the doors to close. David's apartment was on the third floor.

David opened his door just as Anna walked up to it, as if he had been waiting there for her, listening for a visitor's footsteps.

"Come on in. I'm almost ready," he said.

Anna walked in, leaving the drab, mauve-wallpapered hallway behind. She headed straight for the blinds on the far side of the room. His apartment always seemed gloomy and sad to her.

"I don't know how you do it. You know it would be good for you to let a little sunlight in every now and then," she said, as she opened the blinds.

The sun now illuminated the room, and the sudden change in brightness made Anna squint.

She walked over to a row of pictures on a bookshelf.

"This picture is new," she said, looking at a framed photograph of David and his wife, Judith.

His wife had died about ten years ago, and David had never remarried.

"Oh, yes..." David said, walking out of his bedroom with a soft brown sweater in his hand.

"I was going through some old boxes of stuff and found it. Wasn't she beautiful?"

"She always was," Anna said with a smile.

David's apartment hadn't changed much for as long as

Anna could remember. If you didn't know better, you would look around and think his wife was just out running some quick errands and would be back at any moment to walk through the front door and give David a big hug.

Anna had known Judith well. Her mom and Judith had been best friends, just as David and John had been.

Anna missed Judith as much as she missed her own mother.

"You brought a sweater, right? It's always cold in there," David said, gesturing in Anna's direction with the sweater in his hand. He pulled the sweater over his head, messing up his wispy gray hair.

"I have one in the car. I'll be fine," she said, as she continued looking over the items on the shelves.

Anna ran her hand along an antique box that she had always admired and loved to look at. It was a little bigger than a shoe box and, as far as she knew, had belonged to Judith.

The box was metal with an intricate pattern engraved on all sides, and it had a small cast iron lock on the front. The face of the lock was very worn, but you could tell that it used to have a beautiful engraving similar to those on the box itself.

There were small words on it that could barely be read anymore. The words looked like they said 'Omnis cognitionis intra,' which Anna assumed had to do with the person who had made the old, obviously handcrafted box and lock. She always wondered what was in it—jewelry? Photographs? Old love letters perhaps?

"I know I have told you this before, but that box is yours when I'm gone. I'll even make sure you get the key," David said, as he watched Anna admiring it, just like the many other times that she had been there. Always adoring it.

"Thank you. It's beautiful," Anna said. She started to walk to the front door, realizing that David was waiting for her.

They took the stairs down to the street and got into Anna's car. The traffic had eased a little and they made it to the restaurant in a decent amount of time.

The two talked and reminisced, laughing during the entire journey to the restaurant. David had so many funny stories about himself and John. He was an amazing window into her father. Talking to David was a way to relive her father's stories, even in his absence.

The restaurant wasn't busy, so the two sat down right away and ordered. Anna always got the same thing, so she didn't need to look at a menu. David, who was always looking for something new, was torn between dishes.

The waitress, a new face at the frequented restaurant,

took their order. She started with Anna's and then turned to David, who in his indecisiveness, told her to surprise him. Everything on the menu was a marvelous culinary experience; David knew she couldn't make a wrong choice.

"Remember when you were little and you had that Polaroid camera? You used to take pictures of everything," David said with a smile.

"Yeah, I still have some of those pictures," Anna said.

Her distant gaze made it clear that she was viewing some of the pictures in her mind. She smiled.

"You must have cost your father a fortune in film!" David said with a laugh.

"Yeah, thank God everything is digital now."

Anna loved taking pictures, but unfortunately, she always filled what little bit of free time she had doing other things. If she could, change careers and be something creative, like a professional photographer, she would.

It was an idea that she sometimes entertained.

"Your father was a good man. I miss him a lot," David said, looking out the window at what seemed to be thousands of strangers walking by.

"I know. I miss him too...every day." Anna sighed.

"How's work going?" David changed the subject.

"It's good," Anna replied with an all-but-convincing smile.

"How about that one patient we talked about? How is that going? I know that you have been frustrated by the lack of progress with his case," David asked with concern.

Since Anna went to David for professional, scientific advice, he knew about Bern's case, although the actual identity of the patient remained anonymous.

"Yeah, that one really has me stuck. He still has nightmares and no memory recall. It seems like I've tried everything. I've had the poor guy on every new drug that looks promising and I'm still making little progress, at best. It's definitely one of the most challenging cases I've ever had," Anna said with an exhausted look on her face.

"Well, don't give up. You will eventually find something, and that's when all your hard work will pay off. You are very good at what you do, just like your father was," David said with a smile.

"Thanks for the vote of confidence. I really need it lately, especially with that case," Anna said.

"I remember when your father had a patient that he worked with for almost five years with little progress. Then, one day, there was a huge breakthrough. The patient started remembering again. It was amazing! To this day, the other doctors still don't know how or why, but I give the credit to your father for his sheer persistence. Sometimes, that's what it takes and is the only thing that can be done," David said, looking her in the eyes while patting her hand. "And that one single event led to many discoveries. Even though they don't know what triggered the return of his memory, they were still able to learn from it and make huge advances. You never know what little things are going to come along and change the world around you. If your father had given up after three or four years, we wouldn't know some things about the brain and memory that we do today. All I can say is, don't ever give up on that patient."

David was an excellent neurologist and a brilliant scientist. He was the person to whom Anna turned since her father's death. Anytime she had a question or idea, she would go to David for his input. He was a huge inspiration and was always very encouraging.

"You remind me so much of your father. He would be proud," David added with a smile.

"Thanks so much. So, how are *you* doing?" Anna asked.

"I've been good. I'm going sailing next week," David said with excitement. You could tell that he was picturing the open ocean waves splashing the boat. He was already smelling the breezy ocean air, while still sitting in a Thai restaurant in the city.

"Wow! That's exciting! You're going to have a great time!" Anna exclaimed. "Have you ever been before?"

"Nope, never. It's going to be an adventure," David said excitedly.

"Where are you sailing to?" she asked inquisitively.

Anna had traveled to many parts of the world and had been on large cruises, but she had never been sailing. To her, the thought of sailing seemed exotic and alluring.

"I have to fly to St. Thomas, and then will be sailing down to St. Barts and then some other islands in that area."

"That sounds incredible! I would love to go sailing sometime. If you like it, maybe we can go on a short sailing trip together in the near future," Anna said, as she imagined the sun and the open ocean—the feeling of true freedom. Exhilarating.

"Let's do it. We'll plan it when I get back," David said without hesitation.

"Okay! It's a date."

"Anna, if there's one thing I have learned over the years, it's that life isn't going to wait for you to be ready for it. I should have gone sailing with Judith. Why did I wait so long? I can't go back and change it, but I wish I had done more with her when I had the chance."

"I know you miss her. I do too," Anna said, as she put her hand on top of David's.

"Promise me that you'll start living your life, my dear," he said in a very serious tone. His eyes were a brilliant blue with a hint of a sparkle.

"I promise," Anna said, getting up from her seat to hug David.

They finished dinner and had a couple drinks each, enjoying a wonderful night of reminiscing. Once again, Anna relived her father's life through David.

"Well, I'm ready to get out of here. You know there's a baseball game tonight. You want to go? The field is right there." David pointed out the window.

Normally, this would have been a quick decision for Anna. She had to work the next day; she didn't want to get home too late.

Besides, she wasn't really a sports fan, and wasn't too interested in seeing a game. She did love the nostalgia of baseball, however, mostly because of her father and his love of the game. She could think of at least a dozen reasons to go home.

But Anna quickly thought about what David had said earlier, and, for tonight, she decided that she wasn't going to care. For David, she was willing to do almost anything.

"Let's go!" Anna said, to David's astonishment.

Anna could see the joy on David's face. Just the idea of having someone to go to a baseball game with made him seem to glow.

Anna and David walked to the field and watched the game. They cheered, laughed, and had an amazing time. It reminded her of going to baseball games with her father when she was younger.

After the game, Anna dropped David off at his drab apartment building.

"Good night. Thanks for a night of wonderful company. We'll plan that sailing trip when I get back," David said, as he got out of the car.

"Definitely! Good night, David. Love you."

Anna waved as she pulled away.

Chapter 5 – A New Outfit.

The next day was the same as usual for Anna. She went to work, did her job, and straightened the untouched books at the end of the day. Another uneventful, mundane day; the kind that seemed to be happening so often lately.

Tonight, though, she and Bern had planned to meet up after work—something to look forward to. Bern would be out in the city near Anna's house, so she said she would pick him up.

She pulled up to the tall unfamiliar building, the address Bern had given her, and put her car in park.

'I'm here,' she texted Bern.

A few minutes later, he walked out, talking to a tall, gorgeous, brown-haired woman. She was dressed in workout clothes, like she had just gotten out of yoga class.

Anna watched as they both laughed at something Bern said. The woman bit her bottom lip flirtatiously and touched Bern's chest as she laughed.

Anna couldn't hear their voices from inside the car, but she wished she could.

The woman kissed Bern on the cheek, gave him a hug and waved goodbye.

Bern pulled open the passenger-side car door and ducked inside.

"She's new," Anna said with a grin.

"It's nothing," Bern responded. "She bought one of my biggest paintings, and it was delivered today. She dropped fifty grand on it, so I figured I should show up and kiss her ass...you know...so she'll buy more. I didn't even do anything; I just met the guys with the truck here and watched them hang it." Bern rubbed his eyes and put on his Wayfarer sunglasses.

"What's the most you've ever sold a painting for, if you don't mind me asking?" Anna inquired.

"Remember that big gray-and-red one you liked about awhile back?" Bern asked.

"Oh that huge one? I loved that one!" Anna said, as she pictured the painting in her head; it was a large abstract painting that Bern had finished about a year ago. Anna had always commented about how much she liked it. The painting had a lot of grays and reds swirled together. Anna thought they looked like twisted clouds.

"Well, I sold that painting for one hundred and fifty

thousand dollars."

"Wow! I had no idea! That's incredible!" Anna exclaimed.

"It pays the bills," Bern said with a smile. "Thanks for picking me up, by the way. I could have just caught a cab to your place."

"It's fine; now we can go get something to eat. What do you feel like?" Anna asked, as she headed in the direction of some of the best restaurants in the city.

"I don't know. How about that Japanese place on Belmont?" Bern suggested.

"Sounds good!" Anna replied. "So, what's up with you?"

"Not much. I've still been having these crazy dreams over and over… different ones, but they repeat almost every night. They become more and more clear each time, and I can remember more about them every time I wake up."

"What are they about?"

"Well, it's different dreams that are repeating. One of them is the house fire one that I told you about before. In another one, there are doctors talking about my mind, asking me questions. I'm agreeing to let them do something, but I can never figure out what."

"Am I in it? Am I one of the doctors?" Anna asked.

"No, I never see you."

"Gasp! You're not cheating on me with other doctors, are you? How could you?!" Anna said, faking an emotional outburst followed by a laugh. They pulled up to the restaurant and parked. Bern fed the meter.

They sat down at a table and ordered a couple drinks and some food. The ambience of the restaurant was noisy. The background was filled with the clinking of glass, the clanging of silverware and the loud talking of patrons starting to fill up the bar for an after-work drink.

"How is your ankle?" Anna asked.

"It is pretty much better. It only hurt really bad that day."

"That's good." She smiled and looked back down at the menu, in silence, for a few more minutes.

"Hey," She looked at Bern as she set the menu down. "I want to ask you something...and you can say 'no' if you want. I won't be mad," Anna said cautiously.

"Uuummmm...O...kay..." Bern said, with a puzzled look on his face.

"Will you go with me to a cocktail party?" Anna stayed stone-faced and wide-eyed.

"Of course I will. Did you think I wouldn't?" Bern asked almost instantly.

"Oh my God! Thanks! I don't know…I was scared to ask you. I just didn't want it to be weird…like I was asking you out," Anna said with a relieved sigh.

"Look, you are my best friend..." Bern said.

"I'm your *only* friend..." Anna interrupted with a smile.

"Well, that's true, but you're still my favorite…and…I'm *your* only friend…so don't get cocky!" Bern said with a laugh.

"Thank you so much! It's this Thursday."

"This Thursday…like day after tomorrow Thursday?" Bern inquired with an unsure tone and a tilt of his head.

"Yeeessss," Anna replied with a wince. "I'm sorry; I know it's short notice."

"Wait, I just thought about this…you…" Bern pointed at Anna, "…you…are going to a cocktail party?" He cracked an unsure grin as he thought about the nonsocial Anna at a party. If it was anything like the ones he went to, she was going to be in over her head.

He continued, "Oh my God! What are you going to wear? No offense, but you dress like a schoolteacher that I had in the fourth grade; she used to beat the children." Bern laughed.

"Shush! I do not!" Anna replied defensively with a soft punch to Bern's arm.

"Well, okay you don't, but I have definitely never seen you in anything that is…ummmm…cocktail party worthy."

"So…can I ask another favor?"

"Of course! Let me guess…clothes?" Bern said.

"You know I don't have anything to wear to a cocktail party! You just said it yourself! I dress like an old, abusive librarian." Anna pouted her bottom lip.

"Not a librarian—a schoolteacher…but like, from the early 1930s." Bern kept laughing.

"Shut up, Bern! This is serious!"

"I know, I know… We'll go to my place after dinner, and you can look. I'm giving up getting laid by my fantasy woman for you again…so you owe me!" Bern said with a pouty grin. "I was supposed to meet up with her Thursday night."

"What?! Tell me more!" Anna said.

"More about how this isn't going to happen for me now?" Bern shot Anna a sarcastic glare that she'd seen a million times.

"No! About this fantasy woman! Who is she?" Anna asked enthusiastically.

"Just a woman I met at a party. You know, you should really come to one of my parties with me sometime. It would be good for you; maybe you'll meet someone," Bern said with a wink.

"I'm not going to one of your crazy parties. Now, tell me about her!"

"I will tell you...if you promise to go to one of my parties," Bern negotiated.

"Okay, fine! But I'm not dressing slutty!" Anna said with a laugh.

"Whatever... Anyway, I met her at a party. She didn't really seem to know anyone there, but we hit it off. We spent the whole night in this beautiful, enchanting pool, drinking and flirting. She has a near-perfect body, some beautiful tattoos and she was wearing the sexiest red bikini I had ever seen."

"Ha! Lust at first sight! Nice! Tell me more," Anna said with complete attention.

"We drank under a waterfall that spilled into a beautiful natural stone pool. We laughed all night in a romantic tropical oasis. She was one of the hottest women I've ever met. She has some very sexy tattoos on her side. I probably already said that. I should have gotten a picture of her. You should have seen her... Anyway, we were talking about going back to my place..."

"Well, did you?" Anna interrupted inquisitively.

"Shhhhh! Just wait for it; I'm getting to the best part..."

Bern said with sarcastic enthusiasm.

"Go on."

"So, I went to get a couple more drinks while she went to the bathroom. I'll spare you the boring details, but I grabbed my phone off the towel and saw something like ten missed calls and twenty frantic text messages from my friend, and it was an emergency, so I had to leave right away. I never got her number and never got to say goodbye or anything. I left in a flash; I even got dressed, into dry clothes, at a red light."

Bern smiled ear to ear, as he watched the dawn of Anna's realization.

Anna's face sank and she said, "Sorry... That's why you had a wet towel in your car when you picked me up? Ugh, I'm so sorry."

"Well, next time you have a flat tire in a bad part of the city, call a tow truck." Bern laughed and poked Anna's shoulder across the table. She frowned. "Whatever. You know I'm here for you no matter what. You can always call me anytime," he continued with a smile.

"Thank you," Anna said softly. "So, wait...if you never got her number, then how did Thursday get set up for me to ruin? Is it a different fantasy woman now? Are you getting them all mixed up?" Anna looked puzzled.

"No, it's the same woman. Such a coincidence. I just ran into her yesterday at the store. Third time's a charm for sex with my fantasy woman, right? I'll still have a fun night at a cocktail party with my fantasy BFF... right...huh...BFF?" Bern said with a goofy smile, as he nudged Anna.

"You're an idiot sometimes," she said, as she rolled her eyes.

"Ahhhhh, that's my girl. Let's get out of here," Bern said, signaling the waitress for their check.

As she drove home, Anna looked over at Bern and said, "I know I have asked this before, but how did you get that scar on your forehead?"

Bern ran his fingers down the bump on his forehead.

"Is it that noticeable?"

"Not really. I'm just curious."

"Ummmm, I don't remember," Bern said, puzzled. "You, of all people, should know not to ask me about things that happened in the past." He shook his head jokingly.

They pulled up to Bern's building, and Anna parked on the street out front. Bern unlocked the front door to his artistic warehouse dwelling.

"Hi, Nickels!" Anna said in a high-pitched voice. Bern turned the alarm system off while Anna dropped to her knees to greet the dog.

Bern walked to his guest bedroom with Anna, who was now up from the floor, following behind him and Nickels behind her.

"Well, have at it," Bern said, as he pointed inside a large walk-in closet he'd opened.

"I still think it's kind of weird that you have all this stuff," Anna said, as she walked in and started looking at the classy women's clothing.

"That's the good thing about having memory problems. I don't even remember what crazy woman they belong to. I don't have to deal with the memory of exes. Trust me, I have heard your breakup stories a million times. I'm glad I don't remember any exes! I just need to give all the clothes away. I'm pretty sure that no one is coming back for them," Bern said, looking at all the hanging dresses.

"Well, you know I've tried my best to take them off your hands. They just aren't me," Anna said. "I'll never wear any of this."

"I know they aren't but they are your only choices unless you go shopping."

"Ugh, I know."

Anna never kept clothes she didn't wear. She had already looked through all the clothes that Bern had and nothing was really her style, so she hadn't taken much. She was way more casual than any outfit in that closet.

Sometimes, she wished she felt sexy enough to wear some of the clothes. She grabbed a few dresses.

"I'm going to try these on."

"Okay, I'm going to take Nickels for a walk while you do that. Take your time!" Bern called out, as he walked out of the room, closing the door behind him.

Anna had picked a short black dress to try on first. She slid out of her jeans and pulled her shirt over her head. She put the black dress on and reached behind her, zipping it up. The dress was strapless, but Anna had left her bra on.

"I don't know," she mumbled to herself.

She didn't own anything strapless and didn't really like the way it looked, so she took the dress off and set it aside.

Next up was an even shorter black and white dress. It was made up of four alternating black and white sections. It reminded Anna of a giant chessboard. Anna held this one up to herself and looked in the mirror.

"Nope," she said softly, as she set it aside.

The next dress was longer than the previous two, ending just above the knees. It was black, tight, and had small, black triangular-shaped studs around the neckline.

"Uggggghhhhhh," Anna groaned, as she held it up to her. She liked the length, and at least it wasn't strapless, but the neckline plunged much lower than she would have liked.

She looked at her body in the mirror, dropping the dress away for a minute. She then went back to the closet, still holding the third dress. She started to look at all the women's shoes.

She figured that maybe the right shoes would make her like the dress a little more.

She finally found the pair that she...disliked the least. They were, very tall high heels that were white, pink, and black with triangular studs. A surprising choice for her.

She liked them—just not really for herself. The fact that they were the opposite of anything she normally wore and contrasted with her shy personality was one of the reasons she ended up picking them—again trying to follow David's advice.

Anna walked over to the mirror that was by the bed and set the shoes down. She looked at her body in the mirror one more time and then slipped the black dress over her head.

It was very snug, so she had to work it down her body a little, shifting her hips back and forth. She slid the shoes on and looked back at the mirror.

"Wow!" Anna whispered. "It's gorgeous."

She thought about her reflection in the mirror after the rainstorm, and how it had made her feel...desirable.

"I can do this," she said to herself, as she nodded.

The dress was tight and snug against her slim body. The shiny black studs brilliantly reflected the light in different directions. The snugness of the dress pushed her breasts up and together in a way that looked seductively restrictive.

It felt equally as good as it looked, as if a pair of hands was grabbing her breasts from behind. The sensual feeling sent chills throughout Anna's entire body.

The neckline of the dress swooped down and exposed her perfect cleavage. Her milky white skin was almost overexposed, looking like one of her old overdeveloped instant pictures. The cream color made it stand out vibrantly against the ebony dress. The brilliance of the dress drew more attention to her beautifully radiant skin.

For a second, Anna felt sexy—not quite like the reflection of the mysteriously sensual woman in the mirror during the storm; but she thought the dress made her look unusually alluring.

Anna wasn't dauntless like that other woman. She wasn't assertive like her. She wasn't sensual like her. She wasn't sexy like her. She wasn't that other woman she saw in the mirror.

Anna looked at her hair in the reflection. "What am I going to do with this?" she asked herself, staring at her ribboned ponytail.

She heard Bern come back in with Nickels.

"I'm almost done!" Anna yelled.

She took the dress and shoes off and got back into her normal clothes.

Anna put the rest of the dresses back and picked up a small, black studded clutch that complemented the selected dress perfectly.

She walked out of the guest bedroom and found Bern sitting on the couch in the living room, watching TV. Nickels was curled up on the floor by his feet.

"That was fast! I made popcorn," he said, pointing to a bowl on the coffee table. "Do you like what you picked?" he asked, looking at the shoes, purse, and dress in her hands.

"Yeah, I found something," she said nonchalantly. She tried to hide the grin brought on by the memory of the way the outfit made her body feel.

"What are you watching?"

"A documentary about Bonnie and Clyde. It's pretty good so far."

"You know I'm a sucker for a documentary that I haven't seen yet," Anna said, as she set her new outfit down, put her glasses back on, and took a seat on the couch next to Bern.

Bern turned the TV volume up a little as they sat and watched intently.

"On November 22, 1933, Bureau of Investigation records revealed that a trap was set by the Dallas, Texas sheriff and his deputies in an attempt to capture Bonnie and Clyde near Grand Prairie, Texas. The bold couple was able to escape the officer's hail of gunfire. Seeing that they were clearly outnumbered, they fled the area. They kept the pursuers at bay until they were able to hold up an attorney on the highway and take his car. They abandoned that car in Miami, Oklahoma. Bonnie and Clyde were again running free, and now their crimes were about to get drastically worse..."

"Can you imagine?! That's nuts!" Anna exclaimed. "I couldn't live like that...always on the run."

"I think I could. I mean, live on the road, minus all the murder and robbery...every day would be an adventure!" Bern said, sounding more serious than usual.

"You're crazy too!" Anna replied with a laugh.

They watched the rest of the documentary together, with Anna falling asleep at the very end.

"Nickels, you want to go outside, buddy? Come on," Bern said quietly, as he got up from the couch.

He walked to the kitchen and got a small wooden box down from the bottom shelf of one of the cabinets.

He set the box on the counter and opened it. Inside were three joints. He took one out and double-checked that he had his trusty Zippo lighter in his pocket, like he always did.

"Come on!" Bern said to Nickels, as he patted his hand on his thigh.

He walked Nickels out the front door and around the right side of the building. There was a patch of grass about the size of a couple of basketball courts. Nickels would always go there first and then walk in the opposite direction around the block.

Bern followed behind, lighting the joint that he brought with him. The smoke was thick and white.

The night was amazingly beautiful with a bright moon and a cool breeze.

Bern got his phone out and set his house alarm from an app on it. He knew Anna wouldn't wake up.

As if on a schedule, Nickels was done and ready to walk in the opposite direction around the block. Bern followed, still puffing trails of thick, white smoke.

They rounded the end of the block and stopped when

they were back at the front door.

Bern walked in and turned the alarm off while Nickels headed straight for his water bowl.

Bern went into the living room and looked at Anna. She was still sound asleep. She had gone from the sitting position, that she'd fallen asleep in, to lying down across the full length of the couch.

Bern walked over and gently took her glasses off. He took a blanket from off the recliner next to the couch and used it to cover her. Anna turned her head and smiled but never opened her eyes.

Bern knew she would wake up early and go home with plenty of time to get ready for work. She was so routine and predictable.

He smiled down on her with bloodshot eyes. He was stoned. Everything felt surreal; everything felt amazing.

This is my best friend, he thought to himself.

He whispered "Good night " to Anna, and sat down on the floor next to the couch. He watched TV. The cartoons were hilarious. He made more popcorn. He laughed. He too eventually fell asleep, lost in stoned slumber.

Bern barely stirred a few hours later when the alarm on Anna's phone went off, letting her know it was time to go home and get ready for work.

"I have to go. Thanks for the outfit," she said to Bern, even though he didn't seem awake enough to understand her words.

She turned the house alarm off and walked out the front door, leaving Bern asleep on the floor by the couch.

As Anna drove home, she thought about the outfit. She thought about the party. She couldn't help but be nervous.

Since the party was tomorrow night, she decided that she wasn't going to do anything tonight. She promised herself a nice, quiet night at home with her cat, a book, and a glass of wine.

Serenity.

Chapter 6 – One Hell of a Night.

Bern opened his eyes just a crack.

It was bright in his bedroom. An intense white glow let him know that it was well past morning; he just wasn't sure which morning it was. As he opened his eyes a little more, it took him a minute to collect his thoughts. His head was killing him. He rubbed his eyes and moaned. Yesterday was a blur in the past that Bern didn't remember.

He barely even remembered Anna leaving for work yesterday morning and didn't remember talking to her after.

He was in his bedroom in his own bed. His mind felt fuzzy and confused. He thought he remembered meeting up with Alice last night but after that...absolutely nothing.

Bern rolled over in his bed to find he was the only one in it. He wasn't even sure if he really expected anyone else to be there, but either way, he was definitely alone.

Bern started to remember a few things — different pieces of the previous night — but he remained unsure whether they were real memories or just things his mind was fabricating. Perhaps they were all fragmented pieces of different memories that his mind was trying to piece together, to make into one complete memory.

After lying in bed, trying really hard to remember, for what felt like hours, the very last thing Bern *thought* he remembered was smoking a joint with Alice and seeing the blurry image of a spellbinding woman rinsing in his shower

He slowly sat up and looked around the room. It was destroyed. His clothes from yesterday were strewn everywhere, with hints of bright red lipstick dabbed on them here and there. Small items that normally sat on the dressers and side tables were now scattered across the floor.

Bern himself was naked. He walked to the bathroom and found a heart drawn on the mirror with red lipstick. He could still smell a scent that reminded him of strawberries.

"Stick heart...ouch!" Bern smiled and grabbed his head. His smile had made his ears ring, and his head seemed to hurt even more now. He rubbed his eyes and looked at himself in the mirror.

Yep, he'd definitely had sex. His body was covered in marks only a woman's mouth could have made. He had red lipstick on his cheek and light scratches on his chest.

"Holy shit! It looks like I had fun," he said to himself, rubbing his eyes. "Wish I remembered."

Bern walked out of the bathroom and looked around the bedroom again, with fresh eyes, at how much damage had actually been done. He only had vague memories of Alice.

Surveying the landscape of his bedroom, it looked like they must have had sex on just about everything in the room.

"She liked it rough, I guess! I wish I could remember it," he said out loud to himself.

A small dresser was now leaning over with clothes falling out of it.

Bern imagined Alice lying on her back on top of the dresser. He was standing between her legs, holding one of her ankles in each hand. "Oh my God!" she screamed with excitement. Ecstasy.

Bern was slamming against Alice's body so hard that the dresser lurched forward. He lost his balance and fell backwards, pulling Alice with him. Her nearly perfect naked body landed on top of his.

They could fix the dresser later...

This is what Bern was imagining had happened, but he honestly had no idea. He barely remember any of it. What he did know was that he had a killer headache, a lot of cleaning to do and felt like he had been hit by a truck.

Bern walked to the kitchen to start a cup of coffee. He was surprised to see that the mess wasn't limited to his bedroom. There were empty drink glasses and liquor bottles all around the house. Spilled liquor had left sticky spots on the counter and floors.

"Whoa! I really don't remember any of this," he said, as he looked around at the rest of the house bewildered, trying to recall any of the previous night's events.

He started a cup of coffee and went back to his bedroom, flopping down face-first on the unmade bed. The messy sheets still smelled like sex.

He looked at his phone; 10:34 last night was the time of the last message he had received from Alice.

'You look fucking sexy tonight!' the message read.

'Did we have fun or what?!' Bern sent a new text to Alice, hoping for a response that would shed some light on the night's events.

Bern texted Anna next. He remembered that she'd taken the day off to go to the dentist. 'Do you want to come over for lunch?'

Anna replied quickly 'Sure. I'll be over sometime. The dentist was fast, so I'm done already.'

Bern wanted nothing more than to stay in his bed and

fall asleep in a sea of soft, fluffy pillows. Instead, he made himself get up and deal with the mysterious disaster.

Still naked, he walked outside to the pool, grabbing his warm, fresh cup of coffee on the way. He had three sips before setting it down on the patio table.

The day was hot and bright, as the sun hung in a brilliant blue sky. It was such a beautiful day, but he could see a dark storm looming far off in the distance.

Bern dove into the deep end of the pool. The cool water shocked his body. As he came to the surface, he instantly felt more awake. He ran his fingers through his hair, once again contemplating a haircut. He looked at his reflection in the glass door.

"Maybe this weekend," he said to himself out loud.

He got out of the pool, dried off, and then went inside and put on a tee shirt and his favorite jeans. After finishing his coffee and taking three aspirin, he started cleaning up the kitchen—an empty vodka bottle, an empty gin bottle, an ashtray with what was left of two joints in it...all remnants of a night he didn't remember.

Bern went to quite a few wild parties and indulged in numerous vices, but it was rare that he blacked out or didn't remember anything the next morning.

As his mind wandered, looking for any hint of a

memory from the night before, he heard a soft knock on the door.

"Come in; it's unlocked!" Bern called out.

Anna walked in, happily greeted, as usual, by Nickels.

"I didn't start lunch yet," Bern said.

"That's fine. I probably won't be hungry for at least another hour anyway," Anna assured him. "Oh my! What happened here? Looks like you had a fun night!" Anna exclaimed.

"Ummmmm...I think so. I don't really remember. I woke up this morning and found everything like this, but I don't remember any of it. I was trying to clean up before you got here." Bern rubbed his face with his hands.

Anna sat down on the couch.

"So, tell me what you *do* remember," she said inquisitively.

"I remember meeting up with Alice at a bar."

"And?" Anna prodded.

"That's it. I remember meeting Alice at a bar." Bern honestly couldn't remember anything else.

"Alice, the dreamy bombshell that I ruined you scoring with...twice? Did she come home with you?" Anna asked, cocking her head.

"Yes, that Alice, and I guess she came home with me. I definitely didn't do all this damage alone."

"Where is she now?" Anna asked, looking around.

"I don't know. I woke up, no one else was here, and the house was wrecked. She hasn't replied to my texts this morning."

"Did you get laid?" Anna asked with wide eyes, intrigued by the whole mysterious situation.

"I don't know; I don't remember, but I'm pretty sure I did. I have scratches and hickeys on my body, and my bedroom is destroyed."

"I get accused of messing up your chances with your fantasy woman on multiple occasions, and then you don't even remember it when it finally happens?!" Anna said with a half laugh.

"Whoa...so...what's all this about?" She pointed to a small mirror that was lying on the coffee table. The mirror was dusted with white powder and had some rolled-up twenty-dollar bills next to it.

Bern looked at the mirror. "I have no idea. I really don't remember any of this."

"Maybe that right there is why you don't remember anything," Anna said, still pointing to the mirror.

"I'm pretty sure that I didn't do coke last night...or this morning. You know I stay away from drugs like that,"

Bern defended himself.

"Well then it looks like your perfect fantasy lay did a bunch on her own!" Anna said, picking the mirror up to have a closer look. "And you don't know where she is?"

"Nope. I don't remember her leaving...or being here, for that matter." Bern sighed.

"I'll just keep my eyes peeled for a tall, sexy blonde with a nosebleed," Anna said sarcastically.

"Ha, ha." Bern wasn't amused.

"What's this?" Anna asked, pointing to the playing card with Alice's phone number on it. She picked the queen of hearts up and closely examined it.

"Oh, that's what Alice wrote her number on when I ran into her at the store the other day."

"How peculiar," Anna said, puzzled by the unconventional use of the royal suit.

"Come look at my bedroom." Bern gestured for Anna to follow him.

"Wow! I can't believe it!" Anna said, looking around the bedroom. "You guys really trashed it! Did she like it rough or what?"

"I don't know! I don't remember! I wish I did!" Bern said, as he leaned in the doorway.

"It looks like there was a serious struggle. I'm pretty sure you killed her. Do *not* ask me to help get rid of the body. I don't have time today," Anna said with a laugh.

"You're soooooooo funny! I didn't kill her," Bern said, secretly wondering if there was a chance that maybe he had.

"Maybe it wasn't her. Maybe it was a prostitute or multiple prostitutes...like two or three of them. Maybe there is more than one body. I definitely don't have time for *that!*" Anna's eyes grew exaggeratedly large.

"Nobody got killed, okay?!"

"How do you know? You don't even remember if you nailed your dream woman or why there's cocaine on your coffee table." Anna pointed out the obvious.

"I don't know! Not remembering is soooo frustrating! You are my memory doctor! You're supposed to be helping me."

"Do you want me to help you clean this up?" Anna asked.

"No, I got it; it's my mess. And...I'm not really sure what I might find under all this stuff," Bern said, as he moved some clothes around the floor with his foot.

"Like a body?" Anna asked, trying not to laugh.

"No! Not like a body!" Bern said, rubbing his face. His

head still hurt, but not as badly as it did earlier.

"Fuck! This is so frustrating!" Bern growled. "What if this starts happening? I can't do it! Losing your memory is a horrible feeling! Mostly because you know that you have lost something. If I didn't know, it would be just like starting over. Knowing that things happened last night that I don't remember scares me. After I lost my memory the first time, it was hell. You know, that's when you met me. It was really fucking hard."

"Yeah, I remember. You were a mess. I couldn't even imagine." Anna had started folding clothes and stacking them in a pile. "It looks like she took a lot of those women's clothes from the closet. Less for you to have to try and get rid of."

"That's great. It means I was also robbed then. Fantastic." Bern said with sarcasm. "At least it was stuff I didn't want."

"Bern, how long have we been friends now?" she asked.

"Counting when I first started out as your patient, about two years, I guess," Bern replied.

"It seems like longer than that, doesn't it?"

"Yep."

"Well, during that time you've shown no signs of additional memory loss. In fact, your brain is very healthy." Anna spoke factually, as if she were sitting in her office with Bern as her patient.

Bern stared at the floor.

"You are going to be okay. I know a really good doctor," she said with a smirk.

"I know. I'm just afraid that I will keep losing memories or wake up tomorrow and not remember anything at all...again. I would rather die!

"What would you do if all of a sudden I didn't remember you or anything we have ever done together? I'm not fucking ready for that!"

"Bern, calm down. Look at this place; you obviously got really messed up! It's not like there isn't evidence of enough cocaine, pot, and alcohol consumption to make a small elephant forget last night! I would be concerned, however, if you just woke up, everything else was normal, but you had no memory of last night. Bern...look at this place! You are fine!"

"I guess you're right. You want to hear a morbidly positive thought?" Bern asked.

"Probably not," Anna said with a sarcastic wince.

"Well, too bad. The good thing about my original memory loss is that after the fire, I didn't remember my parents. I never had to mourn over them and I don't miss them. It would be like you reading an obituary of someone you never met or spoke to. You don't have feelings for them. I'm sure I would have been devastated had I not lost my memory and found out they hadn't made it. I'm sure I loved them. The positive thing was that, without those memories...I didn't really care."

Bern was referring to the accident that caused his initial memory loss. When he was visiting his parents, staying with them in their house, there was a raging fire that consumed the building while the family slept. Unfortunately, his parents didn't make it out. Bern was found by the firefighters, unconscious, by the back door just inside the house.

He woke up in the hospital with no memory. Doctors believe the memory loss was from the lack of oxygen to his brain for an extended period of time—carbon monoxide poisoning.

"Morbidly positive...I'll give you that," Anna said. "Speaking of morbid...if there is a dirty needle in this stuff and I get stabbed, I'm going to be really mad at you!"

"Fuck you! You know that I don't do anything like that!" Bern said laughing. "And...that coke wasn't mine."

"Well, I got my eyes on you! This better not be the beginning of some kind of downward spiral into darkness!" Anna warned.

"Oh stop!" Bern replied, rolling his eyes.

Anna and Bern cleaned up his house while joking and laughing like only the best of friends do; it helped to make the time fly by.

"Thanks so much for helping!" Bern said, looking around at his cleaned-up house after a couple hours of work

"You're welcome."

"Man, what a mess that was. I wish I remembered if it was worth it."

"Well, next time you are with a fantasy woman, try and remember it for me. I want to hear all about it. You owe me for helping you clean up. You know I don't go out, so I have to live vicariously through you," Anna said with a grin.

"Okay, you'll be the first to know. Let's go get something to eat. I'm starving, and I sure don't feel like cooking anymore."

Bern and Anna had a late lunch. After lunch, Anna dropped Bern off and went home to start getting ready for the cocktail party that was planned for tonight. Just thinking about it made her nervous and gave her butterflies.

Chapter 7 – A Cocktail Party.

Bern stepped out of the shower and grabbed a towel. He looked in the mirror at his now shorter hair and beard, which he had just trimmed before getting in. He had already picked out what he was wearing—a dark gray suit with a light purple button-down shirt...no tie.

Getting ready didn't ever take Bern very long, so he sat outside by the pool and read for about an hour.

Earlier in the day, he had insisted that he would drive; he secretly didn't want Anna to have any reason not to drink. Hopefully some alcohol would help her loosen up a little. He wasn't going to let her get through this cocktail party without having a good time.

When it was almost time to go, he got dressed and let Nickels outside one last time. Once Nickels was back inside, he locked the house up, got into his car, and sped off toward Anna's house.

Bern pulled up to Anna's building and found a parking spot right out front, which was almost unheard of. He got out of the car and took the elevator from the lobby to Anna's floor. He checked the time on his phone as he walked up to her door and lightly knocked.

"Just a minute," he heard from the other side of the door. Anna opened the door with curlers in her hair, and wearing a fluffy, white bathrobe.

"Sorry, am I too early?" Bern asked uncertainly.

"No, you're fine; I'm just finishing up. Give me a few minutes," Anna said, as she nervously closed her modest robe more tightly. She turned and walked back to her bedroom, quickly shutting the door behind her.

Bern walked to the living room, took a seat on the couch, and grabbed the television remote control from the end table. Ruff jumped up on the couch next to him, purring and rubbing his head on Bern's arm, begging to be petted.

"It's always so quiet in your house. It would drive me crazy!" Bern said loudly, as he stroked the length of Ruff's back.

"I like it that way!" Anna yelled from her bedroom, as she took the rollers out of her hair, leaving beautiful brown waves.

Anna looked at herself in the mirror as she let the white robe fall to the floor. She studied her nearly naked body in detail, judging herself more harshly than usual. Looking back at her, from the mirror, Anna saw the flawed woman that she always did.

She didn't wear a thong very often but tonight she felt like she had to because the dress was so tight. She picked a pink one that matched the lacey bra she was wearing.

Anna pulled the black dress down over her head and adjusted her bra, smoothing out all the bumps.

She turned and ran her hands from her lower back down to her thighs, looking closely in the mirror for any signs of her underwear lines showing through. All she saw were the natural curves of her body, so she turned back around to adjust the front of the dress.

The shiny studs along the low, swooping neckline danced in the light, as Anna struggled to make less cleavage visible.

"I hate this," she mumbled, adjusting her breasts so they appeared more even. Anna was wearing a pink push-up bra that made them look full and round. She pulled the neck of the dress up so that she could no longer see any of the pink lace that had been showing.

She went to the closet and slid on the pink-and-white high heels she'd taken with the dress. The height of the heels made her feel awkward and clumsy—more than usual, that is.

She walked back to the mirror for one last look. The woman's reflection was sexy.

Anna felt a thousand butterflies in her stomach, and she could come up with a thousand reasons to cancel her plans and just stay home. She took a deep breath.

"Okay, let's do this," she whispered to herself.

"I need a drink," Anna said, walking out of the bedroom. "I'm sooooooo nervous! I'm going to be a wreck!"

"Wow! You look amazing!" Bern said. "We can go get a drink first...take the edge off before you get there. You can always smoke with me if you want," he said with a grin.

"I hate you sometimes. Let's go get a drink," Anna said, walking to the front door.

"We're gonna have fun!" Bern said enthusiastically, as they walked out the door and took the elevator down to the street.

"Can I drive?" Anna asked

"Of course!" Bern said, tossing her the keys.

"I love your car!" Anna said, running her fingers along the edge of its curvy, cold metal body.

"Me too." Bern replied with a grin.

Anna slid behind the wheel of Bern's glossy black convertible Porsche. She started the car to the sound of a sexy low rumbling. Anna slid her high heels off, put the car in gear, and pushed the gas pedal. The engine revved and they pulled away instantly.

Anna looked over at Bern with a big smile. "I LOVE

it!" she shouted.

"I know a place near the party where we can get a drink. Go to Fourth and Lowry," Bern told Anna.

Anna drove the long way, enjoying every moment, postponing the march of the butterflies one minute at a time.

When they pulled up to the front of the building, a valet came out, opened the door for Anna, and then drove the car to an underground parking garage.

Bern led the way to an elevator in the lobby. They took the elevator to the rooftop, which was on the twentieth floor. The elevator doors opened to a beautiful bar, which was softly lit with a blue hew. Half of the open-air section of the roof had outdoor patio furniture, oversized chairs, and couches.

It was very cozy and comfortable. The other half of the outdoor section had dining room seating with groups of tables.

"Wow! It's amazing!" Anna said, instantly attracted to the adjacent doors, which she exited and then approached the railing at the edge of the roof. "The view was breathtaking!" Anna used her cell phone to take a picture of the city skyline.

"I'll go get us a couple drinks," Bern said, as he started to walk back to the bar.

"Hey, how have you been?" Bern asked, recognizing

the bartender.

"Good. What can I get for you?"

"Two dry candy martinis," he laid a fifty-dollar bill on the counter.

Bern looked at Anna as she peered over the railing in the distance. She looked happy. He wished she would loosen up and do things like this more often.

"Keep the change," Bern said, as he grabbed the two drinks.

"I haven't seen that one around for a while," the bartender said.

"What one?" Bern asked, looking around.

"The woman you're with."

"Oh, no you must be thinking of someone else. That's my reclusive, hermit, cat lady friend. She doesn't go out...ever. I always try though! Trust me, it's like pulling teeth."

"Well, she's pretty hot for a reclusive hermit cat lady," the friendly bartender joked.

"Well, she looks absolutely nothing like this normally. That dress she's wearing actually belonged to one of my exes."

"You're kidding?!" the cheery man said with a laugh.

"True story. You have a good night, man," Bern said, raising the two glasses.

"You too, Bern. See you around."

Bern walked over to Anna without her even noticing. She looked magnificent as she leaned over the railing in the black dress. She was fixated on the sights of the city below. It wasn't very often she got to see it this way—the nightlife.

On the far corner of the roof, a man sat playing a grand piano. The live classical music filled the air with beautiful notes that were as brilliant as the city lights below.

Bern leaned against the railing and handed Anna a drink.

"Beautiful, isn't it? I love this place. I told you that you should get out more. You would see more things like this."

"I know," Anna said with a sigh. "I want to; I just have a hard time being comfortable in social settings."

"You should smoke pot," Bern said with a wink.

"I'm not going to smoke pot."

"Why not? It will take the edge off."

"Because, I think that as a professional neurologist, I shouldn't." Anna said in a serious tone.

"What? Code-of-ethics-type stuff? Come on, your best friend is a patient; isn't there something against that in your ethical code of conduct?" Bern asked sarcastically.

"No, because we are just friends and not in a relationship. Also, we have drug tests at work. I can't fail one of those," Anna offered her back-up excuse.

"Sometimes, I think you're awesome; but, most of the time, I think you're lame," Bern said with a smirk, nudging Anna with his shoulder.

"Whatever. Socially challenged or not, I'm not going to smoke pot."

"Fine, when you are old and reflect back on your sad life, you can't say I didn't try to de-hermitize you," Bern said, as he lit a cigarette and watched the smoke float away gently. His eyes followed the cloud until it disappeared against the backdrop of the dark night sky.

"See all the people down there?" He said as he leaned over the railing. "Do you ever wonder what they're all doing? Where they're going? What they're thinking? Every mind down there is thinking something different. Thoughts are like snowflakes; no two are ever the same. They could be thinking about what they're going to eat, a loved one who died, if they remembered to let the dog out, or if the present they ordered for someone is going to arrive in time."

Bern pointed to different people below them. They all

looked so tiny from so high above. "A view like this makes me realize how insignificant most things in my life really are. I imagine myself on the street, with someone else looking down at me. I'm just another body to them—going somewhere unknown, thinking something unknown...all irrelevant to a person who is just viewing me from far above."

"Yeah, I guess when you put it that way, most things are pretty insignificant," Anna said, nodding.

"Yeah, like a lame professional code of ethics and drug testing," Bern said, as if he had just won an argument.

"I hate you," Anna said, as she walked away to one of the plush outdoor couches.

She sat down and Bern followed, taking a seat across from her. Their drinks were already halfway gone.

"Are you going to want another drink before we go?" Bern asked. "The bar is getting busy so I'm going to go order now."

"I don't think so. I'm starting to feel this one already," Anna said. "Let me finish this and see how I feel then."

Anna and Bern chatted and laughed for a couple of hours, each having another drink.

Anna was really loosening up. This was a side of her that Bern rarely saw. She was sexy when she was confident. Not that she was now confident, but she was just buzzed enough to not care—liquid courage.

"We should probably get going," Bern said. "The address is close, so I'm just going to leave my car in the parking garage here and we'll walk."

Bern led them out of the bar and down to the street. They took their time walking the few blocks to the private residence where the cocktail party was being held.

They arrived at the address and stared up at a tall, magnificent building full of luxury condos. They went into the lobby, entered the elevator, and headed for the suite on the fortieth floor.

The elevator arrived, opening its doors so the two could get off.

There was only one door in front of them. A metal sign on it read 'Suite 40RF.'

Bern was about to knock when he turned to Anna and said, "Oh my God! What if this sucks? What if this is the worst thing ever? You know there are people in there, right? I'm scared."

"Shut up! I'm fine," Anna said, playfully leaning her tipsy body into his with a smile.

Bern knocked lightly.

An elegantly dressed woman opened the door. She was wearing a short red dress with red high heels.

"Anna!" she exclaimed. "I'm soooo glad you made it!"

She hugged Anna and then stepped back to look at her. "Wow! You look amazing! I love those shoes! Come in, come in."

"This is my friend Bern," Anna said.

"Nice to meet you. I'm Mary." She daintily shook Bern's hand. "Okay, drinks are being made outside on the patio. I hired a bartender so you don't have to make your own."

They followed her into the expansive, beautiful penthouse. There was gorgeous marble and wood adorning almost every corner. There were large sliding glass doors looking out to an expansive patio and rooftop pool.

"Your place is beautiful!" Anna exclaimed.

"Thank you! I'll just give you a quick tour and let you guys get some drinks. The nearest bathroom is down that hallway. There are two more on the other side of the house too. Just walk through the living room and take that hallway left or right. There is a bathroom at each end."

Just then, there was a knock on the front door. "Oh, please excuse me while I get that. Go get yourselves some drinks. We have catered food in the kitchen too!"

"Thank you," Bern said.

Anna and Bern walked through the large, open living room, admiring all the intricate decor. On the far wall was a fireplace made of beautiful stones that had fossils in them.

"This place is beautiful," Anna whispered with an awe-struck look on her face.

"You need to get out more," Bern whispered back. "I mean, don't get me wrong, it's nice…but you should see the houses of some of the people who buy my art. They are insane! You will see when you go to one of my parties with me sometime. That was the deal, remember?"

Anna ignored him and ran her fingers along the keys of a baby grand piano that stood alone in the corner. She gently pressed some keys and listened to the beautiful tones as they hung in the air before slowly fading away. She loved the sound of the piano; her mother played almost every night when Anna was growing up.

"Let's get a drink," she said, turning to Bern and ushering him outside.

They walked out onto the large patio overlooking the pool. "I bet the view of the city is even more amazing from here," Anna said.

"We'll find out right after we get these drinks," Bern said, turning to the bartender. "Can I get a straight whiskey and a gin and tonic, both on the rocks?" Always making sure he tipped well, he put a twenty-dollar bill on the table. The bartender finished making the drinks and thanked Bern.

Walking over to the low wall along the roof edge, the most beautiful scene slowly came into view. They could see all the major landmark buildings glowing along the night skyline. Looking in the other direction, they could see the dazzling river reflecting the colorful city lights as it moved slowly.

Everything and everyone looked so busy, but in the most beautiful way.

All the glowing lights were more intoxicating than the alcohol.

"Wow! Okay you got me with this view! This is probably one of the best views I've ever seen...and I've seen quite a few," Bern said in awe.

The two stood next to each other without a word, each one sipping their drink. Side by side.

"I'll be right back," Bern said, breaking the silence.

He came back with two more drinks—the same as the first. He handed Anna the gin.

"Thanks," she said, looking into his eyes.

"For everything...I mean...thanks." She quickly looked away.

"What do you mean?" Bern asked inquisitively.

"Just...for everything. For coming here with me

tonight, for being such a good friend, for always trying to get me to come out with you, and for always being there for me...for everything."

"Aww, of course! I wish you opened up like this more often! I love to see this Anna! I miss this Anna!" he said with a smile and a hug. "How do you feel?"

"Intoxicated," Anna said with a wink.

Bern and Anna talked for hours. They talked alone. They talked with other people. They had more drinks. They had more laughs.

By 2:00 a.m., the majority of the guests had left. Mary, the hostess, had joined Anna and Bern, along with a couple other guests. They were all sitting on the plush patio furniture around a gas fire pit.

The flames licked bright orange and electric blue tones through the broken glass crystals at the bottom.

"Speaking of things I hate..." Mary continued, "I fucking hate those stick-people families that people put on their cars. Am I the only one? Isn't everyone sick of these fucking things already?" Everyone laughed.

Mary pulled out a joint and lit it, passing it over to the guest next to her.

"My wife wanted to put those on our car, and I said 'No way in hell!'" the guest said, as he pulled the smoke into his lungs and passed the joint to the woman next to him.

It made its way over to Bern, who puffed it and swished a mouthful of whiskey.

"What do you think?" he asked, holding the joint out toward Anna.

"No thanks," she said, taking it and passing it back to Mary.

"What about this other Anna I'm with tonight? I think this Anna should let go and just live life tonight!" Bern quietly attempted to encourage some bad behavior.

"Yes! Let's live life tonight! We should get in the pool!" Mary said enthusiastically.

Anna and Bern realized they had fallen out of the group's conversation...and that the group had begun following theirs. All eyes were on Anna as if they longed to hear her say that she would let loose for once.

"How about another drink, and then I will consider the pool again," Anna said, raising her glass.

"Fair enough. I'm keeping the bartender here until long after we're in the pool!" Mary said, raising her glass of rum.

"Soooo speaking of stick figures..." Bern started in, smirking at Anna.

"Oh my God, I hate you," she mouthed to him with a playful look from her glossy brown eyes.

"Have you ever heard of a stick heart?" Bern asked the guests.

Of course, Anna had to explain the whole stick heart thing.

"...like stick people's hearts. It's what I've always called them since I was a little kid," Anna finished saying.

Everyone laughed, including Bern. It never got old.

"That's hysterical!" Mary said, as she started sipping on a fresh drink.

The small group talked and laughed for another hour or so, well into the morning.

"Alright...it's POOL TIME!" Mary shouted suddenly.

For Anna, it was two drinks later, and she was honestly reconsidering getting into the pool.

"I don't know though; I don't have a suit," she said out loud.

"That's fine, dear. Wear whatever you have on under that beautiful dress...or nothing at all, if you want. If it will make you feel better, I'll go in wearing my underwear," Mary said with a wink.

"I'll just sit by the pool and sip this drink for now," Anna said, still inhibited, despite how drunk she was. "You should go in," she said, nudging Bern.

"We can leave anytime you want," he said to her with a look that was both serious and seriously drunk.

"No, I'm having a great time. I just don't want to swim. I would if it was just us, but not with all these people," she said with a long gaze.

"Well, let me know what you want to do or when you want to go," Bern said, not completely convinced she was alright.

"Okay, but right now, I want you to get in the pool and have fun, I'll be right here," Anna said reassuringly.

Now standing over by the bar, Mary unzipped her red dress down the back and let it fall to the ground. She lifted a foot and slid her red high heel off, losing her balance a little in the process. She only got the other shoe off after finally sitting down on an ottoman next to Bern.

Bern and Anna watched as the tipsy hostess walked down the steps and into the pool.

"Well, she wasn't kidding about going in wearing her underwear," Bern whispered to Anna, as he watched Mary's exposed body disappear under the water.

"Go!" Anna said, as she pushed Bern away.

Anna watched as Bern stood up and unbuttoned his dress shirt, leaving behind a tight white undershirt that showed the shape of his well-defined body underneath. He took his shoes and socks off, unbuckled his belt, and removed his pants, leaving just gray boxers on his lower half and the white undershirt up top.

"Wet tee shirt contest!" Mary yelled from the pool, with her drink still in hand.

"Or...I could just take it off and skip the foreplay," Bern said, laughing.

"Yes, take it off!" Anna said, followed by a wide-eyed facial expression that let everyone know she didn't mean to say that out loud.

Bern was thankful that the marks from the night before had almost completely faded. He pulled the undershirt over his head and dove into the deep end.

Anna had always found Bern attractive, but he wasn't her type. They just didn't click like that. Tonight was a little different though. Tonight, she found him unusually sexy. She felt like she couldn't escape thinking about him lustfully. She felt like a different person.

Maybe this was exactly what she needed. She was relaxed.

Anna watched Bern splashing and laughing in the bright blue pool. The colorful city lights glistened off the droplets of water on his nearly naked body. Bern was a crush to pass the time.

Anna wasn't thinking about her dress anymore. In fact,

it was perfect—exposed cleavage and all. Part of her pink lace bra was even visible and she didn't care. She didn't feel awkward. She felt happy.

There was no other place in the world that she would rather be at that moment.

Bern walked up to Anna, snapping her out of a steamy daydream.

Anna bit her bottom lip and looked, doe-eyed, up at Bern.

"Hi," she said.

"Hi," Bern said, cocking his head and looking a little more serious.

"You...okay?" he asked.

"Yeah, I'm great! You just caught me daydreaming," Anna said with a smile.

"You want to go? You're the one who has to get up for work in a few hours."

Anna thought back to her most recent conversation with David. She had been thinking a lot about the things he had said.

Life isn't going to wait for you to be ready for it. She could still hear his voice inside her head.

"You know what? I'm going to call in sick," she said with a shrug.

"What?! That's unheard of!" Bern exclaimed.

"Well, a couple close friends recently told me that I need to start living life...soooooo...I just started."

"I hope you mean it and it's not just all talk because you're drunk."

"I mean it," Anna said convincingly.

"Let's go to your place so I can get in the pool...pleeeeaaaease. I just can't get in here," Anna said, as she grabbed Bern's arm.

"Okay, let me get my things," he said, grabbing a towel to dry himself off.

Anna watched Bern put his clothes back on, sad that the night would be ending soon.

Mary, the gracious hostess, insisted that they stay. The pair assured her that they would come back anytime they were invited.

"I'll bring something to smoke next time. I just didn't know Anna's friends were like that," Bern said to Mary, as he lit a cigarette.

"Yeah, neither did she," Mary said with a laugh.

"Well...I didn't know," Anna looked at Bern, shaking her head as she responded.

They said goodbye and caught a cab in front of the luxury penthouse building. They drunkenly laughed the entire ride to Bern's house.

Inside of Bern's front door, they were greeted, as usual, by Nickels. As Anna knelt down to pet him, she lost her balance and fell over. As she was laughing, Nickels started licking her face with sloppy wetness. Love.

"Yuck! That's too much. I'm not that drunk, Mr. Nickels!" Anna said, wiping the dog slobber off her face with her hand.

Bern laughed.

"I have got to pee sooooo bad," Anna said, as she got up and headed to the bathroom. She finished up and washed her hands and face, making sure she was slobber-free. She dried her face and looked at herself in the mirror.

The woman in the mirror was sexy. The neckline of the dress was lower now and showing quite a bit of her pink bra along with her overexposed cleavage. She adjusted her bra and fixed the dress a little, hiding just some of the pink and leaving the rest still exposed.

Anna turned to go out the door and stumbled a little bit. She was way more drunk than she was letting on.

She walked to the kitchen where Bern was standing. While she had been in the bathroom, he had made two delicious-looking martinis.

"Hi," Anna said, looking at Bern.

"Hey, I made you a drink," Bern said.

"Will you get in the pool with me?" Anna asked, as she pulled the olive off its toothpick with her mouth.

"Sure," Bern answered.

Anna and Bern walked outside together with their new drinks. Anna set her drink down on the wrought iron table. She made sure Bern was looking as she slowly unzipped the black dress, exposing the pink strap of her bra.

With her heels still on, she slid the dress down to the ground, exposing the pink lace thong. Its color matched her pink shoes and bra perfectly.

Bern couldn't help but watch as Anna bent down to pick up the dress, keeping her legs as straight as possible the whole time. When she stood back up, she lost her balance a little, cross-stepping one foot in front of the other, almost losing a shoe, and twisting her ankle. She threw the dress over by the table.

"Whoa, killer," Bern said, lighting a joint that he got from the cigar box he'd left out earlier in the day. "You're pretty drunk."

"Come get in. It's sooooo warm!" Anna said, already waist deep in the water. Her bright pink heels sat abandoned, appearing to glow against the dark stone at the edge of the pool.

Bern grabbed an ashtray and sat down on the pool

steps.

"Isn't Anna usually asleep with her cat by nine? What's up with that? How are you feeling?" Bern asked. He had never seen Anna this drunk before.

"I'm good! I feel amazing! You're right; I really should do this more often," Anna said, as she twirled in the glowing blue water, illuminated by soft underwater lights. "David has been telling me the same thing. If I don't go to work tomorrow…or today…I guess I should say, 'So what?' Tonight was worth it!"

"That makes me happy. It's about time you let loose for once. You looked amazing tonight, by the way," Bern commented uninhibitedly.

Anna's phone broke through the silence with a loud chiming sound. It lit up on the table just a short distance away.

"Can you get that for me? It's strange that anyone would be texting me at this hour," Anna said, scrunching her face.

"Ha! It's strange when you get a text at any hour!" Bern said with a laugh.

"Shush! People text me…like you and David…and Stan sometimes. Ouch, that was mean!" Anna stood in the water with an exaggerated pouty bottom lip.

Bern walked to the table where Anna had set her purse and phone. He grabbed the phone and brought it, along with a towel, to Anna.

Anna dried her hands and looked at her phone. Bern watched her face change as it glowed white from the light of the screen.

Anna almost instantly burst into tears.

"Oh my God, what's wrong?" Bern asked.

A crying and speechless Anna handed Bern her phone.

'Something happened to David. He has been taken to Blake Memorial Hospital. I'm on my way there now,' the text message from Stan read.

"Oh my God! I'm so sorry! I'll call us a taxi. I put a couple of towels on the chair. I'm going to grab you some comfortable clothes and we will head to the hospital."

"I think I'm going to throw up," Anna said, unsteadily climbing out of the pool. She was sobbing heavily and seemed to be having a hard time catching her breath.

Bern quickly doubled back and wrapped her in a clean, dry towel. He walked her to a chair and helped her sit down.

"I'll be right back. I'm going to grab a few things. Okay?"

"Is this real, Bern?" Anna asked in a soft, distressed voice, every word interrupted by a sob.

"Anna, look at me. Stay right here. I will be right back. I promise," Bern assured her.

Anna buried her head in her hands and continued to cry.

Bern grabbed some sweat pants and a tee shirt — the most comfortable ones he had. He also grabbed some quick essentials like a bottle of water and a couple of aspirin. He then started a cup of coffee.

Bern hurried back out to Anna with everything in hand, setting it all down on the table where she was sitting.

He slid his soft shirt over her head and helped guide her arms through the sleeves. He pulled the soft cotton shirt over the wet pink bra. The lacy material was cold to the touch. He couldn't help but think about how good Anna smelled. Closing his eyes to escape the situation for a few seconds, he breathed in deeply.

Bern helped Anna stand so they could get his comfortable sweatpants on her almost naked lower half. He knelt down as she leaned on his shoulder. She lifted a foot and Bern helped get the first leg in. He then did the same with her other leg. Anna wobbled as she tried to keep her foot off the ground. Bern's hands slid up her thighs, his fingers brushing her silky skin. It was so soft and smooth. His hands stopped at her waist, pulling the shirt down over her bottoms.

"What happened Bern? Why is he in the hospital?"

"I don't know. We will go find out,"

Bern tightly wrapped his arms around Anna. She loudly burst into tears again from what had become a quiet, intermittent sob.

"I'm right here," he whispered.

Bern held Anna close, giving her time to calm down. When he thought she was ready, he called for a taxi to take them to Blake Memorial Hospital.

They sat on the steps in front of Bern's warehouse. Anna leaned against his strong shoulder for support.

The two sat in silence.

Waiting.

Chapter 8 – Blake Memorial.

Anna and Bern burst into the emergency room of Blake Memorial Hospital, where Stan came rushing up to meet them.

"What happened?!" Anna cried out.

"Anna, somebody shot him!" Stan said.

"Oh my God! David?! Why David?! What is wrong with people, Stan?"

"I don't know, Anna, I don't know," Stan said, staring at the floor, his eyes full of tears.

"I don't understand at all. How did it happen?" Anna asked, wiping tears from her face.

"The police got a call from his house that was just dead air, nothing but silence, so they sent an officer out. They found him shot in the chest at home. They wouldn't tell me anything else," Stan said.

"He was going to go sailing, Stan...he was going to go sailing...it's not fair!"

"I know. It was supposed to be next week..." Stan

stared off into the distance. His voice trailed off as he wiped his sad eyes and hugged Anna. The older security guard was in as much shock as she was.

"Where is he now?" Bern asked.

"He is down in the last room, but we're not allowed down there," Stan said, pointing with one hand and wiping tears from his face with the other.

"I'm going to go have a smoke. You wanna join me?" he held a cigarette toward Bern.

Stan looked tired and worn out. His eyes were bloodshot, puffy, and still watering slightly.

"No; thanks for asking though. I'm going to stay with Anna. I don't want to leave her."

"Okay, I'll be back," Stan replied with a nod, as he wiped his eyes with a tissue Anna handed him from a box on the counter.

"Thank you," Anna whispered to Bern, as she took a seat in one of the old, uncomfortable, hospital chairs.

Anna sat nervously in the hospital waiting room; a pile of used tissues had accumulated next to her. On her other side sat Bern. They were just waiting…waiting for any sign of an update…waiting for someone to tell her that David was okay.

Waiting.

Anna leaned her head on Bern's shoulder and wrapped her arm around his. She felt dizzy and exhausted. Still drunk. She started to fall asleep.

Stan came back in and sat across from the two with his head in his hands.

About an hour passed when a doctor finally walked into the waiting room. He had papers in one hand and a clipboard in the other.

"You are here for David Oxford?" he inquired, confirming what the nurse at the front desk had told him.

"Yes." Anna nodded.

"He is currently still in a coma. We are trying to keep him stabilized. He was shot in the chest right about here." The doctor gestured to his chest on the middle right side.

"He was rushed into surgery right when he came in; one of his lungs had collapsed. We repaired as much damage as possible and stopped the internal bleeding. He has gone into cardiac arrest twice since he was brought in. He is stable for the most part but still in very critical condition. Unfortunately, I can't let you see him until he remains stable and is off the critical list. We won't know more until later this morning. I suggest going home and getting some good rest and then coming back."

Anna looked at Bern, burst into tears, and collapsed into his arms where he sat in the chair next to her.

"I'm sorry," the doctor said. "If you leave us your phone number, we will let you know if there are any updates."

"Thank you," Bern said, nodding his head. "555-9275, Anna Smith," he recited, as the doctor wrote on the chart.

"I'll be talking to you soon. If you have any questions, please let us know. Here is our number." He handed Bern a business card with all the hospital information on it.

"Thanks," Bern said with a nod.

"Thank you, doctor," Anna mumbled with her head still buried in Bern's chest.

Bern and Anna sat there, waiting to wake up from the nightmare...waiting for David to call saying there had been a mistake...waiting for the shock to wear off.

Waiting.

Bern held Anna tight. He rubbed her arms as she continued to cry.

"I'm scared," she said quietly, barely lifting her head from his tear-soaked shirt.

"I know," Bern said, kissing the top of her head. "Let

me take you home to get some sleep."

"Don't leave me alone," Anna whispered.

"I won't," Bern reassured her. "You're going to my house with me."

Anna stood up without another word. Bern followed, letting her lean on him as she walked. She seemed very weak and exhausted. Still tipsy.

The two said goodbye to Stan, who walked them out, taking advantage of the opportunity to smoke another cigarette. Stan decided he was going to stay at the hospital instead of going home. He felt he had to be there.

Bern stood outside, next to the curb, where they caught a cab. Anna laid her head on Bern's chest in the backseat of the car. The entire ride was silent.

She stared wide-eyed out the window as the world passed by.

Bern could only imagine how much Anna's mind was racing. He wondered what she was thinking. He pictured her thoughts as sadly broken, melting snowflakes.

He knew that David was such an important person in her life, just as her father had been.

They got to Bern's house and he walked her inside. Nickels' greeting was unusually silent and subdued, as if he sensed something wasn't right. He came up to Anna and licked her hand, lovingly showing his concern for her.

Anna walked to the couch and sat down for a few seconds. She then stood up again, biting her nails as she paced. She seemed to have a renewed, adrenaline-fueled burst of energy.

"Nickels, go out back," Bern said, opening the back door.

On his way back through the kitchen, Bern poured a glass of ice water and grabbed a couple of aspirin. He walked over to Anna, who was still pacing and chewing her fingernails, and handed them to her.

"I'm freaking out," she said. "Bern, I'm freaking out."

"I know. I'm sorry, dear. Let me know if I can do anything else for you. I can get you anything you need. Do you need anything from your place?" Bern asked.

"Bern, no! You are not leaving me! You can't leave me! Please!"

"I'm not going to leave you. I will be right here...all night...I promise." Bern walked over and hugged her tightly.

Anna sat down on the couch. Her short-lived second wind seemed to be wearing off. Bern walked back to the kitchen, returning with a handmade ceramic ashtray and a joint he'd grabbed from inside the cigar box. He lit the joint, puffed it once, and then set it in the ashtray on the coffee table.

He sat down next to Anna and started to rub her shoulders. He could feel the tension in her muscles. He thought that this was the least he could do to try to relax and comfort his best friend.

Anna sat with her face in her hands.

"Why David?" she asked. "It doesn't make sense."

"I don't know. David is a really good guy. Who would want to hurt him?" Bern asked, as he grabbed the joint from the ashtray and puffed the thick smoke, exhaling away from Anna. He set the joint back in the ashtray and went back to rubbing her tight neck muscles.

Anna abruptly grabbed the joint and put it to her lips. Bern watched the end glow bright orange. He could hear the dry crackle of the crystal-covered leaves as they burned. He looked closely at Anna. He looked carefully at all the tiny details. Her eyes looked sad and tired. This broke his heart into a million pieces.

Couuuuughhhh!

Anna lunged forward. Bern handed her the glass of ice water and patted her on the back. She quickly drank almost half of the glass and then set it back down.

"Thank you so much! Wow, that burned!" she said, coughing a few more times. "I wasn't really ready for that."

Anna sat and leaned back on the couch as she felt the tetrahydrocannabinol start to affect her brain.

Still seeing the world as a scientist, she knew that the THC was now starting to bind to her cannabinoid receptors. She imagined being inside her own head and watching the neurotransmitters speed up and slow down.

Within a few minutes, everything seemed better. All Anna's cares seemed to melt away, as her short-term memory started to fail her.

"Can we watch TV?" she asked Bern, staring at him with bloodshot eyes. I need a distraction."

"Sure," Bern said, turning on the TV and handing Anna the remote.

She found a documentary about the theory of the universe. Anna sat fixated on the TV. She felt as if things were more colorful. She wasn't focused on what she was actually watching; instead, she was mesmerized by the colors and shapes and how they moved. In the middle of that feeling, however, she was still paying attention to the documentary. The feeling was nothing like Anna had ever experienced before.

She picked the joint up again, inhaled again, and coughed again.

"Are you okay?" Bern asked, as he puffed the joint she handed over to him.

"Oh, what?...Sorry...the TV...I'm really high," Anna said, giggling a little. "I want to watch cartoons."

She wasn't thinking about David in the hospital; she wasn't thinking about why it happened; she wasn't worried about anything at all. She just wanted to watch cartoons and get some sleep.

Anna looked at Bern with a smile. "I know what you're thinking. Yes, I smoked pot. A really good friend told me, not too long ago actually, that I should start living my life. Life is short." She smiled at Bern sleepily.

After the documentary ended, Anna found an older cartoon from their generation. A childhood classic. "Oh, remember this?"

"I don't...remember that. If I remembered my childhood, we wouldn't even know each other. I would have never needed you as a doctor," Bern said jokingly.

"Oh yeah. I forgot, that you forgot." Anna laughed.

"Will you unhook my bra? "she asked, lifting her shirt up in the back.

Bern unhooked it without saying a word. He was thinking how this was the absolute worst timing. Bern wanted to touch her back where the bra had been. He wanted to touch her body, her skin. He let her shirt fall back down.

They sat and watched the mystery-solving cartoon

gang on TV. The gang solved the mystery with the help of their canine companion. Of course, it was Old Man Jenkins in the ghoul costume. It usually was.

Anna, now lying on the couch, looked at Bern intently. She touched his hair with her fingers.

"Don't leave me," she said, as her eyes started to close.

"I won't. I promise," Bern whispered, as he watched Anna's eyes stay closed for longer and longer periods of time, only opening with what seemed like a quick check to make sure he was still there.

She soon fell asleep. Once Bern saw that she was sleeping peacefully, he quickly followed, slumped over on the floor next to the couch where Anna slept.

Chapter 9 – A Bright Blue Light.

Bern woke up on the floor next to the couch. It was light outside. He looked at the clock—8:04.

The TV was still on, playing cartoons.

Bern sat up and looked at Anna. She was still asleep, curled up in a ball on the couch. He grabbed the blanket and covered her back up. He knew it was going to be a long day, and he wasn't going to wake her up this early.

Bern quietly let Nickels out the back door and got a drink of water. He walked back to the couch, grabbed an unused pillow, and resumed his spot on the floor where he'd been when he'd promised Anna he wouldn't leave her.

Bern thought about the Anna who was with him last night—the different Anna. He thought about the way they talked, the way they laughed, the way they had an unusual spark. As horrible as it may sound, he wished that was how she was most of the time.

He looked at her bra, now hanging on the armrest of the couch, and he smiled. He slowly drifted back to sleep.

Bern awoke a couple of hours later to the sound of Anna stirring on the couch. He sat up and looked at her, squinting from the bright, late-morning sun outside. She turned her head toward him and smiled.

"Hi. You didn't leave."

"Hi. I didn't leave," he replied, returning the smile.

"What time is it?" She squinted as she tried to make out the numbers on the clock.

"It's about ten...something. You want breakfast? It's going to be a long day."

"If you're making something, sure, but don't go out of your way for me."

"I wouldn't consider it!" Bern said, walking to the back door. Nickels was lying in the bright yellow sun, happily watching the birds and sniffing the morning breeze.

"Come on, buddy!" Bern said, as Nickels got up and ran inside, heading straight for the couch.

He ran to Anna and started licking her face. "Good morning, Nickels! I love you too!" she said, rubbing his head.

Bern headed to the kitchen and started to make some blueberry pancakes. He knew they were Anna's favorite.

"I slept really well. Thank you for everything. I can always count on you," Anna said from the couch. Nickels was now lying on the floor next to her, taking over Bern's spot and keeping it warm.

"You know I'm always here for anything you need. What time do you want to go over to the hospital?"

"We should probably call first," Anna looked at her phone to confirm that the hospital had not called already.

"I can't believe all this," she said, shaking her head.

Bern handed her the business card that the doctor had given him.

"Where did you get this?" Anna asked, as she started to dial the hospital's number.

"The doctor gave it to me."

"Oh, I didn't see that," she said just as the hospital receptionist answered on the other end of the line.

"Blake Memorial Hospital, how can I assist you?"

"Hi, I just wanted to check on someone who was brought there last night."

"Name please?"

"David Oxford"

"Let me page the doctor. I don't see an update. Please

hold."

The hold music started before Anna could even say, "Okay." She turned her speakerphone on so Bern could hear too.

"Hello," the doctor said, picking up the line.

"Hi. My name is Anna Smith, and I wanted to check on David Oxford."

"Hello, Anna. Well, the good news is that David's condition hasn't gotten any worse. The bad news is that his condition hasn't gotten any better. Nothing has really changed. If you come down soon, I will make sure you can go in to see him."

"Thank you so much. I will be down there soon," Anna said before hanging up the phone.

She got up and grabbed her pink bra from the arm of the couch.

"I don't even remember taking this off," she said, barely loud enough for Bern to hear.

Bern smirked without a word as he started making two cups of coffee.

Anna went into the bathroom. Her once elegantly beautiful, wavy hair was a mess. She grabbed a hair tie, which she had left there a couple days ago, from the counter. She pulled her hair back and put it in a ponytail. She looked a little rough, and she felt even worse.

Anna put her pink bra back on and then washed her hands.

She emerged from the bathroom as plain old Anna— the one Bern had been friends with for a couple of years now.

"Well, I guess I smoked pot. So that was a thing...that happened," Anna said with a hint of uncertainty and regret.

"Don't worry about what happened last night! You needed help relaxing. There is only so much you can take before you just need to escape for a little bit. And you have definitely held strong for longer than most people could have."

Anna barely smiled. She was distracted, now thinking about what David was going to look like. She was trying to mentally prepare herself for seeing that reality. She had no idea what to expect.

She looked up at Bern. "You helped me be stronger. You have no idea how grateful I am for that."

"I would have never let you go through all of this alone."

Anna smiled at him. "I know." She said with the most humbling acknowledgement.

"Speaking of being grateful; here's pancakes," Bern

said, finishing the last one and putting it on top of the others. They sat stacked on top of a small plate next to the two cups of coffee he had put into travel mugs with lids.

"Bern, I don't know if I'm ready for this. I don't know if I can see David like this. What if he doesn't make it?" Anna said while putting one of the pancakes on a small plate.

"He's a strong man. I think he's going to be okay," Bern said reassuringly.

Anna picked her pancake apart, moving the pieces around her plate but not actually eating much.

"Thank you for always taking care of me. I don't know what I would do without you," she said, sipping her toasty, comforting coffee.

"You're welcome. Let me know when you want to go and I'll call a cab for us."

"Oh, that's right; you still don't have your car..." Anna remembered leaving it at the bar, the night of the party, when they had too much to drink.

"It's okay. I'll get it later, after we go to the hospital. No big deal," Bern replied. "Let me know when you're ready."

"Okay, just a few minutes. I'm still trying to prepare myself mentally and emotionally...you know?"

"Of course. Do you need anything else?"

"Nope. I'm okay."

Anna got up and walked to the sliding glass doors. She stood and stared outside. Dark clouds hung low in the sky; it looked like it was going to storm.

"Why can't today be a beautiful day? What do you think we would have done today if this hadn't happened?" Anna asked, still staring off into the distance.

"I don't know; anything we wanted. There's a new exhibit at the art museum I've been wanting to see."

"That would have been nice..." Anna said, turning toward Bern. She still had a distant stare, and she seemed hollow when Bern looked into her beautiful brown eyes.

"I'm ready when you are," she said, taking another sip of her coffee.

Anna went to the front door and put her shoes on. Bern walked over and handed her a bottle of aspirin.

"Take a few," he said.

"Thanks."

Bern called a cab and took Nickels outside for a quick walk. Anna followed them out but sat down on the steps, looking at the dark clouds above them.

"It's going to rain," she said.

Nickels finished up and Bern took him back inside. He grabbed his coffee and a sweater for Anna, thinking that hospitals were always cold.

Bern set the alarm and walked outside, sitting down on the steps next to Anna. He got out his Zippo lighter and a cigarette. He put the cigarette in his mouth, lit it, and closed his eyes while the smoke filled his lungs. He was tired.

Anna leaned her head on Bern's shoulder. They sat quietly listening to the rumbling of the distant thunder. Aside from that, there were no other sounds.

Silence.

Anna was visibly nervous. She hadn't spent much time at hospitals. They made her feel uneasy, and this time, unfortunately, she was going to be sober.

The cab arrived a few minutes later, and they climbed inside.

"Blake Memorial Hospital," Bern said to the driver.

Anna took a deep breath as she looked at Bern. He patted her knee.

"You're going to be okay," he reassured her. "I'll be right beside you for as long as you need me."

"I'll always need you," Anna whispered, as she

slouched in her seat next to Bern and laid her head on his chest.

Bern looked out the window. He watched the people walking as they drove by them. As it started to drizzle, he could see three different kinds of people out there.

The taxi pulled up to the hospital and Anna sat up and stared out the window at the tall building in front of her. She opened the door and got out of the car.

Anna gazed up at the top of the building; the dark storm above made it look very menacing. It was one of the older buildings in the city; it had been built with old brown bricks and beautiful masonry. The building looked very old and gloomy from the outside.

This was the last place Anna wanted to be.

Bern got out behind her, after paying the driver. He walked up behind Anna, put his hands on her arms, and rubbed them gently.

"Are you ready?" he asked softly.

Anna nodded.

Bern knew that she must have been terrified. She had already lost her mother and father. Now the most important person to her was barely hanging on to life, in the building they were standing in front of.

Bern had also lost his mother and father, but since he didn't remember them, it never affected him. He had never lost anyone...no one he could remember anyway.

It was hard for him to relate to Anna on this level, and it killed him.

It started to rain harder. Anna was still looking up at the building in front of them, thinking about what she would have to face when she walked inside. She closed her eyes as the rain started to hit her face more steadily.

"Let's get out of the rain. You know it's going to be cold in there. I don't want you to be wet."

Anna opened her eyes and looked at the automatic sliding doors. She slowly started walking and Bern stayed right next to her.

Swoosh!

The sound of the sliding doors opening as they approached them made Anna shiver.

They walked to the front desk, where Bern asked the nurse what room David was in.

"Let's see. Oh, he is in the intensive care unit. I'm sorry, we don't allow visitors in there."

"But I talked to the doctor one the phone. He said—"

"Oh, the doctor called? Let me see...he may have authorized it. What is your name, dear?"

"Anna Smith."

"Oh yes, I see it on here. Okay, I will buzz the door open. Go straight down the hall and he will be at the very end on the left-hand side."

"Thank you so much," Anna said.

Bern and Anna walked toward the red steel door. As they got closer, they heard a loud buzz and a heavy click. Anna took a deep breath and grabbed Bern's hand. He could feel her hand trembling in his.

He gently squeezed it to let her know that he was right there with her.

They walked through the door and saw rows of beds and machines, some with curtains around them and some without.

As they walked past the first few beds, they found that it was hard to ignore the unfortunate souls surrounding them.

They heard a low, raspy voice saying, "Heeeeelp meeeeee."

Anna didn't look over; she stared at the floor and kept walking.

"Can you get the doctor?" another stronger voice said, as they continued past more beds.

Bern looked over at the man. His head was bandaged in a white dressing with blood soaking through it. His left arm was missing from halfway below his elbow.

The end of his arm was also wrapped in the same white dressing. Bern could see hints of blood soaking through the end, where the rest of his arm used to be.

"I will send him over," Bern said with a nod as they kept walking.

Coooough! Cough!

The gurgled noise of the air rushing out of a person's lungs sounded horrible. The patient in the next bed continued to cough and spit as Bern and Anna walked by.

Anna still hadn't looked up; she was becoming more and more unnerved. She looked over at Bern with watery eyes.

She doesn't look too good, Bern thought.

They passed a bed across the room that had an old man asleep in it. The thin, gray-haired man twitched as if he were having a horrible nightmare. He was connected to a machine that was breathing for him. His face was sad, old, and contorted into a painful grimace. Something inside his mind was torturing him.

As the pair continued to walk, now almost in the middle of the long room, a bright blue light illuminated above a bed that had curtains pulled around it.

There was a long, steady tone.

Beeeeeeeeeeeep!

A nurse came running, quickly disappearing behind the curtains. The overhead speaker blasted a loud announcement.

"Code blue! Intensive care unit 20! BLUE ICU 20! Code blue! Intensive care unit 20! BLUE ICU 20!" the voice overhead blasted the words down on them.

A couple more nurses and a doctor came running in, pulling the curtains around the bed open and out of the way so they could work on the woman lying in the bed. The crew immediately started the life-saving techniques they had all been trained to perform.

Anna closed her eyes and buried her head against Bern's shoulder. She didn't open them or look up again until she felt him stop walking.

Terrified, she knew they had gotten to David. She knew that this was it. She slowly and hesitantly looked up.

David lay in bed, surrounded by an overwhelming number of machines, just like all the other beds they had passed. He had small tubes going into his nose and a larger tube in his mouth going down his throat. Anna put her hands up to her face, covering her mouth. She looked over at Bern as tears streamed down her face. She was speechless.

The woman dying ten beds down faded away into the

background. All the beeping, two shocks from a defibrillator, the loud voices—it all disappeared.

Bern didn't know what to do. He didn't expect this and neither did Anna.

"Oh my God! Why?!" Anna wailed.

She ran forward to the edge of the bed. Reaching over the cool silver bedrail, she grabbed David's hand. It was limp and cold.

"I'm here, David. It's Anna."

She brushed his gray hair back with her other hand.

"You have to get out of here so you can go sailing. We have a date, remember?" Anna's face was soaked, and her tears were now dripping onto her hand that clasped David's.

Bern touched Anna's shoulder blade right here," he said, stepping back to give her a little privacy.

She talked to David for a while. Bern watched her, from a distance, and wished he could relate.

After about twenty minutes, Anna walked back to where Bern was standing.

"I think I need to go," she said, looking pale and ghostly.

Bern nodded silently.

They walked back over to David's bedside.

"Please get better, David," Anna said, grabbing his hand one more time.

"David, it's Bern. We know you're strong. We're going to be praying for you."

Bern didn't believe in prayer or God, in that sense, but he knew that David probably did. He thought that if David could hear their words, the thought of prayer would be comforting and might give him some peace.

"Bye, David. We'll be back," Anna whispered, brushing his gray hair back with her hand one last time.

Anna turned to Bern and buried her head against his shoulder again.

This whole scenario was what Anna determined to be her worst nightmare. This was her hell.

They started walking back toward the big red metal door, which was the only way out. It seemed so far away.

Anna winced as she heard all the voices and noises— the sound of coughing and choking, the sound of pain and suffering.

If there is a hell, it must be something like this, Bern thought.

Bern saw that the one bed that had previously had the bright blue light above it was now empty. The woman was gone. It sat cleanly made, with bright white linens, waiting for the next unfortunate damaged body to arrive. He couldn't help but wonder how many people had died on that very bed.

Bern didn't like the place, no matter how detached he made himself feel.

The two pushed though the red door and out into the waiting room. Anna looked up only when she recognized the sound of the door opening.

"I need fresh air," she said, gasping.

She increased her pace to a near sprint.

Swoosh!

The automatic doors slid open to a rainy sky, filled with dark clouds—darker than they'd been before they'd gone inside.

Anna hit the sidewalk and fell to her knees. People on the busy sidewalk unsympathetically went around her, like water flowing around a large stone in a river.

Bern caught up and helped her to her feet. He walked her to a covered bench and helped her sit down.

"I'm dizzy," she said, covering her face with her hands.

"You need to eat something. Let's sit here for a while

and then go get you some food."

Anna nodded.

They sat there on the bench in front of Blake Memorial Hospital for almost an hour. As they watched people on the street walking by, they could see three different kinds of people, all of them thinking about completely different things.

Each one unique...just like snowflakes.

Chapter 10 – A Bowl of Soup.

Once Anna had calmed down, she and Bern left their bench behind and went to get something to eat.

It had stopped raining, and the dark clouds had moved on to the horizon. The sun was shining, and the cool air started to warm up a little.

"Can I do anything for you?" Bern asked, as they slowly walked up the street.

Anna shook her head.

"I have the perfect place to eat," Bern said, countering Anna's silence.

Bern knew a small restaurant up ahead that had amazing soup. He thought that warm soup would be comforting for Anna and that she might actually eat some of it.

They continued to walk side by side against the flow of all the people on the busy sidewalk. The backdrop of the usual city sounds seemed noisier than usual— footsteps and trains, honking and yelling. All the sounds that they had learned to block out over time now seemed louder and more obnoxious.

The streets were wet with the rain that had fallen, and the cars splashed water from the puddles as they drove by. The two continued to walk in silence, unfazed by the wetness.

"We're almost there," he said, putting his arm around Anna's shoulder and squeezing her.

After one final block, they got to the restaurant—a quaint, cozy-looking little diner with a 'Mom and Pop' feel to it.

"They have the best soup," Bern said, as they walked inside and grabbed a table.

"It smells so good!" Anna said.

Bern smiled.

The waitress came up and greeted the two. She was young, cute, and courteous—exactly what you would expect from such a homey place.

"The chicken noodle sounds really good. I'll have that. Oh, and just ice water to drink," Anna said with a smile, handing the menu back to the girl.

"Same for me, but can I get a root beer also?" Bern asked.

"Of course. I'll go put those in and be right back with your drinks."

"Thanks," Bern said.

"So, what are we going to do? We can't really visit him for very long," Anna said, with a soft voice that cracked at the end.

"Well, we can go see him again and then go home and relax for a while. We'll do whatever you want to do," Bern answered.

The rest of lunch was mostly silent. Anna's mind was running away with what seemed like thousands of thoughts all at once. Like a blizzard in her mind, the thoughts—the snowflakes—were cold and overwhelming.

The somber Anna ate half of her warm soup.

After lunch, they slowly walked back to Blake Memorial Hospital, neither of them in a hurry to get back to the hell they had left behind for a warm bowl of soup.

The day had become bright and sunny. The storm clouds could no longer be seen. The thunder could no longer be heard. It was very deceptive, but they both knew they were going back to a dark, sad place. Anna kind of wished it was still storming.

"This day shouldn't be sunny," she said quietly, as she silently wished the storm would come back.

As they got closer, Anna felt uneasy and nervous, like a million butterflies were inside her. She did not want to go back into the tall, menacing building that had David inside.

Swoosh!

The sliding doors opened. Anna and Bern reluctantly walked in together.

"Hi, we're back to see David Oxford," Bern said to the nurse behind the counter, who was a different one from before.

"Okay, let me see. He is in Room 310. Take this hallway down to the elevator and take it to the third floor."

"Wait...he was in the ICU just a few hours ago," Bern said, pointing to the big red door.

"It shows he was just moved to a room. The doctor determined that he was stable enough."

"That's good news!" Bern said, smiling at Anna.

She was speechless. She'd been hoping for something like this. David might not be in heaven, but at least he was no longer in hell.

"Let's go!" she said excitedly.

They briskly walked down the hall to the elevator and took it up to the third floor.

When they found Room 310, Anna stopped and took a deep breath. She walked in the room first. There was one empty bed, which was closest to the door. David was in the second bed, next to the window.

There weren't as many intimidating machines as there had been in the intensive care unit. The room was more peaceful. The only sounds were a couple of beeps and the 'woosh' of an oxygen machine that was helping David breathe. Anna walked up to David's bedside.

"Hi, David. We're back," she said, brushing his gray hair back and grabbing his hand.

"You look better. You are in a regular room now. That is really good news for us to find out." Anna wiped her tears away. She realized that she still was not going to get any response from him. He was still in a coma.

David's hand felt warmer, and his skin had more color to it than earlier. He looked completely different— almost like he was just peacefully sleeping. It was good to see that change. It gave his friends hope.

Anna talked to David for hours. She told him stories. She reminisced about things they had done in the past. She talked about her father.

She talked about going sailing.

"I miss you, David," Anna said quietly, as tears rolled down her cheeks.

Bern sat behind Anna on the small, stiff hospital love seat and watched and listened. He hoped that David could hear her words.

"We should probably go soon," Anna turned and said.

"Whenever you're ready. I'm not in any hurry. Take all the time you want," Bern said. He was determined to make sure Anna got all the time she needed with David.

"Visiting hours are almost over, and we've been here for a long time. Anyway, maybe David is sick of hearing my stories by now."

"I doubt that, but if you're ready to go, we can," Bern said with a smile.

"Yeah, I think we should. I'm hungry," Anna said, with her hand on her growling stomach.

She turned to David. "We'll be back tomorrow." She then leaned forward and kissed his forehead, brushing his hair back once again and grabbing his hand. Anna had one last thing to say.

"I love you, David."

She turned to Bern and they walked out of the room. Anna wiped the tears from her face and sniffled.

"What do you want to eat?" she asked Bern.

"I don't care; you pick. What sounds good to you?"

"A big, juicy burger," she replied

"I know a great place. We can stop on the way home and eat or just get something to go."

"I would rather just go home and eat. We can get it to go."

"Better than that—they deliver! We can order now, and when we get back to my house, it won't be long until it's delivered."

"I need to stop by my place sometime. I need to feed Ruff and get some clothes."

"Let's go back to my place first and I will drive you home. Then you can take care of everything there."

"Okay," Anna said, as they waited for a cab to stop.

They were now standing by the street in front of the hospital. Everything that the rain had soaked was now dry. The late sunset had passed. The storms hadn't returned that day. It was a beautiful night.

They got into the first cab that stopped. Bern was about to tell the driver his home address when he said, "Shit, I forgot! I don't have a car."

"Okay, so let's go to that parking garage," Anna said.

Bern gave the driver the directions to the garage where they'd left his car before the cocktail party.

Bern and Anna got out of the cab at the garage and walked toward Bern's car.

"Wanna drive?"

"No thanks," said Anna.

Wow! That's unheard of! Bern thought. He knew that Anna truly was broken on the inside.

They got into his car and drove to the gate at the pay booth. Bern put his ticket into the machine.

The screen lit up showing a hundred-dollar fee.

"Ha ha!" Bern laughed. "A hundred bucks? That's ridiculous!" He inserted his credit card and paid. The gate went up.

"Your house first, or do you want to eat first?" Bern asked.

"I guess my house first. We will eat later if that's okay."

"I'm fine with that," Bern said in agreement.

They drove to Anna's house and parked out front on the street.

They went up to her apartment, which always smelled funny to Bern. He always tried to talk her out of them hanging out there. To him, it smelled like what a grandma's house should smell like—old, sticky peanut brittle and cats.

"Hey, Ruff!" Anna said enthusiastically. She knelt down and petted the fluffy calico cat.

The cat rubbed against Bern's leg.

"Oh hey, Mr. Ruffles! You look very fancy today!"

Bern could see what he undeniably felt was discontent in the cat's eyes, for taking Anna away from him. Bern stared back. He wasn't really a cat person.

"Okay, let's go get your things!" Bern said, walking Anna forward, as if to herd her away from the cat.

"What do you need? I'll help you get whatever; just tell me."

Anna went over the things she needed, collecting the items with Bern's help. She fed Ruff and changed the litter.

"Okay, I'm good. We can go to your place and eat," she said.

They got to Bern's place and ordered a couple of burgers for delivery. Bern and Anna sat together outside, listening to the city sounds.

They talked very little.

The burgers came, and while they ate, they talked even less.

Bern tuned to a streaming radio station on his phone—something quiet and soothing.

"Remember me fondly..." the song played quietly.

Anna was exhausted but was at least somewhat content. David was doing better, the night was beautiful, the storms had passed, and her burger was good. It was one of the best burgers she had ever eaten.

Chapter 11 – Where the Hell Is Heaven?

"I'm glad you ate something," Bern said, referring to Anna's burger, which was now completely gone.

"Yeah, I feel better. The day really turned around. Hopefully, tomorrow will get even better," Anna said optimistically.

"Amen to that!" Bern said, as he lit a joint and put it to his lips. He inhaled deeply, filling his lungs with smoke like he had done probably a thousand times before.

He held it out toward Anna. To his surprise, she plucked it from his fingers and put it up to her lips. The joint quietly crackled as it glowed and smoked. Anna set it down in the ashtray and slowly exhaled, watching the thick smoke twist and swirl from her mouth up into the air. The shapes it made were beautiful, Anna thought. It was too bad it only lasted a couple of seconds before the smoke faded and disappeared.

"I just want to forget about today," Anna said, looking at Bern. Her eyes told the day's story without words. Normally bright, brown, and cheery, they now looked dark, sad, and exhausted.

Bern picked the joint up and took another hit.

"Let's forget about today then," he said, as he handed the joint back to Anna again. She took it and smoked. Her eyes felt heavy now. She passed it back to Bern as she coughed little.

"I did talk to Stan today; that was good. I haven't heard from him as much as I thought I would have. He has texted a couple times to check on me, but that's about it. I think he's having a really hard time with it. I don't think he can stand to see David like that," Anna said sadly.

"None of us can," Bern replied.

A few minutes of silence passed. Bern and Anna both sat quietly, each thinking their own stoned thoughts.

"What do you think about God?" Bern asked inquisitively, breaking the silence as he inhaled another lungful of smoke.

Anna sat silent for a minute, looking dazed.

"I don't know...I'm not sure anymore," she stated.

"Me either. All the suffering and pain we saw today...to me that was hell. We walked through hell. It isn't a place underground with fire and brimstone; it's all around us every day. Why would a god let those kinds of things happen to people...especially good people like David?" Bern coughed a little and passed the joint to Anna.

Anna stared at the floor.

"...and if that was hell and it's all around us, where is heaven? I mean think about it...people used to think heaven was in the sky or in the clouds. We don't even know where our universe ends; so far it is proving to be infinite. If the universe is infinite, then, where the hell is heaven?!"

"Where the hell is heaven..." Anna repeated to herself softly. The play on words made her smile.

"I don't know. I guess if hell is all around us, then heaven must be all around us too," Bern said.

Anna thought about her life and tried to think of any time she might have seen heaven. *The cocktail party*, she thought. She felt happy, carefree, and very loved that night. That, to Anna, was heaven.

"I guess heaven is happiness. It's not a place. It's any of those happy memories you have from certain times in your life. Maybe that is as close to heaven as we can ever get. Maybe sailing was going to be David's heaven," Anna said, closing her bloodshot eyes.

"I think you're right," Bern agreed, as he thought about his life...at least the short span of time—a couple of years—that he could remember. He thought about being in the pool with Alice. That whole night, minus the abrupt end, was his heaven.

"Heaven is in your mind," Anna said, opening her eyes. "Heaven is your perception. I guess anything could be heaven if you want it to be. For Bonnie and Clyde, robbery, police shootouts, and murder...those times must have been their heaven."

"Well, I guess we found where the hell heaven is," Bern said with a laugh. "We solved that philosophical question pretty quick. Now, on to life's next big mystery...where the hell is my lighter?" Bern said, as he looked at the joint, which was no longer burning. He felt in his pockets and down along the cushions of the couch. "Huh? I just had it."

Anna giggled. It was in her hand. She handed it back to Bern.

"What were we talking about?" he said.

"I don't know. God or heaven or something," Anna answered.

"Ha ha ha...fuck the man," Bern said, as he relit the joint.

"What?!"

"There is a song that says 'heaven's pearly gates have some eloquent graffiti like..."fuck the man"...and "we'll meet again." 'The Trapeze Swinger'...you should listen to it sometime." Bern passed the joint to Anna. She puffed it and then put it in the ashtray.

Bern had gotten out a small bag of weed and some rolling papers. He started rolling joints and lining them up in the empty cigar box.

Anna grabbed her phone, looked up the song Bern was talking about, and they listened to it together.

"I like it," she said, closing her eyes and leaning her head back on the couch.

Anna felt good.

Forgetting about all the horrible things from the day and leaving just the good memories, Anna was in heaven.

She climbed on the couch and curled up. "We found where the hell heaven is," she whispered to Bern.

"I know," Bern whispered back.

Anna smiled and fell asleep to the sound of cartoons and Bern's laughter.

Chapter 12 – A Day Nobody Expected.

Anna awoke at around 10:00 a.m. It was a beautiful, sunny morning.

She quietly got up from the couch and went over to the sliding glass doors. She looked outside. Everything was glowing bright yellow in the warm morning sun.

Anna walked to the coffee machine. Picking a light roast breakfast blend, she made a cup of coffee for herself. Bern was still sleeping on the floor next to the couch.

Anna turned the house alarm off and went out by the pool. She sat down on the edge of the pool, dangling her feet in the cool water, as she sipped her hot coffee.

The day was amazing. It was bright. It was colorful. It was perfect. Anna sat and appreciated this heaven for as long as she could.

The bliss was uninterrupted until Anna heard her cell phone ring from inside.

She ran inside for her phone. It was the hospital.

Anna's heart sank.

She hesitantly answered, unsure if she wanted to know why she was getting the call.

"Hello, this is Anna," she said.

"Hello, Anna, this is Doctor Fisher. I just wanted to update you on David Oxford's condition. He had some complications overnight, and we rushed him into surgery. The surgeons found more internal damage that they hadn't seen before, and he had started bleeding internally again."

"Is he going to be okay?"

"From what we can tell, it looks like everything went well, and they expect him to be sent to the recovery room shortly. We will be monitoring him closely while he is in there."

"Are we allowed to visit him?" Anna inquired.

"I am going to make sure they will allow you to see him while he is in there, but only for a few minutes. Just tell them that I authorized a visit. They will see it on his file," the doctor answered.

"Thank you so much," Anna said with deep sincerity.

"If you need anything else, you have our number here. We will let you know if anything changes. Have a good day, Miss Smith."

"Thank you for the phone call, doctor," Anna said.

Bern walked over to Anna. Her conversation had woken him up from his spot on the floor.

"What's up?" he asked.

Anna sadly explained what the doctor had told her.

"Well, thankfully, it sounds like they got him into surgery in time. We can go down to the hospital as soon as you're ready," Bern said as he ran his fingers through his hair. "I just need to change clothes."

"I'm not in a hurry," Anna said, staring back outside. It was still such a beautiful day.

She went back outside and sat with her legs in the pool again. She swirled them around, disturbing the water's perfectly smooth surface. The cool water made her feet start to feel a little numb.

Anna wished that *she* was numb.

Bern watched her from the kitchen for about fifteen minutes until she abruptly stood up and walked into the house.

"Hey," she said.

"Hey." Bern sipped his coffee.

"I'm almost ready," she said, putting a slice of bread in the toaster.

"I'm ready when you are," Bern said, having changed clothes while Anna had been outside.

Anna rubbed her eyes and sighed, waiting for the slice of toast, which seemed to be taking forever.

"You okay?" Bern asked, walking up behind her and squeezing her shoulders.

"As good as I can be, I think." Anna turned around and gave Bern a half smile.

Click! The toast was done.

Anna grabbed some butter from the fridge and the golden toasty bread from the toaster. She stood at the kitchen counter, ate the toast, and finished her coffee. She stared outside without saying a word.

Bern could tell that she wasn't staring at anything in particular outside. She was completely inside her head, thinking deeply about everything that had happened over the last couple of days.

Anna finished her toast and gently put the plate and coffee mug in the sink.

"Let me go change quick," she said, as she walked to the guest bedroom.

She looked at her reflection in the mirror. She had dark circles under her tired, sad eyes. She was as exhausted-looking on the outside as she felt on the inside.

Anna changed out of yesterday's clothes, which she had slept in, and put on a pair of jeans and a button-down shirt that she had picked up from her apartment yesterday. She tied her hair back in a ponytail with a red ribbon. She washed her face in the sink. The cool water was refreshing.

Anna could taste the smoke from the weed last night mixed with the cup of coffee from this morning.

"Blah," she said, as she stuck her tongue out at her reflection. Her tongue was white and cottony-looking. She drank some water from the faucet and then brushed her teeth.

She felt better...good enough for a hospital visit at least.

"Okay, let's get going," Anna said, walking out of the bathroom to the front door. She put her shoes on and looked at herself one last time in the mirror, that hung by the door.

Bern let Nickels inside—the last thing he had to do before they left.

They got in Bern's car without a word. They didn't need to talk; they both knew what the day had in store.

About halfway to the hospital, Anna broke the silence.

"What do you think it will be like?" she inquired in an attempt to prepare herself. "I imagine it won't be as bad as ICU, but probably not as good as yesterday.

"Yeah, that's what I'm guessing," Bern said with a nod. "By the way, you know that I've dropped any plans I had so that I could be here for you...right?"

"Yes, I know that, and I'm very grateful," Anna said, patting Bern's knee.

"Well, I only say that because tomorrow night I have an appointment that I need to try to keep. I just want to bring it up ahead of time. Don't get me wrong, if you really need me, I will cancel it and be there for you, but I would really like to try to go," Bern explained carefully.

"Is it Alice?" Anna asked.

"No, of course not. I wouldn't ditch you for that right now. Someone is buying the big painting that I've been working on. They're giving me a lot of money for it. I have to go to their house and see where they want to hang it and finalize the sale. It should only be a few hours."

"Oh, of course! I don't have any problem with that. Wait, speaking of Alice, whatever happened to her?" Anna asked.

"I don't know. She never replied after that night with the coke, and then messages to her phone started failing. I even tried to call her, and it told me that the number was no longer in service. She just disappeared."

"Oh, that sucks. I'm sorry," Anna said partially sympathetic, partially relieved, hiding her true feelings inside. Although, as much as she tried to hide it, a hint of jealousy peaked through. Luckily, Bern didn't notice.

"It's fine. Maybe I'll run into her again someday," Bern said, as he thought back to that night, drinking in the pool with Alice.

"A one-night stand for Bern? Do you feel used?" Anna asked with a smirk.

Bern didn't mind the comment. He knew that it was just Anna talking to keep her mind busy. She was trying to hide the thought of the grievous unknown that lay ahead, just a short car ride away.

She rambled on, mostly about Alice. Bern responded and answered questions. Bern could tell that Anna wasn't listening; it was all just noise. He just played along with the fake conversation.

"Hey," Bern said

"...so that's why I think she…" Anna stopped mid-sentence and looked at Bern, almost as if she just realized what she was doing. "Oh, what?"

"You need to slow down. I know you're nervous. I'm right here. Take a deep breath. You're going to be okay." Bern tried to calm her down.

Anna took a deep breath and closed her eyes for a few minutes. When she opened them again, she realized that they were pulling into the hospital parking garage. She shivered for a second.

"Don't leave me," she said, looking at Bern as he pulled into a parking spot.

"You know I won't." He smiled, reassuring her that he wasn't going anywhere.

They got out of the car and took the elevator to the lobby.

"We are looking for David Oxford. The last we heard is that he was in the recovery room. The doctor authorized us to see him."

"Name please," the nurse said in the most monotone voice Anna had ever heard.

"Anna Smith."

"Okay, go down the hall to the right." The nurse pointed in the direction of a long, empty hallway. "Take the elevator to the fourth floor."

"Thank you," Bern said, as the pair turned and headed in that direction.

Anna's heart dropped as the elevator doors closed. The elevator dinged, the number four button flickered off, and the doors slowly opened back up.

In front of them was another desk with another nurse.

"We are here to see David Oxford. My name is Anna Smith. The doctor authorized us to see him."

The nurse looked up the file on her computer, and

said, "He is right here in the first bed on the left." She gestured to a door on her left side.

Anna took a deep breath and stared at the door; the last thing she wanted to do was walk through it.

Bern walked in front of her and opened the door. He held his hand out, without looking back, waiting for Anna to grab it.

Anna hesitantly grabbed Bern's hand and let him lead the way. The curtains were drawn closed around the first bed—David's bed. Bern led them between the curtains and next to the bed.

Anna gasped, though the gasp itself was near silent. She stared at David's face, which was now bruised on the right side.

There were swirled hues of purple and blue.

Tears rolled down her cheeks. She looked over at Bern and silently mouthed, "What the hell?!"

Bern shook his head. He didn't really know anything about medicine. Even if he did go to college, he didn't remember any of it. Sometimes, he wondered if he was different before the fire. His mind wandered...

Anna grabbed David's clammy hand that was closest to her. She ran her other hand gently down his face, looking more closely at the large, dark, swirled Van Gogh-esque bruising. She shook her head in disbelief.

On the other side of the bed, a nurse pulled the curtain open.

"Oh, I'm sorry! I can come back," she said, as she looked at David's hand in Anna's.

"No, it's okay," Anna insisted. "Can I ask you a question? Why is his face bruised like that now? It wasn't like that yesterday."

"Well, it probably was an injury that he came in with. He had lost so much blood that there was little bruising. They also found internal bleeding in surgery today, so that internal blood loss may have kept the bruises less visible for longer. Now they will start to show up as he stabilizes. It's actually a good thing in his case," the nurse assured them.

Anna winced. "It looks so terrible though."

"It's good; it's color. If he was pale white, I would be worried. I'll be out of here as soon as I change this IV," the nurse said.

Anna was thinking that no amount of convincing was going to make her think that David looked good right now.

The nurse finished up and left the three alone.

"Bern!" Anna said, crying. "Look at his face! Look what they did to him! I want to kill the person who did this to him!"

Anna looked so broken. She stared intently at David's face. He seemed content and at peace.

Suddenly, there was a loud tone and a bright blue light started flashing above them. Anna and Bern both jumped at the shrill noise. The overhead speaker blasted the announcement: "Code blue! Recovery room unit 1! BLUE RR 1! Code blue! Recovery room unit 1! BLUE RR 1!"

Before Anna had a chance to process what was happening, two nurses abruptly pulled the curtains open. A third nurse followed, took Anna by the arm, and briskly walked her away from David's bed.

"I'm sorry, but we need the room," the nurse said commandingly.

Bern had already backed out of the way. He followed Anna, watching her try to pull away from the nurse's clutch. In her eyes, you could see that she was done— ready to just let go. Anna didn't *want* to fight anymore but she did because she knew she had to.

"Let go of my arm. Tell me what is happening." Anna demanded as she shook her arm free.

The nurse walked them out the door and into the waiting area, then said "I am not sure yet. The doctor is already with him. We will let you know as soon as we have an update."

Bern sat down in an old hospital chair. Anna paced,

tears continuing to flow. She bit her nails and watched the door, waiting for any sign of it opening. She finally sat down next to Bern. He rubbed her back gently.

"I'm scared!" Anna whispered.

Anna and Bern sat there for what seemed like an eternity. They listened for any sound—any noise that might give them a hint about what was happening just on the other side of the door. Finally, the door opened and a doctor in the usual, white, sterile attire approached them.

"Hello. You were just in there visiting David Oxford?" the doctor asked.

"Yes," Anna replied with worried eyes.

"I'm sorry. Mr. Oxford didn't make it. He went into cardiac arrest and his heart stopped. We couldn't get him back this time. We did everything we could."

Anna ignored the words, as she wondered how many times a week this doctor had to give a similar speech...to a mother, father, brother, daughter—"We did everything we could..." over and over.

Anna was in shock. Stunned.

"Can I see him?" she asked quietly.

The doctor seemed a little surprised. "Well, yes, you can. They will be taking him away in a few minutes."

"Thank you," Anna said.

She looked back at Bern, and then turned and followed the doctor through the door. Bern didn't know what to do, so he just stood there.

Anna walked up to the side of bed number one in recovery room at Blake Memorial Hospital. Most of the machines around the bed had already been turned off. A nurse was disconnecting the last of the wires and equipment.

Anna just stood there, staring at David. He still looked content. He still looked like he was at peace.

Everything seemed so tranquil. Time slowed to a crawl. Anna didn't hear a single sound. Deep down inside, she knew it was good for David to finally let go.

She hoped that David found his heaven and that Judith was waiting there for him. She pictured them doing all the things they never had the chance to do. Anna pictured them together again in their heaven.

Anna was very sad about the incredible loss, but, at that moment, she experienced a sense of stillness that was like nothing she had ever felt before. This was the first time she had experienced death up close. It wasn't like in the movies. It wasn't scary or dreadful; it was the most peaceful time that Anna had ever experienced in her life. Excruciatingly hard to comprehend but peaceful nonetheless.

She put her hand on his. It still had some warmth to it. She whispered, "Goodbye, David," and slowly, with tears streaming down her face, walked out of the recovery room.

Bern was standing on the other side of the door, waiting. He had let her go in alone for privacy, figuring he would go in after a few minutes to check on her. He was shocked to see Anna composed. Tearful but composed. The hysterical Anna, the one Bern expected to see surface in a situation like this, was nowhere to be seen.

Puzzled, Bern didn't know how to react; he just stood there.

"Okay...we can go now," Anna said, as she walked up to Bern. She looked and sounded completely drained.

Bern hugged the exhausted woman, and then, without another word, the two walked to the elevator and took it down to the parking garage. His arm wrapped around her.

Bern opened the car door for Anna, and she slid into the passenger's seat. He got in, put his hand on her knee, and patted it gently. He wasn't really sure what to do or say.

"I'm sorry," he said. "I know this is repetitive, but if I can do anything, anything at all, let me know."

"Let's just go home. I want to get some sleep. Does it

sound horrible to be glad that all this is over?" Anna asked, feeling a little guilty. "Is that selfish?"

"No, not at all," Bern said, looking over at the brokenhearted, worn-out scientist named Anna.

"Bern, it was really strange. It was so peaceful...so calm. I can't even describe the way it felt." Anna stared out the window, tears still falling.

"You're going to be okay," Bern said sincerely.

They got to Bern's house, and he walked Anna inside. Nickels was waiting at the door, as usual. Anna fell to the floor, and Nickels climbed all over her, nudging her face with his nose. She petted him and kissed his head.

"I love you, Nickels," Anna said.

Anna got up and headed to the couch; her pillow and blanket were still on it from last night. She yawned as she lay down. She pulled the soft blanket over her head.

"Bern, can you do me a favor and get me some different clothes? Something more comfortable?" Annas muffled voice rose from the blanket.

Bern went to his bedroom and returned with a soft tee shirt and a pair of his boxers.

"Here you go," he said, setting the clothes down on the coffee table.

"Can you help me?" Anna asked, pulling the blanket off her head as she sat up, facing away from Bern.

"Sure." Bern wasn't really sure what he was supposed to do, so he hesitated and sat down next to her.

Anna unbuttoned her shirt and slid it off, leaving just a lacy black bra.

Bern put the shirt that he had brought over her head. She reached back and unclasped the bra with one hand. Anna slid the black straps off her arms, letting the bra fall to the floor next to the couch, where Bern had slept last night.

Bern stared at Anna's naked back. He could see faint red lines—the shallow indentations where the bra had been. Her skin looked so soft and smooth. Anna got goose bumps and the hair on the back of her neck stood up. She shivered for a second and then closed her eyes.

She put her arms in the sleeves. Bern watched her bare back disappear as he pulled the tee shirt down.

Anna lay down on her back and undid the top button of her jeans. She unzipped them and lifted her body off the couch as she slid them down her legs. Bern grabbed both of the pant legs as she rested her body back on the couch. He pulled the dark denim the rest of the way off.

She lifted her legs up so that Bern could help put the

boxers on. He could not help but notice her black lace underwear. They were a perfect match for the bra that was now lying on the floor.

Bern slid his boxers up Anna's naked thighs and past the ebony lace. His fingers felt the sensual lace brush them as they slid past.

Anna smiled at Bern and closed her eyes. Almost as fast as her eyes shut, Anna was sound asleep.

Chapter 13 – A Small Painting.

Bern awoke to the sound of Anna's voice. It was the next morning. He had painted all day while Anna had slept, and then he'd fallen asleep on the floor next to the couch, after getting stoned while watching cartoons again.

"Hey, I made us breakfast," she said.

"What? Why?" Bern was surprised.

"I woke up early and didn't go back to sleep. I decided breakfast was the least I could do for everything you've done for me," Anna said, kissing Bern on the top of his head. "Come eat."

"You still shouldn't have, but thank you!" Bern got up and shuffled to the kitchen.

"It's soooo bright outside!" he said, rubbing his eyes.

"I know! Isn't it beautiful?" Anna said enthusiastically.

"Yeah, it's so beautiful it burns!" he said, as he grabbed his sunglasses from the counter. He put his sunglasses on, poured a glass of orange juice, and sat down at the table.

"So, I called and found out that David already has

funeral arrangements. He and Judith made them before she died. Everything is already taken care of. The service is going to be tomorrow evening."

"Well, that's good. I mean, good that you don't have to do it. Wouldn't that be hard?" Bern scrunched his face.

"Yeah, not something I would have looked forward to," Anna said with a shudder.

"Wait, how long have you been up for?" Bern asked inquisitively.

"I don't know…a couple of hours…and a couple cups of coffee," Anna said, as she put a plate of pancakes in front of Bern.

"I made blueberry ones because I know they're your favorite," Anna said, smiling.

"Thank you!" He figured that this whole mood change was probably part of her grieving process. A coping mechanism. As odd as it seemed, he didn't want to interfere, so he went along with everything.

He sat and ate the blueberry pancakes while he listened to stories about David. Anna talked about the times he spent with her family and the fact that they had talked about going sailing. Bern listened as she told stories about his amazing wife, Judith, and about the time they went to a baseball game, just the other night, which was the last time she got to see David 'alive.'

She told Bern that, in retrospect, going to that game was one of the best decisions she had ever made.

"I called my boss this morning and told him I needed a couple of weeks off. He understands…" Anna said, finally changing the subject.

"That's great."

"Can I ask you a favor? Will you paint something small for me?"

"Of course!" Bern responded immediately.

Anna handed him a picture. He examined it, looking at the colors, shapes, and shades.

"Is this all? Do you want it to look like this?" Bern lowered one eyebrow.

"Pretty close, but with that beautiful Bern Andrews' abstract style that I know you will add," Anna said with a smile.

"Is this for tomorrow?" Bern asked, assuming that it was.

"Yes." Anna nodded.

"Okay, I guess I should get started. I'll get it done in plenty of time," he reassured her.

He found his cigar box on the kitchen counter. He took a joint out and lit it.

"You smoke a lot," Anna pointed out.

"Yes, and I also paint a lot," Bern said, raising his head to look at her with a smile.

He was now going through a box of paints, looking for the colors that he would need, and setting them aside as he found them. The joint now lay in an ashtray, smoking all alone.

Bern went to the far end of the living room and started looking at the canvases he had.

"How big?" he asked.

"I don't know...pretty small. Like this big." Using her hands, Anna made a rectangle that was about the size of a cookie sheet.

"Like this?" Bern lifted up a canvas that was 16" by 20". "I don't have any that are much smaller, but I could make one."

"What about that one?" Anna pointed to a perfect sized canvas, facing backwards, leaning against the wall.

"Oh, that's not blank." Bern flipped the canvas around.

It was a mess of dark colors. Bleeding and swirling. Mixing and blending. It looked like agony captured in oil based paint. Despair presented in broken technicolor. It looked the way Anna felt.

"I started this a long time ago. It just sits there. I'm never going to finish it. It's just really dark."

"Can I use it?" she sheepishly asked.

"You mean paint over it?" he asked squinting his eyes.

"Yes." She said quietly as she pictured what the colorful paint might look like overtop the dark colors. It would transform the agony and despair into joy and happiness. Changing the negative emotion of the painting into something positive. "That painting is how I feel."

"I think that would actually be perfect then." Bern knew exactly why she wanted him to use it. She wanted to see a transformation. And he couldn't agree more.

Bern put the dark painting on the easel, and next to it, he put the picture that Anna had given him.

He started with a pencil, drawing on the painting some of the major shapes in the picture. He grabbed the ashtray and took a drag off the joint.

Anna watched intently. "Do you mind if I just hang out with you today?" she asked.

"Of course not! I don't even know why you would ask," Bern said lowering his eyebrows over his bloodshot eyes.

"Well, I've kept you right next to me for the past few

days. You are probably sick of me," Anna said with a frown.

"No way!" Bern exclaimed. "But I do have that appointment tonight, so you will be on your own for a couple hours if that's still okay."

"Of course that's fine! I'm okay; just glad it's over," Anna said, trying not to sound selfish or heartless.

"I just think of David with Judith, now reunited in some beautiful place. She was his heaven, and as long as I can imagine him there with her, I can let him go. It would be selfish of me not to. I'm still brokenhearted, but I'll be okay," Anna explained the complex feelings she was experiencing.

"Good point," Bern said, agreeing with her.

"I bet that they're sailing together right now."

Anna imagined David and Judith on the bow of a large sailboat, with the wind blowing through Judith's hair as the boat sliced through the water, its sails filled with a perfectly gusty wind.

The water was a dazzling, crystal blue and a beautiful island, which looked like the depictions Anna had seen of the Garden of Eden, quickly came into view. David steered the sailboat closer and anchored it in the shallow water. He jumped off the boat and into the water.

David reached up for Judith and helped her down,

kissing her on the cheek once she was in the knee-deep water with him. He reached up and grabbed the basket, which she had set down on the edge of the boat.

Together, they walked hand in hand to the beach. They sat down for a picnic. They could stay here for all eternity if they wanted.

This was heaven.

"He is in a beautiful place," Anna said confidently, smiling at the comforting thought that was unique like a snowflake.

"I know he is. He deserved it- they deserved it," Bern said with a smile, happy to be part of this special painting.

Bern painted for a while, only stopping briefly to turn some music on and get a drink.

Anna watched him paint, admiring every brushstroke.

"I don't know how you do it," she said, "...taking a blank canvas and making it into something so amazing. I wish I could."

"You can," Bern said, as he stopped painting. He walked over to his canvases and grabbed another small one. He put it on his other easel and handed Anna a brush.

"There," Bern said. "Paint something."

"I don't know what to paint."

"Exactly! That's the best part. It can be anything you want it to be. You are the creator; now bring something into existence. Don't worry about what it looks like. The longer you just sit and look at it, the longer it will stay nothing for."

"Oh, I have a picture I took on my phone. That would be cool to paint. I think I'll do that." Anna got out her phone and found the picture, showing it to Bern. It was a picture of the city skyline at night, taken on the rooftop at the cocktail party.

"Oh that's a great picture! That would be really cool. Remember though, it doesn't even need to be of anything; just start painting."

"I don't know how to paint...not like you." She pointed to his painting with her brush.

"Just feel it out. Get some paint on the brush and put it on the canvas. See what it feels like. You will learn," Bern said, as he continued painting.

Anna picked a dark purple color. She pulled the brush across the canvas, leaving a plum-colored trail.

"Now see how that feels doing it softer and then harder. Pay attention to how the paint looks different when you change the pressure."

Bern watched Anna paint. She seemed different today. Bern couldn't put his finger on it. She seemed unusually carefree.

"Show me how to paint up and down like that," Anna said with an up-and-down hand motion, as she watched Bern finish a long stroke.

"Like this. Let your wrist move at the top." Bern stroked his brush upward, bringing his wrist back at the end of the stroke. Anna tried with an awkward, T-Rex-looking arm movement.

"No...like at the top of the stroke. Let your wrist flick up slowly. No...let me show you." Bern walked up behind Anna.

He put his brush down on her easel. He grabbed her right hand—the one with the brush in it—and put his other hand on her stomach, pressing her body against his.

He moved her arm up and down in a silky, smooth motion, slowly flicking her wrist at the end.

"Like this," he said quietly, his soft lips barely touching her ear.

His words gave Anna chills. She closed her eyes and continued to stroke the paint onto the canvas, letting Bern guide her blindly. She was creating something that hadn't existed only a few minutes before, and she loved the way it made her feel. Overall, she felt different today. She felt free.

Bern stepped back and watched. "You're a natural! I

mean that! You picked it up like you've been doing it forever."

Anna smiled and enthusiastically continued to paint. It made her feel good.

Bern stood next to her, painting with a definite purpose. The pair stayed mostly silent the rest of the time. Music played softly in the background, and Bern occasionally offered encouraging words.

They stood side by side, painting and enjoying every moment. They painted for hours, stopping only for some lunch and a quick afternoon swim.

Side by side, the pair painted into the evening. For part of the time, they talked and laughed; the rest of the time, they said nothing at all.

They didn't need to say anything at all.

Today, they had both found heaven. Amongst all the sadness and pain, it was still there; they just had to find it. They had to open their eyes to be able to see it.

"As much as I would love to stay and never, ever stop painting, I have to go get ready for that appointment," Bern said, as he started to finish up the part of the painting he was working on. "Are you sure you're going to be okay?"

"I'll be fine. I could probably use some time alone now that everything is over anyway," Anna said reassuringly.

"Okay, I'll only be a couple of hours, and you know you can always get a hold of me on my cell," Bern reassured her.

He watched Anna painting. Her brushstrokes looked natural and, for a first-time painting, the scene she had done so far looked amazing.

"I promise I will call frantically if you are about to get laid by a gorgeous woman. It's what I'm good at," Anna said with a smirk.

"You're so funny," Bern replied to her sarcastic comment.

"I'm going to keep painting. I like it."

"Good, I'm glad!" Bern smiled back.

He walked to his bathroom and took a shower. He got out and dried off, then picked out the clothes he was going to wear—an expensive designer suit pants with a relaxed, light green, button-down shirt.

"Wow, that's very casual but snazzy at the same time!" Anna said when she saw Bern in the outfit he had chosen.

"Snazzy? You just said I look snazzy?" Bern laughed.

"Yeah snazzy casual. Snazzual!" Anna said, laughing.

"You are crazy!" Bern said, laughing. "Will snazzual get me a $100k sale?" he asked, laughing at Anna.

"Of course it will! You look like a hundred thousand bucks," Anna answered with a wink.

"Thanks...I think," Bern said, as he grabbed a sport coat from the closet and set the alarm on the way out the door.

"Good luck!" Anna said, as he shut the door and said goodbye.

Anna smiled. She painted for another hour or so as time quickly flew by, and then she went to the kitchen to pour a relaxing glass of wine.

Anna couldn't help but notice the old, wooden cigar box sitting on the counter. She stared at it while she poured the wine into the glass, almost letting it overflow. Anna grabbed the glass of intoxicating crimson liquid and walked over to the box, never taking her eyes off it. She slowly opened the box. The old hinges creaked. The box contained four joints and a small box of matches.

Anna took a joint out and carefully examined it. The thin, white paper that held the crystalized leaves had been twisted and creased ever so carefully. She looked down at the small box of matches. They had the name and address of an Irish pub in the city.

Anna was contemplating. Should she?

She thought back to David's words and her promise to him.

'Promise me that you will start living your life my dear.' She could still hear his voice, tucked away in a memory that she wanted to keep forever. The voice in her memory sounded exactly like David's. An exact copy. A perfect memory.

Anna took the joint and put it to her lips. She took the matches and struck the red end of one of the wooden sticks against the edge of the small box. The end sparked and ignited into a glowing, dancing flame. Anna raised the flickering match to her face, staring, mesmerized, at its magnificent glow.

The dancing flame burned the end of the joint as Anna inhaled. She shook the match out, extinguishing the flame, and then set it on the marble countertop. She grabbed the ashtray and went back to her easel, coughing a little along the way.

Anna set the ashtray on a small side table next to the easel. After all, the main purpose of this side table was probably to hold Bern's ashtray while he painted and smoked.

Anna didn't think about what the THC was doing to her brain or how certain chemicals worked the way they did. She wasn't Dr. Smith, the scientist, tonight; tonight, she was Anna. Anna the artist.

She smoked the joint and continued to paint. The drug made her love everything around her.

Anna thought about Bern and hoped his appointment

was going well. She thought about how thankful she was to have him in her life, especially now that she was feeling like she was finally finding herself in the middle of this incredible loss and emotionally trying time.

After a couple more hours, Anna finished up her painting and left it to dry. She looked out the sliding glass doors at the dark pool. She reached over and flipped a light switch, making the pool come alive with a brilliant blue glow. It was beautiful.

Anna grabbed the ashtray, with half of the joint still in it, and the pack of matches that had been left lying nearby. She disarmed the alarm on the back doors and walked outside. She sat at the edge of the pool, dangling her legs in the cool water.

The water felt incredible. She could feel it swirling around her legs as she swayed them in a different way than when she was sober.

Anna sat in another deep state of contemplation. *Should I?* she asked herself.

She lit the joint and puffed the smoke, setting it back in the ashtray when she was done. It still glowed.

She thought back to David's words again and how much better her life had been since she'd started listening to his advice more. *Why shouldn't I?* she thought. And for that question, Anna didn't have an answer.

She stood up and slowly pulled Bern's boxers down from her waist. Underneath, Anna was wearing a small pair of orange lace underwear.

She stood outside, next to the glowing pool, in just a tee shirt and her orange lace panties. The night was calm and beautiful. The sky was dark and lightly sprinkled with dazzling stars.

Anna pulled the soft shirt up over her head. She wasn't wearing a bra. Her breasts were perky, and her nipples were hard from the thought of getting in the cool water. She shivered for a split second.

Anna put one hand inside the waist of the orange lace underwear, which sleekly hugged her hips. She slowly pushed them down on one side, still contemplating.

Why shouldn't I? she thought again.

Again...Anna didn't have an answer to that question. She had no reason not to; nothing was stopping her but herself. Nothing was holding her back, other than her own mind.

She slid the brightly colored lingerie down her thighs to her calves, and then bent down and removed her legs one at a time, slowly stepping out of the sexy orange lace.

Anna stood there, at the edge of Bern's pool, completely naked. She felt unbelievably good! She felt uninhibited. She felt free.

Anna bent down, picked up the glowing joint, and took a long drag. She walked over to the pool steps and slowly walked down them, taking her time to feel the cool water on every inch of her naked body.

Anna felt the water go from her legs up to her waist, to her breasts, and then up to her neck. It felt so sensual when she was high. She took one more hit of the joint and set it on the edge of the pool.

Anna held her breath and dove under the water. She felt weightless. This was the most amazing sensation she had ever felt in her entire life. Her mind let go of everything—every memory, every worry, and every care. Anna had stripped everything away until the only thing left was…simply existing. She found, without a doubt, her favorite version of heaven that night.

Anna wanted to swim forever. The water felt so amazing on her silky, bare skin. Her shadows, from the pool light, playfully danced on the brick wall of Bern's warehouse home. The waves made the light bend beautifully in all different directions.

Anna loved every second, and thankfully, to her compromised state of mind, every second felt like it lasted forever.

Anna spent what seemed like a couple of hours in the pool smoking, swimming, and splashing in its seductive glow. Her naked body was illuminated as the light in the pool bounced off it.

Eventually, Anna grew tired, her eyes became heavy, and she decided to go inside.

She slowly walked up the steps and out of the pool. The water glistened and sparkled in the light as it rolled off her lovely, exposed body.

Being unusually spontaneous—not to mention stoned—Anna had completely forgotten to grab a towel. She stood naked, like a white pillar in the night, biting her nails and contemplating what to do with her wet body.

Still dripping with water, Anna opened the sliding glass door and quickly walked to the bathroom. She slipped on the tile a little as her wet feet almost slid out from under her.

She got to the bathroom and grabbed a towel, drying her body off in the dark.

The light in the bathroom was off, but the light from the living room shone in, just barely illuminating everything. The soft light made the curves of Anna's body look exquisitely seductive. With bloodshot eyes, she looked at her reflection in the dark mirror. Instead of seeing that other usual mystery woman, she saw herself. She saw Anna. She was sexy, she was seductive, and she was amazingly sensual. Anna didn't wish she was anyone else.

"I know who you are," Anna whispered to her reflection. "You are sexy."

Anna thought about the women's clothes in the closet of the guest bedroom, and with a defined purpose, she walked across the house. Still naked, but now dry, she left the towel in the bathroom behind her.

Anna opened the closet doors and looked at the hanging row of beautifully alluring dresses. They appeared sensuous and irresistible in a way Anna had never seen them or felt before. She took down the familiar short black-and-white dress—the one that she had refused to try on for the cocktail party. It was made up of four alternating black and white sections that reminded Anna of a giant chessboard. She held the previously dismissed dress up to herself and looked in the mirror.

Anna unzipped the back of the dress and slid it over her head. The soft satin fabric inside felt amazing as it brushed over her bare breasts.

She smoothed the dress out against the sensual curves of her body, sliding her hands slowly down her thighs.

"Wow!" Anna said, looking in the mirror. Her reflection looked stunning! Her hair was half-dry now, but still messy from the pool, adding to the mysterious allure of this newfound Anna. A woman she now recognized as herself.

Anna went back to the closet and grabbed a pair of vintage-looking black-and-white high heels. She walked to the attached bathroom and sat down on the toilet, putting the shoes on and buckling the strap that went across the top of her foot. As she leaned down, the neckline of the dress fell away from her body, exposing the soft, smooth skin of her bare breasts.

Anna stood up and looked down at her feet, admiring the shoes and smoothing the dress out over her flat stomach. She walked back to the full-length mirror in the bedroom. She admired the outfit and felt different—like a new Anna. She glowed with a large smile that seemed to stretch from ear to ear.

Anna spun around and fell face-first onto the bed. She was asleep within minutes, peacefully dreaming, off in another world, still wearing a flirtatious black-and-white dress and a sexy pair of vintage-looking high heels.

Bern finally got home, later than he thought he would. He walked into the house, surprised not to find Anna asleep on the couch. The house smelled like weed and wine.

He walked over to Anna's painting and looked at what she had done. It looked unbelievably good. The color, the strokes, everything about it was near perfect.

Bern noticed the pool light on, and he walked outside, Nickels following behind him.

He saw the orange lace panties lying next to his ashtray. An empty wine glass sat as if it longingly wanted to be refilled and emptied again. Everything he saw by the pool was abandoned. Outside, there was no sign of Anna—only the few items she had left behind.

Bern bent down and picked up the lingerie, noticing how soft the orange lace felt in his fingers. He grabbed the ashtray and the empty wine glass, along with his tee shirt and a pair of his boxers, and then he walked back inside. Nickels still followed closely behind. Bern set down everything on the kitchen counter, except the clothes.

He still saw no sign of Anna.

"She disappeared Nickels."

Puzzled, he started looking in other rooms for her. He was drawn to the guest bedroom when he saw that a light was still on in there.

He found Anna, now lying on her back, with her feet tucked up next to her shapely body and her knees in the air. One of her bare breasts was almost completely out of her dress as the neckline had been pulled to one side when she'd rolled over.

Bern was confused by the seductive outfit, the kind that Anna loathed, and the way her body was suggestively positioned. Her hair was wild-looking; unlike her usual ponytail, it looked disheveled, but in a sexy way.

Anna's skin was so soft and smooth-looking…nearly perfect. Bern stared at her legs and slowly followed them up to her perfect thighs and perfectly curvy hips.

He could now see part of the way up the short dress. Bern peered past the shadows, cast by the dress, to the space between her thighs.

He could see the plump, fleshy, light pink edge of Anna's barely exposed, neatly shaven wonderland.

Bern pulled the dress back over Anna's naked breast. Brushing her milky skin with his fingers, he made sure she was no longer awkwardly exposed.

"Hey, sleepyhead," Bern said quietly, as he gently touched Anna's head. "Did you go out somewhere or something?" He set the clothes, which he had picked up from outside, down on the bed.

Anna stirred a little, and her knees started to drift apart. She spread her legs slowly while Bern watched lasciviously. He could now see everything, pink and smooth, soft and wet. Thank God he was sober, or his mouth would be all over her body, making bad, friend-destroying decisions.

Bern quickly became more and more aroused. His mind filled with lustful thoughts.

"What?" Anna asked sleepily, as she put both her legs together and down to one side as she rubbed her bloodshot, brown eyes.

"No, I stayed here," she said, barely awake.

Anna was a little confused. As she slowly started to wake up a little more, she looked around, appearing slightly bewildered.

"Did you see my painting?" she asked, smiling sleepily at Bern.

"Yes, I did! It looks amazing!" Bern sat down next to Anna on the bed.

Bern was still picturing Anna's exposed body—white, pink, and silky smooth. He wanted to kiss and lick every part of that surprisingly seductive body. His mind wandered with erotic thoughts, each unique like a snowflake.

"You can have it," Anna said with a smile. She lay back on the bed and put her knees up the way Bern had found her.

"Excuse me?" Bern was shocked.

"I want you to have it. It's all yours!" Anna said, reassuring him. Anna rolled to her side, causing her round breasts to almost fall out of the dress. Anna looked down at them, but she didn't fix anything; she left them uncovered, and Bern noticed. She smiled, looking Bern in the eyes.

"What?" Bern replied, cocking his head to one side and scrunching his eyebrows.

"I'm serious, Bern. You have to take it. I'll be mad if you don't! It's the least I can do to thank you for everything," Anna said insistently. "Unless you don't really like it and you're just being nice. It is my first. I get it."

"Huh?", Bern said, as he was now completely lost. He wanted everything that he saw laying on the bed, but he wasn't about to admit that.

"My painting, Bern. If you don't want it, just tell me, but I really want to give it to you. Don't be afraid to be honest," Anna said sincerely. "What did you think I was talking about? Are super you high?"

"Oh yeah, of course I want it! It really is good! I'm going to hang it up. No, I'm not super high; my mind was just wandering…sorry," Bern said with a grin.

"Why are you dressed like this?" Bern inquired, quickly changing the subject. "I found your…I mean my clothes outside by the pool, minus the orange lace panties…those aren't mine," he said with a laugh, as he pointed to the clothes on the bed.

Anna blushed as she tried to open her eyes a little wider. "Sorry about that," she said, slightly embarrassed. "I don't remember falling asleep at all. I was just trying on this dress."

She sat up next to Bern, adjusting the neckline of the black-and-white fabric.

"I actually really like that outfit! Those shoes with that dress, both black and white…it looks stunning!" Bern complimented Anna.

"Well, thank you! I like it too! I owe you

accompaniment to one of your parties, remember, for you telling me about Alice? Maybe I will wear this then."

Anna looked down at her feet, still in the vintage-looking heels she had fallen in love with hours ago.

"Are you going to bed?" Bern asked.

"Well, I need to get out of this thing first, but I'll stay up a bit," Anna said, rubbing the dress with her hand, up and down her thigh.

Anna stood up, pulled the short dress down a little, and took the orange lace panties off the bed.

"Sorry again..." Anna said, blushing as she took the shoes off.

She turned and looked at herself in the mirror. She bent down and put her legs through the openings in the orange lace.

Still looking at herself in the mirror, she stood up and slid the panties up her thighs and under the black-and-white dress.

Bern was fixated. Anna looked back at him in the mirror and grinned. "I went swimming naked," she said.

"I know," Bern replied, still a little shocked. "Well, I'm going to go smoke. You should join me," he said, standing up to leave the room.

He watched for a few more seconds as Anna reached back and started to unzip her dress.

Bern turned and walked out the door, reaching for the knob.

"You can leave it open," he heard Anna say behind him.

Bern let his hand fall away from the doorknob, leaving it open while Anna's dress silently fell to the floor behind him. Never looking back, but imagining what he would see if he did, he walked to the kitchen and got a joint from the cigar box.

Bern filled a glass with ice and poured his favorite whiskey over the cubes of frozen water.

"You want a drink?" he called out toward the guest bedroom.

"Maybe one more glass of that red wine!" Anna yelled back.

Bern got a bottle of red wine out of the wine cooler and poured Anna a glass.

"I'm going outside," he said, just as Anna came walking into the kitchen, again wearing the tee shirt and boxers from earlier. Her hair, pulled back in a ponytail, was mostly tamed now.

"Thank you so much!" Anna said, taking a sip of wine. "It's cool! You opened a new bottle? You didn't have to do that!"

"Shall we?" Bern said, gesturing toward the pool outside, ignoring her comment about the wine.

"We shall," Anna replied, as they walked outside and sat down together at the edge of the pool.

"I sold my painting," Bern said.

"Oh my God! I completely forgot! Congratulations! That's awesome!" Anna said with a tone that made it obvious that she felt bad for not asking.

"Thank you!" Bern said, lighting the new, fresh-smelling joint.

Bern and Anna talked and smoked well into the morning. They watched the sun as it started to rise over the city skyline. It was a magnificent sight and an incredible feeling. Neither of them would have admitted that they didn't want it to end. Neither of them wanted to be the one who ended it.

Such a perfect morning.

Chapter 14 – An Unexpected Film.

Bern and Anna slept for most of the next day, after staying up until early morning. They only awoke later in the evening to start getting ready for David's funeral.

They sat down at the table and quietly ate leftover blueberry pancakes.

In the silence, their minds independently wandered through completely different thoughts of what the funeral would be like. Each thought was like another unique snowflake in a world that had been turned upside down and shaken like a snow globe.

Bern hoped that Anna would be strong enough. Anna hoped that she would be strong enough.

They dressed in their funeral clothes. Anna wore a black dress that she had brought from her house. It was long and slinky, covering everything from her neck to her wrists. It was full, all the way up to the high neckline, and, even though it covered most of her skin, it still hugged her body in a way that gave it some credible sex appeal. Anna had never worn it and never intended it to be a funeral dress, but it was actually perfect for the occasion.

Bern wore a black designer suit with a dark gray shirt and a black tie. Individually, they both looked very attractive, but together they looked breathtakingly stunning.

The drive over was quiet; Bern drove while Anna bit her fingernails and stared out of the passenger-side window.

Anna and Bern hesitantly walked into the funeral home. Inside it was cold and funny-smelling, like an old church. The room was divided into two seating sections split in half by an aisle. A greeter welcomed them in and handed them a folded program.

Anna walked down the aisle, tightly holding the special painting. She headed toward the casket that was against the far wall. A picture of David was sitting on top. Anna started to cry as she got closer.

She found a spot, down in front, where no flowers had yet been placed. She took the painting and leaned it against the stand on which the coffin rested. She stepped back and wiped her eyes, admiring Bern's work. The beautiful painting was perfect in every way, an artistic tribute to David. A warm sun was setting on the horizon of a vibrant, blue ocean. In the foreground a sailboat caught a silent breeze that swiftly pushed it ahead on its journey. The old darkness, that lied under the new painting, would never be seen again. Anna had chosen the perfect canvas.

She kissed her finger and touched David's framed

portrait, sitting on top of the casket. She then walked back over to Bern and the two took a couple of seats near the front.

Anna looked at the beautifully made program. On it were some pictures of David, a brief biography, and some song credits.

"Awwww look," Anna said, wiping her eyes again. She pointed to the bottom of the program where it read, 'This service was prepared in loving memory of David Oxford by his devoted wife, Judith Oxford.'

Anna smiled at the thought of David and Judith together again, doing anything they wanted for the rest of eternity.

"That's really nice," Bern said with a smile.

Anna looked over as someone took the empty seat on the other side of her.

"Hi, I'm so sorry Anna!" Stan said, hugging her in her chair.

"Stan! Hi, how are you holding up?" Anna asked. She had been worried about Stan.

"I'm okay. I have had better days, I can tell you that," Stan said, shaking his head. "How are you doing?"

"I'm pretty good, actually," Anna said, staring at the painting that she had placed up front.

The three quietly watched everyone taking their seats as the room quickly filled up. Anna looked around and recognized more people than she thought she would.

The room fell silent as the funeral director walked to the front and addressed the guests.

"Thank you all for coming out tonight. We have a special presentation for you..."

Suddenly, there was a loud series of rings from the back of the room. A man, whom Anna didn't recognize, got up quickly from the back row and started fumbling through his pockets to find his phone.

"Hello..." he said, answering his phone as he quickly walked toward the door behind them.

"Are you kidding me?! Who the hell does that?! What did he come here for? That makes me so mad! Show some respect!" Anna whispered to Bern, disgusted and angry.

"Ridiculous," Stan said quietly, shaking his head.

Bern looked back and saw the unknown man out the window, walking around, still talking on his phone.

"What a dick! And where did he get that ugly suite from? A thrift store?" Bern whispered.

Anna laughed and put her put her finger to her lips making an almost silent *ssshhhhhh* sound.

"I guess on that note, I should remind all of you to turn your phones off please," the funeral director said.

People around the room checked their phones, turning them off or silencing them as needed.

"This funeral was put together by David's loving wife, Judith, years before she left us. Without further introduction, ladies and gentlemen…the life and memory of David Oxford."

The lights dimmed, and a screen off to the left side of the room was brightly illuminated by a projector positioned at the back.

The screen went black and said, 'Welcome' in bold, white letters. Soft music was playing in the background. The words faded out and were replaced with much larger ones: 'David Oxford, 1951–2019.'

The name and years slowly faded away.

On the large screen, old photos were displayed, each representing a happy memory from David's life.

It started with a baby picture of David lying on a blanket in the sun outside. His tiny face had a big grin, and his pudgy cheeks almost hid his eyes. The film continued through a couple more baby pictures, all bringing smiles to the audience, as intended by the filmmaker, Judith.

The next photo was of what looked like David's first day of kindergarten. He stood in a yard with his knapsack, wearing new school clothes. He looked happy.

The film swiftly progressed through David's life, touching on big events. The film caused soft laughter and whispers, as people remembered being a part of some of the events.

A more recent photo came up. It was a picture of David taken during a birthday party at his house. He was standing in front of the pool and smiling, wearing a party hat. He held a glass of whiskey in one hand and in the other, a cigar. The large numbers on the cake, which sat on the table next to him, read '45.' David honestly could not have looked any happier than he did in that picture. The picture slowly faded away.

"That's such a great picture!" Anna whispered.

The next picture faded in; it had been taken just a few seconds later than the previous one, and it looked almost exactly like it. The most notable difference was that it showed Judith coming into the frame. David stood in the same spot, still smiling and starting to look towards Judith.

The photo faded away.

The next photo faded in. It was the same scene. David looked like he had stepped back; his mouth was now open, as if he were talking. Judith's arm was outstretched, and her hand was buried in the middle of the cake.

The picture faded out. The audience whispered softly.

The next picture of the same scene faded in. Judith's arm was now outstretched toward the other side of the frame, with a handful of frosting and cake. David's head was turned, and white frosting was smeared down the side of his cheek. Judith still appeared to be headed toward him.

The picture faded away.

More whispers and now soft laughter could be heard from the audience.

"I remember this," a soft, unrecognizable voice said from the middle of the room.

The next photo faded in. Again, it was the same scene as the last, but a few seconds later. David's cake sat on the table with a fistful missing from the center, and the numbers four and five had been knocked over. David was pulling Judith by her arm toward the pool behind them. He was laughing, with white frosting still on his face.

"I was there," a woman behind Anna and Bern could be heard saying.

The next photo faded in and showed water splashing in all directions. Judith's and David's legs could be seen above the water in the pool. Everything else was covered by the white water that churned as their bodies hit it.

The picture faded away.

The final photo was a close-up of Judith and David in the pool, their arms resting on the edge as they looked up at the camera. They were both laughing in their soaking wet clothes from the previous photos. David still had a small line of frosting on his cheek, which the pool water had failed to wash off with the rest. He was wearing a wet party hat and holding a glass of pool water in one hand and a soaked cigar in the other.

The audience smiled, laughed, and talked quietly while the last picture remained displayed longer than the previous ones had.

"Their heaven..." Anna said so softly that it was barely audible. "They were each other's heaven."

The screen faded to black, and the soft music disappeared. The audience became silent almost instantly.

"Hello, everyone. Thank you for coming today! I hope you all enjoyed those memories," a middle-aged Judith said, as she faded onto the screen.

"Many of you here shared some of those memories with us. We hope they made you smile."

"This may be strange to see for some of you, but when David and I got married, we talked about prearranging our funerals. We decided to record what we wanted to say, so that we could still be there for each other even if one of us couldn't make it. What we wanted from today was not a funeral at all. We wanted to share our memories with you and celebrate the life that we lived together."

"We are here today to remember my husband, David, the most amazing person I have ever met. David is my entire world. I know that many of you can say he touched your lives in some way, and that makes me proud to call him my other half. David, I love you with my whole heart. I loved you the moment I met you, and I will love you until the end of time. All of you are here today because you shared our life with us in one way or another, and we wanted to thank you for that. We are grateful to have known every one of you. We hope you are all still smiling and that you all keep smiling. David, did you want to add anything?" Judith said, looking off camera.

"Sure! Hello everybody." David came into the frame next to Judith.

"I'm sure this is even more odd to see me talk at my own funeral, but I did just want to take a moment to thank everyone again. Our lives wouldn't have been what it was without all of you. Please don't cry for us; there is no need for that. Be happy in the thought that Judith and I have already found each other again. Right now, we are probably off on adventures through eternity. There's a good chance that we are both so busy together that we missed our own funeral. Sorry about that, but look us up when you get here. We love all of you. You are all friends and you are all family. Thank you."

David and Judith kissed each other as the screen faded to black.

Soft music started to play in the background as a slideshow of more photos started.

'The End,' the screen read in large white text, as the photos changed behind it. The audience sat and watched, not quite sure what to do.

'The End' slowly faded away.

New words faded onto the screen

'...but also just the beginning.'

A photo of David and Judith came up. They looked young, maybe in their late twenties. They were standing on top of a mountain, with hiking gear on. They looked like the two happiest people to have ever lived.

The film faded to black.

The audience was silent for a minute or two.

Then, someone in the back started quietly clapping. The other guests looked around at each other, the majority still not sure what to do. One by one, they eventually started clapping quietly. The room filled with soft applause that continued for a couple of minutes.

"Oh my God. I forgot how amazing they were together. I forgot how much that changed for David after she died," Anna said to Bern.

"They loved each other so much! Nothing could keep them apart! That is how my dad and mom were," Anna said, smiling at the memories of her parents. "Even with David and Judith both gone, they are still here together. I mean, Judith presented David's funeral! That was intense and powerful!"

"I have never seen anything like that! I never knew Judith, but she seems like she was an amazing person too," Bern said.

"I remember a lot of those times," Stan whispered with a nostalgic look in his teary eyes. "Man, that hurt."

The lights in the room slowly brightened back up. The audience continued to talk. The darkness slowly faded away.

At this point, it was odd to see a casket sitting there in front of everyone. With a dark stigma, it represented a traditional funeral, agonizingly dreadful and sad. A combination of a boring sermon and some dry hymns. Depressing and upsetting.

The coffin represented tragedy and sorrow. An ending. It represented everything that the film was not. David and Judith thought that funerals always seemed to focus on the death and not on the life that was or the eternity that might be.

The film had made the audience momentarily forget that they were at a funeral home, at a funeral…just like the filmmaker had intended.

Chapter 15 – The Detective.

Anna awoke to the sound of her phone ringing. It was the day after the funeral.

"Hello," she said sleepily.

"Hello, Miss Smith. This is Detective Thatcher."

"Oh hello!" Anna said, sitting up quickly, almost as alert as if she'd had a shot of caffeine.

"I was wondering if you could come down to my office to answer a few questions. Mr. David Oxford had you listed as the next of kin, so we can also release his belongings to you then as well."

"Oh...ok. Sure, of course. What time?"

"Whenever you can. I will be in the office all day. Just ask for me when you get here."

"I will detective. Thank you."

Anna hung the phone up and gently nudged Bern.

"Bern..."

She nudged Bern harder when he didn't respond.

"Bern, that was a detective. I have to go down to the police station." She shook Bern by his shoulder as he slept.

"What?" He sleepily tried to open his eyes.

"A detective called. He wants me to come down and pick up David's belongings and answer a few questions."

"Okay, I can be ready in a couple of minutes," Bern said, as he got up and headed to the bathroom.

Anna and Bern got ready to go and then called a cab that took them down to the police station.

Detective Thatcher greeted them both when they arrived.

He was a solid, muscular man in his late forties. He had a very square, clean-shaven face that held a kind but intimidating look. He stood tall and firm, with a strong build and a rigid stance. Raised by a strict father in the military, the detective was always solemn and serious.

Detective Thatcher was very good at successfully solving homicides due to his attention to fine detail and his 'think outside the box' logic.

The detective escorted Anna into a private interview room while Bern waited outside.

"I just have a few questions for you. Have a seat," the

detective said, sliding a chair out from under the small table.

Anna's shoes squeaked on the white, vinyl-tiled floor as she sat down. Everything, including the air itself, felt cold and sterile. She looked around the small, brightly lit room. Her mind wandered as the detective began to speak.

"As you know, this case is being investigated as a homicide, and since it involves a government agent, the FBI may get involved."

"What do you mean, a government agent?" Anna asked with a confused look.

"David Oxford was a government agent. He has not been active since his retirement, but the FBI may still want to conduct their own investigation based on some confidential information he may have had. I just wanted to give you fair warning of that possibility."

"...a government agent..." Anna said to herself under her breath. "I don't understand. He was just a scientist like my dad."

"He also worked for the government. He was a trained federal agent for over thirty years," the detective said, in a most factual tone.

"Okay...wow! I didn't know this. I'm...I'm...shocked!"

"How did you know David?" the detective continued on past Anna's confusion.

"He was my father's friend growing up. I have known him my whole life. He was pretty much a second father to me, especially after my real father passed away."

"When was the last time you saw David?"

"Um...we had dinner Tuesday...I think it was Tuesday...we went to a baseball game after dinner."

"Did David seem concerned about anyone around him or his safety? Did anything seem out of place?" he asked.

"No. Everything seemed normal."

"This guy that came in with you today, that is Bern Andrews, correct?" Detective Thatcher pointed to the closed door.

"Yes...that's Bern...Andrews."

"He knew David as well?"

"Bern? Yes. They knew each other."

"Did they ever argue that you know of?"

"What?! No! Absolutely not!" Anna frowned, her eyebrows lowered.

"Has Bern ever been in David's apartment that you know of?"

"I don't think so...I'm not sure...wait! There is no way he did this, if that's what you think!" Anna responded defensively.

"I'm not saying it was him at all; I'm just asking. You know we have to look at all the people who knew him as a standard part of the investigation. We are questioning Bern as well. I got a message that my other lead detective has taken him into an interview room." The detective pointed to the wall; the next interview room was on the other side of it.

"He is going to cooperate. He didn't do this! He is a good person! I know him! He is my best friend."

"So, this is the Bern Andrews that is with you, correct?"

The detective slid a photo across the table. It was a mug shot of a messy-looking Bern. His forehead was deeply gouged open. Half of his bottom lip was swollen, and he had a black eye.

'Bern Andrews: 10/31/2010,' the text at the bottom of the mug shot read.

"What is this? It...is...Bern," Anna said, examining the picture closely. She ran her finger over the gouge on his forehead and pictured what was now a scar. It was faint, but she had always noticed it. A scar that he could never explain.

"Just because a person doesn't remember what happened years ago doesn't mean it didn't happen," the detective said, lowering his eyebrows at Anna.

"This picture was taken when Bern got charged with assault and battery along with carrying an illegal firearm. He spent three months in jail. He has also been arrested four other times. He was the prime suspect in his own parents' house fire. It was found that he had caused it accidentally, but it still seems suspicious to me. I'm sure you know all this though...being that you are his best friend." He continued, "To me, as a detective though, it just means he is a little more suspect than some other people would be. We have to ask about him. I'm sure you understand." Detective Thatcher nodded at Anna. "I guess the real question there might be if you *really* know who Bern is."

Anna sat there in the small interrogation room, stunned. She had no idea about any of this. She never heard about any assault charges, illegal weapons, or jail time.

"So, how long has Bern known David?" The detective continued with his barrage of questions.

"Ummm, two years, I guess," Anna said with uncertainty.

"Did Bern and David ever get into a fight that you know of?" the detective asked, as he wrote something down on his notepad.

"Oh no, of course not! They are both so passive...gentle and humble," Anna said in a very animated way.

"Does Bern own any guns?" he inquired.

"I think so," Anna said in a hesitantly unsure voice.

"Do you know what kind of guns?"

"Oh, I have no idea. I'm not a gun person…it's a black one, I think," Anna said, shrugging her shoulders.

The detective reached down and took his service weapon out of the holster. He unloaded the gun and laid it on the table in front of Anna with a thud.

"Did it look anything like this?" he asked.

"I don't really remember. I think so…it was black," she said, as she looked at the gun that, to her, looked almost like every other gun she had ever seen.

"What about you? Do you own any guns?" Detective Thatcher asked, picking his gun back up and reloading it.

"Oh no! I have never even shot one. I have pepper spray that I carry in my purse, but that's it."

"How do you know Bern?" the detective asked, putting his gun in the holster and looking back up at Anna.

"He is a patient."

"And you are a psychologist? Is that right?"

"No…a neurologist." Anna shook her head.

"Where were you Thursday night, Anna?" Detective Thatcher asked, as he stared intently.

"I was at a cocktail party...with Bern. We were together; that's when we found out about David."

"Okay, so you were with Bern. Now, as a neurologist, tell me why Bern is your patient. Tell me why he has been seeing a mental health professional for the past couple of years," the detective said inquisitively.

"It's not like that! He isn't a mental health patient! He is a test volunteer. He lost his memory because of a lack of oxygen to his brain during the fire at his parents' house."

"The suspicious but accidental house fire?" the detective interrupted, reminding Anna of the questionable fact.

Anna nodded solemnly, bothered by the fact that she hadn't known about all of this until now.

"I work with his mind to try and understand memory loss better, to see if we can recover any of his memories and help others. Mentally, he is fine! He wouldn't do anything like this!" Anna was getting visibly frustrated.

"Do you know if he has any history of blacking out or forgetting blocks of time?" the detective pushed on.

Anna hated the way the small, bright interrogation room smelled. It smelled like innocent people sat in there all day and sweated bullets while aggressive cops asked them probing questions. It smelled exactly the way it should, and she hated it.

Anna started to sweat.

The very sharp detective picked up on Anna's hesitation as her mind raced to the thought of Bern's trashed house, the cocaine, and his missing memory of that entire night—a complete blackout.

"No," Anna said quietly and cautiously.

"Why did you hesitate when you answered?" the detective pried, as he tilted his head a little to the left.

"I'm sorry; I'm just really nervous," Anna said, trying to play off the blatant lie.

"So, you just said Bern was your patient, but earlier you said he was your best friend. Tell me about that. Isn't that against a professional code of ethics or doctor–patient confidentiality?"

Anna was getting increasingly aggravated. Her heart started racing; her mouth was dry. Even with her brain in crisis mode on the inside, from the outside she was still able to appear cool and calm.

"Well, we are both. Again, he isn't a mental health patient; he is a volunteer for tests related to the brain and memory loss. Also, we are not dating or romantically involved; we are just friends," Anna said factually, in defense of their complex relationship.

"Would you say that you are protective of your friend, Anna?"

"Of course!" Anna said, without thinking of where the detective was trying to lead her.

"Would you lie to protect him?" the detective pushed further.

"No, I wouldn't. I want to find who did this more than you do! I loved David like a father!"

The detective looked at his phone, reading a message that had just caused it to vibrate.

"Well, thank you for your time, Doctor Smith. Here is my card. If there is ever anything that you think of or need to tell me, please call. I'll let you know as soon as I have any update on the case. Do you have any questions?"

"Yes, I still don't know what happened exactly. Can you please tell me?"

"Well, we think it was just a burglary gone wrong. Probably just some people trying to get money. Most likely some drug addicts looking for a way to get their next fix. They broke in and a ransacked the place. Unfortunately, David was home and they shot him in the chest. It looks like he pulled out his old service weapon on them, but it wasn't loaded. He must have been able to get to the phone because we got a dead-air call from his home. As far as we can tell, that is what we believe happened. We really don't have many leads right now."

"Oh my God!" Anna said, as she covered her mouth. "Thank you. Please find them for me."

"We are going to try, Doctor Smith." The detective stood up, grabbing his files and Bern's mug shot. "Don't forget to see the officer at the desk on your way out. Since David listed you as the next of kin, his belongings that we aren't keeping for evidence are released to you. They will get them for you down there."

Anna left the interview room quietly, finding that Bern wasn't out of his yet. She took a seat and put her head in her hands while her elbows rested on her knees.

Detective Thatcher walked out a minute later. He stopped in front of Anna and said, "Please be careful...especially with people you think you know. You are vulnerable right now. Be careful who you trust...especially when it comes to guys that have a history of criminal violence."

Anna remained motionless and didn't say a word.

The detective walked into the next room and shut the door. Anna looked up to catch just a quick glimpse of Bern sitting across the table from another detective.

"Oh my God," she said to herself.

She was thinking about how devastated she would be

if Bern really was involved. It would crush her entire world. *But why would he be involved?* she thought.

Anna couldn't believe all of this. Assault and battery? That wasn't the Bern she knew at all! But what if he really had some crazy, secret cocaine habit and was falling apart? She thought about his house the other day and how insanely trashed it had been. Was he going to start blacking out and becoming violent? What if she didn't know Bern at all? Her mind numbed under a blizzard of negative thoughts.

It was only a few minutes later when the other door opened and Bern walked out.

"Ready to go?" he asked cheerfully, as if he hadn't just come out of an intense police interrogation.

Anna looked up at him and saw the scar on his forehead. A scar that she had asked about before. She pictured his forehead gouged open, half of his bottom lip swollen, and a black eye, just like in the mug shot.

"Yeah, I'm ready to go," she said, quickly looking away. "We need to stop by the front desk."

The woman at the front desk asked for 'the victim's' name. Hearing David called 'the victim' so bluntly made Anna cringe.

"David Oxford," she responded distantly.

"Sign here," the lady said, pointing to the line on a touchscreen where Anna signed the electronic version of her name.

"Okay, one minute," the woman said, as she went back to playing a card game on her cell phone.

Anna and Bern stood there together in silence. They each had a million questions and wanted to talk about what had just happened, but they both knew that it would be a bad idea, at least while they were still inside the police station.

Suddenly, there was a loud buzz and a barred door opened, letting a uniformed officer through. Bern and Anna both jumped a little at the loud, abrupt sound.

The officer handed a white bag to the woman at the front desk. She scanned a barcode on the bag and signed the touchscreen.

"Here you go. Please do not open the bag in the station. Thank you," the woman behind the desk said coldly, setting it on the counter for Anna and then quickly returning to her electronic card game.

Anna took the bag and walked out of the station with Bern, a convicted criminal, by her side.

"What's in the bag?" Bern asked.

"I don't know…some stuff of David's," she replied, as she started walking more swiftly.

They got in Bern's car and Anna opened the bag almost immediately. One by one, she started pulling items out.

First was a set of keys for David's car and house. There were also a few other unidentifiable keys. They were all grouped together on a ring with a worn brown leather tag that read 'Oxford' in cursive script.

Next, Anna pulled out a piece of paper that was an inventory list of the contents of the bag.

This was followed by David's wallet, which had his driver's license, a few credit cards, and six dollars inside it.

The last two items Anna pulled out were a black handgun and an empty matching clip.

"Oh wow!" she said, handing the gun to Bern. "Here; guns make me nervous."

"It's a .45 caliber semi-automatic. It looks like the magazine holds about eight rounds. This is a pretty mean-looking gun! Don't worry, it's not loaded. I'm sure the police always keep the bullets when they give guns back. They aren't going to hand you a loaded gun in a police station...and we wouldn't have been able to legally drive with it if it was loaded."

"Yeah...that could be like potentially handing a loaded gun to a convicted criminal," Anna agreed, staring at the gun in Bern's hand. "Do you have a gun? I know I have seen one before...but...I didn't know if it was yours," Anna asked cautiously. She wanted so badly to know the truth about a mysterious past.

"Yeah, I do. You should really learn how to use a gun, and then they won't make you nervous. You know what? I'm going to take you to a shooting range someday!" Bern said enthusiastically.

"Okay," Anna said, as she silently thought about the police interview.

She wanted so desperately to ask Bern about the arrests. Sitting next to him in the car and thinking about what the detective said made her feel like she didn't know him as well as she thought she did.

"I found out that David was a government agent. That was a shock," Anna said with a hollow tone to her voice.

"Wow! Really? That's crazy!" Bern said, astonished.

Anna nodded.

Silence fell over the inside of the car, and Anna sat distant and closed off for the remainder of the drive back to Bern's place.

They pulled up to his industrial warehouse home. Anna, having started to fall asleep during the drive, woke up as soon as they arrived.

"Is it okay if I take a nap?" she asked.

"Of course you can," Bern said, patting her on the leg. "We can do anything you need to do. I don't have any plans. You're lucky I don't have a real job," Bern said with an unnoticed wink.

"Thank you," Anna said, still staring out the window.

"I know this is a stupid question with all that's going on, but are you okay?"

"Yeah, I just need some rest," Anna replied, though not very convincingly.

"I'll take Nickels outside while you go lie down," Bern said, as they got out of the car.

Bern opened the front door and called Nickels outside while Anna disabled the chiming alarm.

Bern took the excited dog around the block, smoking a cigarette along the way.

Anna had gone inside and laid down on the couch. She covered her face with the sheet that she had been using when she slept at night.

She began to cry.

She was confused and overwhelmed. In a just a few days, her entire world had been turned upside down, in so many different ways.

She struggled to clear her mind. Over exhausted, she fell fast asleep.

Bern came back in about fifteen minutes later with Nickels to find Anna sleeping.

He felt like writing, so he climbed the stairs to the small loft, slumped on the soft leather couch, and grabbed his notebook and a pen.

After a few hours, Anna woke up. Bern was still writing, but he stopped when he heard the sound of her waking. He came down from the loft to check on her and see if she needed anything.

"How are you doing?" he asked.

"I'm okay…just overwhelmed. My emotions are changing in huge waves," Anna said, as she rubbed her eyes. "Will you go with me to David's place? I don't want to go alone."

"Of course! Anna, you know I will! Anything you need, just let me know and I'm there!"

"Thanks," Anna gave Bern a half smile.

Chapter 16 – A Crime Scene.

Anna and Bern walked into David's apartment, pulling down the fallen yellow-and-black crime scene tape behind them.

Bern had driven them over when Anna was ready, knowing that David's house would be terribly hard for her to visit alone.

Anna walked over to the blinds, just as she had done a hundred times before. She opened them to let light into the stuffy room. The room lit up to a scene that did not feel like David's home anymore. Papers were scattered everywhere, and the contents of drawers and boxes had been dumped out.

"Oh my God! I wonder what they were looking for! It doesn't look like it was money," she said, slowly processing the entire overwhelming scene.

Anna picked up one of the stray papers and looked it over. It was a medical file recording a brain scan and testing.

The patient was not identified by name but was referred to as 'Test Subject #164579.'

"Nobody goes through papers looking for money or drugs. They go through drawers and closets. They didn't take any electronics or anything of value." She gestured toward David's iPad, still sitting in plain view on the dining room table, surrounded by more mysterious report pages.

"These people were looking for something else, and I'm going to figure out what. I have to...for David," Anna said, as she looked over more papers similar to the first.

"I've got your back; we will figure out who did this," Bern said with a nod.

Anna started collecting the papers, putting them all in one neat stack. They were all pretty much the same—brain scans and standard testing...the kind of reports Anna was used to seeing.

"This doesn't make any sense. These documents mean nothing," she said softly. "It's just research."

"That's why they left them. What we need to know is the significance of what they *did* take," Bern said.

Anna looked at the bookcase, one of the few things that went undisturbed. She looked at the pictures on top and started to tear up. She focused on one of her with David and Judith at the beach.

Anna was about seven years old at the time.

"There you go, honey!" Anna's mother said to her.

"Now you won't burn." Anna sat on the beach in the sun. It was a bright, beautiful day. She could smell the creamy sunscreen that her mother had put on her. It smelled good...like coconut. Young Anna sat quietly and watched Judith and David. They were down by the water, splashing and laughing. They were in love.

This was another memory that Anna could relive and feel. It was just like she was there again.

Annas mind strayed out of the memory and back to reality.

"Ugh! There's so much work to do here," she said, wiping her eyes. "This is overwhelming!"

"Relax. I'm going to help. Let's just start by stacking the papers. That will make a huge difference," Bern said, putting his hand on Anna's shoulder.

They stacked paper after paper. There were thousands of papers, most of them very similar to each other. Any papers that they thought looked different or interesting, they put in a separate stack. Anna wanted to look at them more closely later.

Bern and Anna went through David's apartment, looking for any clue—anything at all—that would tell them what really happened there that fateful day.

"I wonder what they were looking for, especially from David. He was just a scientist like my father. What would anyone want from him?" Anna asked, looking at another paper that was just like the hundreds she had already looked at. "And why would he even have all these confidential reports at home?"

"I don't know," Bern said. We'll figure it out though, okay?" he added confidently, as he stared into Anna's glassy brown eyes.

Anna felt confused. Was the man she thought she knew real or just some criminal mental patient? It was a question she felt terrible asking herself about Bern.

The place was finally tidied up and looked almost like it had the other day when Anna had visited.

Both were now tired; they sat down on the couch together, and Anna grabbed the stack of interesting papers and started looking through them. She still did not find anything significant—just more random testing and data.

"I wonder if they found anything or if this was all in vain?"

"We should find out," Bern said.

"What?" Anna raised her eyebrows.

"We should find them and find out what they know. It can't be that hard," Bern said confidently.

"Or, maybe we should just let the police do it..." Anna said, scrunching her face. "It sounds dangerous."

"Anna, they think it was some random druggies looking for money. They aren't looking for the right people. You know that! This looks like something bigger. What if it's a cover up? "

"Why are you so paranoid?" Anna asked, shaking her head.

"You said that David was some kind of government agent that you didn't know about. You don't think that's crazy? He was very close to your family throughout your whole life, and you didn't know that about him? You don't think that's completely odd? These people were looking for information...information that cost David his life. I want to know what that information is, and I want to find the killer," Bern spoke passionately.

"I still think the police should handle the dangerous stuff," Anna said, shaking her head in disagreement.

"It won't be dangerous...just some research," Bern assured her.

"Maybe David was a spy and he was shot by a Cold-War-era sleeper agent who just came out of hiding!" Bern sounded more excited than Anna thought he should.

"Shut up, that sounds crazy." Anna said.

Anna wanted so badly to ask Bern about his own criminal charges, the jail time, the illegal weapons. The questions burned in her mind. She just wanted to wait until things settled down a little first. For now, she just needed to act normal.

"Let's go soon," Anna said. "It looks pretty good for now. I can come back some other time and finish."

Bern was looking over all the unique objects on the bookshelves.

There was a piece of brain coral, a small Buddha statue, framed photographs, various fossils, and a beautiful piece of petrified wood, among many other interesting items.

"Can you grab that metal box there for me?" Anna asked, pointing to the beautiful antique box with the lock that read, 'Omnis cognitionis intra.'

Bern grabbed the box and set it down on the coffee table in front of Anna.

"All the knowledge within," Bern said.

"What?" Anna looked puzzled.

"It's what that lock says. It's hard to read, but that's what it says. Don't ask me how or why I know how to read Latin, because, I don't remember. Procedural memory...I guess. My doctor told me that." Bern shrugged his shoulders.

"Huh, I never knew for all these years. I could have always just looked it up online, but I never did for some reason." Anna rubbed her finger across what was left of the worn words on the lock.

"Isn't it beautiful? I have admired this box for so many years. David said to me, just the other day actually, that it would be mine when he was gone. I wish I had the key. I want to see what's inside!" Anna said rather excitedly.

"I wonder if it even still unlocks. It looks really old." Bern looked at the lock closely.

"I could get it open, but it's definitely antique, and I don't want to risk damaging it," Bern said, admiring the delicate, artistic craftsmanship.

"No, I definitely don't want to risk damaging it either. I'm sure if David had a key, I will find it in here eventually. I have admired it for years; what's a few more days to wait to find a key?" Anna replied, now looking at a couple more papers from the stack.

"I wonder if we can find out who these patient numbers belong to? That could have something to do with all this. I have been writing them down, and so far, there have only been twelve patient IDs on these thousands of papers. I want to know who those twelve people are," Anna said, as her mind ran wild with theories, both realistic and absurd. Every thought was like a snowflake that flurried around in her mind.

"I think we should organize the papers by that patient ID and then by date. We would at least have a full picture of each patient. We could make a simple diagram of how the reports progress for each patient," Bern explained with quick, excited hand gestures.

"Yeah, I think that's our best and maybe only chance," Anna agreed.

Anna and Bern collected all the scattered papers in the apartment. They put them all into one stack but kept them separate from the other, more interesting pile.

Looking at the stack, Bern estimated that it was about 2,500 sheets. In contrast, the stack of interesting papers only seemed to have maybe about 250 sheets.

"I think that's it," Anna said, looking around the apartment.

Anna picked up the beautiful antique box and put it on top of the stack of interesting papers. She grabbed the stack of papers and made sure the box wasn't going to slide off, and then she carried both and set them on the floor outside the door to the apartment. Bern grabbed the rest—the much taller stack—and walked into the hall. Anna locked the door behind them and then picked up the box and the small stack of papers from the hallway floor.

Anna was back to thinking about what the detective had said...back to wondering if she knew who Bern really was...wondering if it was truly safe to trust him. She couldn't imagine it being any different from the way it was now, but she also never in a million years would have thought that he had a secret criminal record.

Anna just needed a little distance and some time to get past everything that had happened. She needed time to mourn and grieve, then heal and sort things out.

Anna decided that she would be staying at her own house tonight.

The two walked down the stairs and out to the car. Bern put the tall stack of papers on the back floor behind the driver's seat. Anna got in the passenger seat, keeping the small stack of papers and the beautiful box on her lap.

She reached back across to the tall stack, keeping one hand on it so the papers wouldn't fall as they drove.

During the ride home, they talked about who "they" might be and what "they" may have been looking for

Some of the theories were outlandish.

"Maybe it was terrorists looking for secrets! Maybe he was a government spy and someone found out!" Anna said.

...and some were realistic.

"Maybe it really was just some strung-out junkies looking for money. Maybe they were just too fucked up or strung out to think about taking the iPad and other things," Bern said.

They got back to Bern's house and decided to order some Chinese delivery for dinner.

"Are you ready to do this?" Bern asked, referring to the stacks of papers and the daunting task of finding some kind of organization in the chaos.

"Yep!" Anna said confidently.

"Okay, let's make a stack for every patient and then a miscellaneous stack for anything without a patient ID," Bern said, pointing to spots on the floor in front of the couch and coffee table. He got a stack of blank papers from out of his printer, and then he handed Anna a black marker.

"Okay, let's just start with the patient IDs. Grab one and start a stack. Write the patient ID on a new blank sheet and put it on top of the stack. Eventually, we will have all twelve stacks, and then we will just need to sort the rest," Bern explained.

He looked at the first sheet that he grabbed.

"193753 Patient #1," he wrote in big, bold letters on a blank piece of paper. He put the patient record underneath, starting the first patient stack on his living room floor.

"738927 Patient #2," Anna wrote on her blank sheet, placing a patient file underneath to start another new stack.

They continued until they had not twelve, but thirteen

patient IDs—thirteen different stacks, not counting the miscellaneous stack. All records were now in either the matching patient stack or the miscellaneous stack.

They stood silently and looked down at the finished stacks of paper spread out across the soft tan carpet of Bern's living room floor.

"Well, we did it," Anna said.

There was a sudden, loud, startling knock on the front door.

Nickels barked.

Perfect timing; their dinner had arrived. They found a documentary about Alaska. Dinner and a movie.

Anna didn't follow the film because she was too distracted. She still had this tiny little seed of doubt, planted by Detective Thatcher.

It was slowly starting to grow stronger, even as she tried to fight it back.

Anna couldn't stop thinking about it all.

Do I really know Bern? she asked herself.

Anna was slowly becoming increasingly uncertain about her best friend.

Chapter 17 – The Secret Life of a Pothead.

"Okay, let's do this!" Bern said, as he finished his sweet-and-sour chicken. "I will take patient...um..." Bern scanned the thirteen stacks of papers spread out before him.

It was like trying to pick the winning lottery numbers. Which patient would reveal more information about a complex, formidable plot?

"Number four...I'll take that one," Bern said decidedly.

"I will take...um...number thirteen," Anna said, picking up the small stack of papers.

"Lazy?" Bern asked with a laugh.

Anna had picked the shortest stack with the least number of papers. Patient Thirteen was the one she hadn't found to write on her original list. The stack of papers for Patient Thirteen was about half the size of the other patients'.

"No, I just like this one because it's different. I figure maybe we will find something significant here since it isn't like the others. Maybe this patient died halfway through the testing or something!"

"I'm going to buy you a pipe, a magnifying glass, and a deerstalker hat," Bern said sarcastically.

"A what hat?" Anna asked, confused.

"A deerstalker...a Sherlock Holmes hat."

"That's what those are called?" Anna asked, thinking Bern was making it up.

"Yep...speaking of pipes, I'm going to smoke."

Bern got up and walked to his bedroom. When he returned, he had a thick, colorful glass pipe in his hand. The pipe was blue and gray with frosted hews and tiny bubbles that had been suspended in time, as the glass had cooled and hardened around them. The colors twisted together playfully down the center. It wasn't just a pipe; it was also a beautiful piece of hand-blown glass art.

Bern had already packed the bowl of the pipe with fresh marijuana, after a thorough cleaning. He handed the heavy glass piece to Anna, along with his lighter.

Anna looked closely at the hand-blown piece of art. She admired the amazing colors and the feel of the smooth glass in her hands.

"Wait? How do I do this? I've never smoked out of a...glass...pipe...thing." Anna looked at it closely, noting how cool, to the touch the thick glass felt.

"Hold it at this end, cover this hole with your thumb, put your mouth on this end, and breathe in while you hold the flame above the weed."

Before Bern even had a chance to start his last sentence, Anna had inhaled a large cloud of smoke.

"Or...you just grab it and do it like you already know how. Sometimes I think you just pretend to be naïve and innocent," Bern said, lowering his eyebrows and grinning.

"What? I had never smoked anything at all before the other night with you. I have never even held one of these glass pipes in my life!" Anna said, playfully defending herself.

"Well, it didn't seem like you needed any help. Maybe you are secretly a pothead. Maybe there is a whole other side to you that I have never seen. Do I know the *real* Anna?" Bern asked sarcastically. He flirtatiously nudged Anna as he looked into her confused brown eyes.

What's wrong?" he asked, when he noticed that her expression had changed. Anna suddenly looked alarmingly serious, as she stared intently into Bern's sparkling blue eyes.

Anna inhaled more smoke.

Do I know who you are? she thought. Once again, Anna was faced with doubt about who her best friend really was. She was also faced with doubt about who *she* really was.

"Are you okay?" Bern asked again, pulling Anna out of her deep thought.

"Yeah, oh, yeah," she said, nervously laughing. She was definitely high. She felt paranoid.

"Well, come on! These things aren't going to chronologically sort themselves," Bern said, pointing to the other eleven stacks of records.

As Bern and Anna put the records in order, they made notes of dates and events. When they finished a patient's stack, they wrote a brief timeline on the top page below the large patient number they had written earlier.

"Patient number three...done!" Bern said, as he finished the next to last stack. He looked out at the stacks in front of him, now each with a brief chronological timeline of events on top.

Anna finished the final few pages of patient number eight, the very last patient.

"Well, nothing jumped out at me—not even with that different patient, number thirteen, with half the number of pages. I really thought that patient was going to be the one," Anna said in a discouraged voice.

"Well, we did it still. Let's put them all side by side and see if we can figure anything out," Bern said, grabbing his keys and walking out the front door. He then went around to the side of his building to a little detached garage, where he unlocked the door with his key.

The small building had lots of interesting old stuff inside it. There was a riding lawnmower; eight boxes, still unopened from when he had moved in; numerous collectibles; an old motorcycle; a large red tool chest, and one large dry-erase board.

Bern grabbed the dry-erase board and walked out, locking the door behind him.

He walked in, carrying the dry-erase board at his side, and Nickels ran over to greet him, curious about what new thing he was bringing back in.

Anna was in the living room, pacing and biting her nails.

"Are you sure you're okay?" Bern asked.

"Yeah, I'm just really nervous or something ever since I smoked that weed. It's making me feel different," Anna said, looking at her fingernail from which she had just bitten a sliver.

"I'll get you a glass of water," Bern said, leaning the dry-erase board against the wall.

"Thanks," Anna said, as she took a seat on the couch.

"So...do you want to call it a night?" Bern asked from the kitchen.

"No. I want to lay this all out. We are so close; why stop now?"

"Okay." Bern brought the water to Anna.

"Thanks," she said again before taking a big gulp.

Bern took Anna's painting down from the easel and set it on the floor.

"I really like it. You did a good job," he said, still looking at her painting. "I would buy it."

Oddly enough, Bern's insignificantly generic words put Anna at ease.

He carried the easel into the living room and set it up in front of the paper stacks, facing the couch.

On the board, they listed the patient numbers and the brief timeline summaries, as well as the number of pages in their records and the date range of the records from first to last.

"The only thing I noticed was that there were some tests kept failing for all of the patients. I didn't understand the procedure that they were having done. Based on where the probes were placed during different tests, they were definitely working with declarative memory and, more specifically, episodic memory," Anna said very scientifically.

"What?" Bern was confused. His stoned mind was completely lost, unable to decipher the scientific terms she had used.

"Remember procedural memory? Well, declarative memory is like, the opposite of that—your memories that are made of facts and knowledge. A subcategory of that is episodic memory. Those are the memories of events, like a brother's wedding, falling off a bike, or a funeral that you will never forget. You can relive those memories and experience the details all over again. This is what they were testing," Anna stated.

"It looks like that short stack 266200, patient number thirteen, had some major event in the middle of the project. From what I can tell, that patient lost all their personal memories...at least all of their episodic memories. The rest had similar events, but not the dramatic brain pattern change that I saw afterwards on this one." She pointed.

"Something happened in the middle there...some sort of brain damage," Dr. Smith continued.

"Something to note is that Patient Five had a similar occurrence, around the same time, but with less memory loss after...maybe two years of loss, judging by the data in the reports. It's almost like they are being forced to lose their memory. Some event in the middle is forcing memory loss.

There isn't anything in the records actually saying that though." She frowned.

"See this test here?" Anna pointed to a specific report.

"This is testing for episodic memories. It monitors how much of the brain those types of memories are using. Something happens right here, and then it drops in size—the equivalent of about two years of memories...completely gone. The other odd thing on this one is that, right after that event, the report shows no memories for about half an hour.
Zero...nothing...complete memory loss. Then it looks like they get restored but are missing those two years. I don't understand that thirty-minute gap...one hundred percent to zero percent to ninety-four percent. That shouldn't be possible, but a few other patients show the same pattern."

"Some of these patients show slight changes or data loss in the frontal lobe during testing. This may mean the patients would have experienced changes in their personalities or behavior afterwards."

Anna rambled on with facts and more big scientific words.

"Okay, so what does all this mean in layman's terms?" Bern asked.

"It means that I think these people had their memories intentionally altered. To me, it looks like the memory loss was definitely because of whatever they were doing these tests for. Memories don't just disappear like that!" Anna explained.

"Some of those patients' memory events line up down to the exact second. To me, that means they were triggered somehow." She spoke in a very serious tone.

"So what does that mean?" Bern asked, still not quite sure if he understood.

"I don't know yet. We need to figure out what procedure was taking place. We need the procedure reports more than these test results. See…doctors will complete a procedure report and then run tests to track any changes. One patient did have some extra testing on them—number six. There were tests that talked about an implanted remote upload device and some kind of data transmission. It was nothing like I have ever seen before and oddly, I don't see any of the memory-loss patterns for this patient, like the others. I do want to read this one more closely." Anna picked up the stack of papers for Patient Six.

She flipped a few pages into the report.

'The mem data transmission device has been functioning as expected. The data has been transferred successfully, in real time, without any corruption.'

"It almost looks like they were testing a device that uploads information directly from the brain," Anna said, as she kept reading in awe.

'The reverse data loss is still occurring. This is keeping the image as an exact copy at all times. We are going to continue advanced testing in an attempt to find a way to only add data, transferring every memory individually. Ideally, a 100% lossless upload device is what we are testing for.'

"Wow, they were! Bern, they were testing some kind of wireless implant that would transmit memory data right from the brain of this patient! Can you imagine that? It's like a constant backup of your brain!" Anna explained.

"That doesn't make sense though! That's not what they were doing! Let me read it," Bern said, taking the report from Anna's hands.

Anna felt offended that Bern did not believe her. She was a neurologist; this was what she did! She didn't question his knowledge of art or illicit drugs.

His outburst did not help the way she was feeling about him at all—the convicted criminal with dark secrets.

"And on that note...I think I'm done for the night. It's getting late; I can look at this tomorrow," Anna said, yawning.

"Yeah, I could use some sleep too," Bern said, also yawning, triggered by Anna's. "You know what I just thought about? There is never a doctor's name in those reports. That's what we need to find—one of the doctors that the reports were for. Maybe we missed something," Bern said.

Anna nodded and said, "I'll look tomorrow. I'm going to stay at my house tonight. I can take a cab home from here."

"I can drive you," Bern said insistently.

"No, you've done enough. Thank you so much for everything." Anna smiled oddly.

Bern noted that she seemed distant tonight.

"Okay, well, let me know if you need anything." Bern got his phone out and called for a ride.

Anna gathered what few things she had at Bern's house and put them in a bag.

She sat next to Bern outside on the steps, waiting for the cab to arrive. They sat in silence. An emotional wave swelled up inside Anna.

She thought about the detective's words once more.

Be careful who you trust...especially when it comes to guys that have a history of criminal violence."

The cab pulled up.

"Have a good night," Bern said, waving.

Anna waved back. The taxi drove her home.

Chapter 18 – The Other Apartment.

"FUUUUUUUUUUCK!" Anna screamed at the top of her lungs.

She had pushed her front door open with her foot, after she'd walked up and found that it hadn't been closed all the way. Under her breath, she blamed Bern the criminal, the last one out the other night, for not shutting it.

Anna quickly backed out into the hallway, fumbling to get her phone from her purse.

Beep! Beep! went the phone's voice command prompt.

"Call Bern!" Anna yelled.

Her phone dialed Bern's number.

"Hey, what's up?" Bern answered nonchalantly.

"Bern! Someone broke into my house!" Anna said, panicked.

"What? Do NOT go in there! Hang up and call the police! I'm on my way!" Bern ran to his midnight-black Porsche and got in. He started the engine, to the sound of a sexy, low rumbling. He slowly pulled out onto the street and then pushed the gas pedal to the floor, making the tires smoke for a split second. With Bern sitting behind the wheel, the beautifully crafted machine was at 60mph in less than five seconds.

It took Bern only about fifteen minutes to get to Anna's house—less time than it was taking the police, who hadn't yet arrived.

Bern found a hysterical Anna in the hallway.

"I can't find Ruffles! I went in there and looked! He's gone!" she said frantically.

"Anna! You were not supposed to go in there! We are waiting for the police!" Bern scolded.

"I couldn't help it! What the fuck, Bern! I lost David *and* Ruff! Bern! Where the fuck is heaven now, goddamn it?!" Anna screamed and walked back into the apartment, dodging Bern's attempt to grab her arm.

Inside, Anna completely lost control. Her arms swung at anything she could get close to. Her stuff was already all over the place, cluttering the floor. Papers, books, and random contents of drawers had all been tossed around by the intruder.

Bern's eyes started to water. His heart broke for Anna, a woman who had already been through so much.

She collapsed on the floor, surrounded by clutter, and

curled up into a ball. Bern sat down beside her. He didn't really know what to do. He stroked her hair as she mumbled and sobbed.

"Ruff...why? I don't understand...Bern, fuck all this..."

"Shhhhh," Bern said, as he pulled her onto his lap. He held Anna tight—the tightest she had ever been held in her life. She continued to sob.

"I didn't call the police," Anna said softly.

"What?! Why?!" Bern asked, baffled by her comment.

"Because this person was looking for something, Bern. They didn't steal anything valuable. I'm scared! What were they looking for?" Anna looked up at Bern with beautiful but defeated brown eyes. She had calmed down quite a bit but was still sobbing heavily.

"I have no idea," Bern said, shaking his head.

"I don't trust the police, Bern. You have to be careful who you trust, and I definitely don't trust them," Anna said, sliding off Bern's lap as she sat up.

"What are you going to do?" Bern asked, as Anna stood up.

"I just want to get out of here. I'll look through this...fucking mess later!" Anna kicked an overturned dining chair.

"Fuuuuuuuuuuuck!!!" she screamed.

She stopped and looked down at the floor, where a glowing light shone through a sheet of paper. Anna moved the paper and found a cell phone. The screen was lit up, but it was locked.

"This isn't mine," she said, looking at Bern with big, watery, bloodshot brown eyes.

Anna swiped the screen with her finger.

"It's got a pass code," she said, disappointed.

"I'm sure there's software that can get past the code. I will get it unlocked," Bern said confidently.

"I bet it belonged to the person who went through my house! How else would it have gotten here? This may even be the phone that belongs to David's killer! OH MY GOD! BERN!" Anna said, swiftly jumping to conclusions.

"Wow! That would be crazy!" Bern said in amazement.

"Let's get out of here so you can break this pass code," Anna said, sniffling.

"This may not be related to David. This probably happened during the funeral. It happens a lot. People will watch the paper for funeral announcements and then break into the family members' homes during the funeral. They knew you wouldn't be here," Bern said, trying to play down the event as a somewhat normal criminal occurrence in the city.

"Why would the same people be looking for something that David had and then search your place? It doesn't make much sense," Bern added.

"But look! They didn't take valuables." Anna pointed to a small side table by the front door. It had some mail, a couple of rings, two bracelets, a necklace, and three twenty-dollar bills.

"I don't know; maybe they were scared off."

"I'm not going to call the police. There isn't even anything missing that I know of. I can't call them because someone came in my house and messed it up. Plus, they think David's murder was a random break-in by a junkie looking to score. They will think we are some sort of crazy conspiracy theorists. They aren't going to see the big picture. They would take that phone and then we couldn't get information from it ourselves," Anna explained between sobs.

"Good point," Bern agreed.

Anna was still very upset. She just wanted to find her cat and then get out of there.

"Will you help me look for Ruff one more time? I want to get the hell out of here," Anna said despairingly.

"Yeah, let's look everywhere." Bern started moving anything that was in the way. They looked under beds, chairs, the couch...anywhere a scared cat may possibly be.

They found nothing.

After about an hour of searching Anna said "I give up. He isn't here. Let's just go." She started to cry again.

"Maybe he'll come back. Has he ever been gone before?" Bern asked, hopefully.

"Nope. He has never gotten out," Anna said.

"I'm sorry," said Bern, losing what little hope he'd had for her.

Anna gathered a few things. As she started to grab a couple of outfits, she began crying again. Most of her clothes had been pulled from the drawers, leaving her to rummage through piles of mixed fabrics lying around her bedroom.

"This is fucked up, Bern!" Anna said. "I feel so violated. I feel like this isn't even my fucking home anymore. Now it's just another thing in my life tainted by David's death. And what am I going to do without Ruffles?!" Anna's crying once again turned into loud wailing and uncontrollable sobbing, making any other words she tried to speak indiscernible.

Bern gave Anna a hug and said, "Come on. Let's go." He knew that the longer she stayed there, the more upset she would get. "We can deal with this later," he added.

Anna shook her head and grabbed the small cardboard box into which she had put some clothes and a few belongings.

Bern put his arm around her as they walked out of her apartment.

Anna carried her small box of possessions down to Bern's car and got in it. She put her seatbelt on and began to cry again. Bern put his hand on her knee. She leaned across the car and rested her head on his shoulder.

Anna's life had changed completely in the past couple of weeks. All her routines, her schedule, her entire world had been shaken and then turned upside down. She hadn't been back to work since David had been taken to the hospital.

"You know, if it wasn't for you, I would be a mess from everything. I know you're the only person who truly cares," Anna said, grabbing Bern's arm.

"Awww, that's not true! What about Stan?"

"I haven't seen him since the funeral and only heard from him a handful of times. It makes me really sad. He has always been there for me. I think he is just having a really hard time with David's death himself. I am probably more worried about him than he is about me. I'm sure he knows that I'm in good hands," Anna said with a half-smile.

"Honestly, you are pretty much the only thing I have left...you and my sanity...until that's gone, which will probably be pretty soon judging by the way my life is going." Anna laughed a little and started biting her nails.

"Ouch!" Anna said, as she bit a nail too short. Her finger started to bleed.

"I don't really have much to lose anymore. I still have a job, but that was my entire life before. I feel like all that has changed. I don't love my work like I used to. I think I was just so content in my routine and my life. I don't think I can go back to that. It reminds me of my ex. Did I ever tell you about my ex?"

"Not really," Bern said. He had gotten used to Anna's mood swings. She had already gone from hysterical to chatty during the car ride home. She would swing back to the sad end when they got to his house; he was sure of it.

"Well, he wanted me to be something I wasn't." Anna went on about her ex-fiancé.

"He wanted me to be more exciting. Imagine that…me…not exciting enough! My parents loved him, but I couldn't take it. I just don't understand how someone can expect you to be something that you aren't. You know what though? I'm not even sure that I knew who I was…or know who I am now, for that matter. I kind of feel like I'm missing and need to find myself, you know?"

"Well, let's start here. What do you love doing?" Bern

asked inquisitively, adding "…besides wearing cat sweaters and being lonely," under his breath. Bern knew that Anna was at the peak of her emotional downswing; joking seemed like a bad idea. She could crash into an emotional wreck at any second.

"Painting! Bern, can I paint with you tonight?" Anna asked with surprising enthusiasm that seemed to come out of nowhere.

"Always!" Bern said reassuringly.

"Thanks." Anna smiled.

"Speaking of exes, what ever happened to Alice?" Anna asked

Bern laughed. "Exes? Ha! I'm not even sure if I had sex with her or not. I never heard from her again. I told you her number stopped working."

"That was it, huh? I'm surprised she hasn't gotten a hold of you. I mean you are a local celebrity artist…not hard to find," Anna noted.

"Yeah. Oh well. I guess coke-binge Alice is gone forever."

Bern made Anna laugh.

Chapter 19 – Who He Really Is.

Anna and Bern walked inside his house. Nickels greeted them, frantically wiggling. His plastic hamburger squeaked in his mouth.

Anna carried her small cardboard box and set it on the coffee table. She stood and looked down into the box, staring at each item that made up its contents—all pretty meaningless. This is what she chose to bring with her. In a way, she kind of felt as if it was all she had left.

Anna continued to stare as tears started to fall inside the box. Finally, she burst into a full-flowing rush of tears.

Bern had already gone and gotten a box of tissues. He knew the minute he saw her staring down into the box that the torrent was coming. She was his best friend, and he knew her well.

Anna sat down on the couch. Bern sat down next to her and put his arm around her. He talked to her until she was calm again.

"Just a few days ago, I was planning on going sailing with David. I thought my life was perfect. And now..."

Anna's crying became harder again. She blew her nose loudly.

"Now...I feel like I have nothing!" Anna covered her face with her hands.

"You have me. I'm right here," Bern said sincerely.

"Thanks," she whispered.

Bern talked to Anna until he had her back on the emotional upswing, telling her that now she would have the chance to find herself. Most people never have that chance, so Bern considered her lucky in a way.

"Can we paint now?" Anna asked, not really wanting to talk anymore.

"Let's do it!" he responded. Bern knew very well from experience how therapeutic painting could be.

He got Anna a new canvas and realized the other easel was still currently being used to solve a mystery. A dry-erase board. He looked at the large board with all the data on it.

"What about all this?" he asked, pointing to the board.

"I don't know. I don't care. I don't even want to think about it anymore! Let's paint!" Anna said persuasively.

"Okay!" Bern said, taking the dry-erase board off the easel.

He set them both up, giving Anna a bigger canvas than the last time. Then, Bern grabbed his ashtray and a new joint from the cigar box.

"Okay, you're ready. Brushes. Paints," he said, pointing to both.

"I'm excited!" Anna said, carefully selecting a brush.

Bern held out the new joint. Anna looked at it and smiled. She took the joint and the lighter, lit, and puffed. She handed the joint back to Bern.

"Bern, you said that you have a gun, right?" Anna asked, as she stroked a long smear of red across the formerly blank canvas.

"Yep," Bern said, dotting yellow areas with brown paint on his work in progress.

"Is it illegal?" Anna asked hesitantly.

"That's a weird question... It's not illegal! But it's not registered," Bern said with a smirk.

"Oh-" she paused.

"Have you ever been to jail?" Anna asked. She had that instant feeling of sheer terror, realizing there was no way to take the question back. What was said was said. What was asked was asked.

"Ha! They tell me I was!" Bern laughed, taking a drag off the joint and passing it back to Anna.

"I don't remember it; I only know the small parts of the stories the police have told me. It was when I was younger. I guess I got into a few fights or something."

Anna was somewhat shocked at his openness.

"Well, didn't you ever want to read your old police reports? Aren't you curious?"

"No, not really." Bern continued to paint. "I don't really care what I used to be like. I am who I am right now, so why look back, you know?" Bern smiled at Anna. "I can't go back to yesterday, because I was a different person then."

Anna could see who Bern really was, and he wasn't those stories the detective had told. He was Bern.

"It must be crazy to not know who you used to be," Anna said, thinking about the whole scenario. "I have so many memories."

"I get by…." Bern trailed off.

They smoked and painted in near silence. Anna was content with the answers she got. She trusted Bern. He wasn't hiding anything. He was her best friend.

Anna looked at Bern and smiled. "I want you to teach me how to shoot a gun."

"We can go tomorrow, if you want," Bern offered.

"We'll see," Anna said, yawning. "I think I'm going to go to sleep. I've had a rough day."

"Well, that's an understatement." Bern responded.

She gave him a hug and thanked him again for everything he had done for her. Then she went and lay down on the couch.

Anna was on her back, staring at the ceiling, as she thought about everything. She thought about David and Ruffles; missing them made her heart ache. She thought about her intruded-upon apartment and how violated she felt. She thought about her job and the fact that it wasn't as rewarding as it used to be.

Anna could hear Bern's music still playing quietly while he continued to paint. She lay silently on the couch and listened to the words.

"...Take your hand away from your face, so I can see everything you are and everything you used to be."

The strum of the acoustic guitar was soothing.

She rolled over and watched Bern paint.

Anna was asleep within minutes.

Bern painted for a couple more hours. He made sure Anna was asleep and then he grabbed his keys, a few large black garbage bags, and some rubber gloves.

"I'll be back, Nickels," he whispered on his way out the front door.

Bern the artist quietly slipped away into the night.

Chapter 20 – The Gun Range.

Bern and Anna woke up fairly early. Bern ordered breakfast from a café that delivered.

The two sat by the pool in the morning sun, eating breakfast and talking.

"I need to go clean my place sometime," Anna said.

"Let me know. We can go anytime."

"Let's take a look at those files again first. I've been avoiding them," Anna confessed.

Anna and Bern reviewed the files again. They found nothing new.

"I want to know what they got or were looking for," Anna said, frustrated. "If only we knew who one of these doctors were."

"I bet one of those doctors is David," Bern said.

"Yeah, but who knows? We don't have anything. I don't know what to think anymore," Anna said in despair.

"Let's take a break and go to my place, if you're up for it," Anna said.

"Let's go," Bern said with a smile. He was always so easy with Anna.

They finished up breakfast, and Bern drove them to her house.

She nervously walked into her violated apartment ahead of Bern.

Anna gasped loudly.

"Bern! What the fuck?!" she yelled.

Anna spun around and punched Bern on his shoulder.

Her apartment was near perfect again.

"It actually wasn't that bad," he said very factually. "It was mostly loose papers. I put all of those in the two garbage bags for you to go through. The rest was mostly just putting your clothes back in the drawers and tidying up."

"Thank you so much! It's like my old apartment again! It still makes me sad, but I'm glad it's not like it was yesterday," Anna said, looking around at everything. Most items were now back in their proper places.

"You are amazing!" she said, kissing Bern on his cheek.

"Well, I guess we can go over and clean up David's place since we really have no work to do here. I brought his keys," Anna said.

The two headed over to David's apartment.

"Let me go in first and look around." Bern said at the front door, putting his hand up to hold Anna back. His fear was, that the scene left behind had the potential to be gruesome. Thankfully, the worst he found was a dry pool of blood.

"Just wait out there for a minute." He called out. He covered the crimson spot on the hardwood floor with an area rug and set the knocked over office chair right side up on top of it. He would call and have a crime scene recovery company come clean it later. There was no reason to even consider Anna doing it.

Bern went back to the front door. "Okay, it's safe. It's just really messy in here."

They got to work. Bern straightened the place up while Anna cleaned out the refrigerator. They ordered lunch, took a break to eat, and then went back to another hour of cleaning up.

"Well, it looks good in here," Bern said, looking around. "You want to go learn to shoot? I grabbed David's gun for you," Bern asked.

"Yes! I don't have bullets though… Do they have those there?" Anna asked.

"Yeah, they will have bullets for that gun. It's a pretty common caliber at this range."

"I'm nervous," Anna whispered, as she bit her lip and looked at Bern. Her seductive brown eyes twinkled.

"You'll be fine. I'll show you exactly how to shoot. I will be right there with you, I promise."

It was about a forty-five-minute drive to the edge of the state park where the gun range was. The location was about as rural as you could get that close to the city. When they got to the range, they could see hawks circling in the distance. They sat for a while in the parking lot and watched the majestic bids as they flew closer and continued to glide directly above them.

"What do you think they're looking for?" Bern asked.

"Prey, I guess."

"Speaking of prey... let's go shoot things! Come on, don't be scared!" Bern said, taking Anna's gun for her.

They walked up to the counter, and Bern set the guns down.

"Hey, Charlie! Can we get six dozen rounds of .9mm and six dozen rounds of .45 caliber?"

"Sure thing, Bern," the man behind the counter said.

He stacked the boxes of bullets on a tray on the counter. Bern grabbed the tray and walked to the first open stall. He set the bullets down on the bench and walked back for the guns. Noticing that Anna was still standing where he had left her, he motioned for her to follow.

Anna was completely intimidated. The place echoed with what seemed like hundreds of loud gunshots.

Bern noticed her expression and handed her a set of protective earmuffs.

"Thank you so much," she said, putting the cups over her ears. The muffling of all the gunshots made her relax almost instantly.

Bern showed Anna how to load bullets in the clip and how to put the clip in the gun. He showed her the safety and explained how to use the sights.

"Now the fun starts," Bern said with a devilish grin.

He stood behind Anna, each one of his arms wrapped around her sides from behind. His hands were on top of hers, the gun grip underneath them.

"So, when you are holding the gun out, you are looking with one eye down at the sights, lining the two up," Bern said, as he steered Anna to the center of the target's chest.

"Now, when you're ready, squeeze the trigger."

Anna could smell Bern. It was a scent that she loved. She closed her eyes for a second and breathed in deeply.

She opened her eyes and lined the sight of the gun

back up with the center of the target's chest.

She pulled the trigger.

BANG!

The gun kicked back fiercely, and Anna was jolted backwards, causing her head to snap forward quickly. She immediately felt Bern's body against her back. She felt his muscles flex as they stopped her body from moving any further. His strong body easily absorbed the impact. He held her tight.

Bern laughed. "Pretty big kick, huh?"

Anna looked at him, and with an astonished gaze, replied, "That was fucking awesome!"

"Let's do it again!" she said with uncontrollable excitement. "I want you to help me again." Her tone was almost demanding.

Bern walked up behind Anna. He could smell her hair—a scent that was calming and inviting. He ran his hands down her arms, leaving goose bumps behind. He wrapped his fingers around her hands.

She held the gun very tightly. The goose bumps that she had gotten from Bern's hands made her tingle. She could feel his body against hers. She stretched her arms to pull him closer. She pressed her back into his chest. It felt amazing. She took a deep breath and aimed the sight on the center of the target's chest.

BANG!

Bern's body stiffened and his muscles flexed, but Anna barely moved. She could feel Bern's arms against the sides of her breasts. He was right there with her, just as he had promised.

She took a deep breath and said, "Okay, I got this."

"Are you sure?" Bern asked, stepping away.

"Yep. It's all about how you stand."

Anna pointed the gun at the head of the silhouette target. She found the center in the sights.

Her heart raced. She pulled the trigger.

BANG!

The gun pushed hard against her hands as it recoiled. Anna was braced solidly and held her shoulders firm. Her body barely reacted to the explosion of the lethal weapon. She hit her mark at the center of the target's head.

Her heart continued to race. She felt more alive than ever before.

Awakened.

She closed her eyes and took a deep breath. The smell was unmistakable. Gunpowder.

"Amazing! I love it," Anna said, looking at the

smoking barrel.

"Very nice," Bern said, as he clapped softly.

"I had a good teacher. Thanks for bringing me," Anna said with a wink.

"You're a natural. I barely did anything."

Anna and Bern took turns shooting through rounds of bullets. They laughed and talked for a couple of hours.

Throughout the afternoon, Anna continued to prove she was a better shot than Bern, much to their surprise. They compared their two final targets, and Anna definitely shot more accurately.

"Man, you are really good! Are you sure you never shot a gun before?" Bern asked, looking at Anna's precisely placed holes in the black silhouette.

"Nope. Never!" Anna assured him with a shake of her head.

"Well, you pick things up really quick. Either way, I'm sure you're going to feel a lot safer now," Bern said.

"Yeah, this was amazing! I'm going to get my concealed weapons permit," she said excitedly.

They packed up their things and headed for the car.

They decided on steak for dinner, so they headed in the direction of a favorite steakhouse. Once they got there, they sat down and started looking at the menus.

"It's really cold in here," Anna said, as she rubbed her arms.

"I'll be right back." Bern got up from the table.

The waitress came and took the drink orders. "Two waters. We're still looking at the menus. Thanks," Anna said.

Anna sat alone and thought about David. He probably loved that gun. She heard him talk about the shooting range a lot. She pictured him at the range, shooting the beautiful piece of mechanical art—a handsomely fatal weapon.

Bern walked back to the table and handed Anna a sweater. "I had it in the car."

Anna put the sweater on and breathed in deeply. The smell was comforting and familiar. It smelled just like Bern.

"Thank you. I mean, for everything—being my best friend, always caring about me, teaching me how to shoot…" Anna said, making her right hand into a gun. "I can't wait to get my concealed weapons permit! I'm so excited!"

As sad as Anna had been for so many days, she finally realized that she was actually free from everything. She could do anything she wanted. Anna thought about how the silver lining of losing everything was the freedom of having nothing to lose. She was on a definite emotional upswing. Bern knew, so he played along.

"Awwwwwwww! No more sleeping at my house anymore! You will feel safe without me now," Bern said, with an exaggerated pouty bottom lip.

"Well, maybe if you ask nicely, I'll still spend the night," Anna said, blushing a little as she bit her lip.

"You're no bother. I like having you around." Bern said with a playful nudge.

Thankfully the two had been able to coexist with little effort. Bern had never had anyone around like that. It made him feel needed. Wanted in a way that was different from past women he had known. Admired for him being who he was. Not for the money. Not for the lifestyle. Not for the fame. Not for the parties.

"Can we paint tonight?" Anna asked quickly, ending the awkward silence.

"You know I paint, like almost every day, right?" You know that's what I do for work don't you? Do you even know me?" Bern joked.

"Shut up." She shook her head and laughed.

"You really love it, huh?" Bern questioned her newfound passion.

"Yes! I do! I feel in control and free at the same time. It lets me escape!" Anna replied enthusiastically.

"Let's go do it!" Bern said, getting the server's attention and requesting the check.

They left the restaurant and went to Bern's house. The paintings that they had started were still on the easels. Anna grabbed the ashtray and the cigar box from the kitchen counter and set them both down on the small table by the easels. She then set the paints up exactly like Bern did.

Bern was in the kitchen pouring two glasses of red wine. He walked over and handed one to Anna.

"Mmmmmm," she said, as she took a sip. "This is so good! What is it?"

"Oh, it's from a small vineyard out in Napa Valley."

"It's amazing! How much was that bottle?"

"Six fifty," Bern said.

"Six fifty?! Like six hundred and fifty...dollars...not six dollars and fifty cents?"

"Yep." Bern nodded.

"Oh my God! How much was that other bottle I drank?" Anna asked in shock, afraid of the answer.

"Oh, that one was only three hundred I think...maybe three fifty," Bern said, trying to remember.

"That's crazy! Seriously who buys a six-hundred-and-fifty-dollar bottle of wine?" Anna asked.

"People who like good wine," Bern said factually.

"Well, it is the best wine I have ever tasted, I'll give it that...but still..." Anna had already finished half of her glass.

"Come on! Let's paint," Bern said, grabbing a brush.

They painted for hours. Bern only stopped a few minutes in to put some quiet music on.

"I love yours!" Anna said, finally breaking the hours of near silence. "Did you see mine?"

Bern had been so focused that he hadn't looked at Anna's for a while.

"Wow, it looks amazing! You are really good. I tell you what...you make eight more paintings that good and I can sell them for probably more than you make in one year now. Then, you could be doing what you love!"

"Are you serious? Don't mess around like that!" Anna scolded.

"No, I'm serious; you really are a natural. I can't believe you've never painted before," Bern said convincingly.

Could she just quit her work that she had loved for so long? She wasn't enjoying it as much as she used to, and with everything that had happened, she didn't have much desire to go back.

Why not paint eight more? After all, I love doing it, Anna thought, as she stood looking at her painting.

"I think I want to sleep in a real bed tonight," she said.

"You can sleep in my bed," Bern said, looking at Anna.

Anna's heart nearly exploded. A million thoughts ran through her head. Anna didn't know what to say. Her mind raced with fantasies. Steamy sexual anticipation. She didn't know if she was ready for this.

"I'll sleep in the bed in the guest bedroom...and you can sleep in my bed," Bern elaborated, as he lit their second joint of the night.

"Oh, yeah, no...you don't have to do that. I'll sleep in the guest bedroom. I like that bed anyway," Anna said, laughing nervously.

"Remember, that lizard in there can be loud sometimes, and it jumps...just a heads-up so it doesn't startle you," Bern said, referring to a golden-crested gecko that was in a beautiful-looking tank in the guest bedroom.

The exotic tank was full of live plants and moss. It was like its own little rainforest ecosystem, complete with a small waterfall. At night, a black heat light shone above the tank, causing a very faint purple glow in the room.

"Speaking of bed...it's late. I think I'm going to go lie down now. I'm exhausted," Anna said to Bern. "But look...I can start painting number three tomorrow," she said with a wink.

"It looks amazing!" Bern said, as he gave Anna a good-night hug, then watched her walk away.

She walked to the guest bedroom and climbed into the bed, in a place that now felt like home. She closed her eyes and thought about the way it felt with Bern behind her when she had the gun in her hand.

"Hey," Bern said , leaning in the bedroom doorway. "I just wanted to say, I really like having you around."

"Awe. I like being around."

"You can toss me my sweater." Bern pointed to the balled up clothing on the bed

"No I'm keeping it. I like it." Anna grabbed it and held it close.

"You're so funny. You can keep it then. Sweet dreams."

"Goodnight Bern."

Anna could still smell Bern on the sweater he let her borrow. She took it to bed so she could inhale the comforting scent while she fell asleep. Anna loved when she borrowed his sweaters. She shivered for a split second, after she inhaled deeply. Chills ran across her body.

She felt different. She felt high. She felt free.

With a smile on her face, Anna quickly fell asleep.

Chapter 21 – The Box.

Anna walked out of the guest bedroom and yawned.

"Well, good morning, sleeping beauty! I thought I was going to have to come in there and make sure you were still breathing," Bern said jokingly.

"What time is it?" Anna squinted from the sun coming through the glass doors.

"I don't know...eleven-ish," Bern said.

"How long have you been up?" she asked as she yawned again.

"A couple of hours. I've been looking at all these papers and the dry-erase board. You know what I figured out?" Bern asked.

"What?" Anna inquired with anticipation.

"Nothing. I didn't find a damn thing," Bern said.

"I hate you!" Anna said, smacking Bern's chest. "I'm going to get in the pool. You coming?"

"Yeah, I'll get in," Bern said, heading to the bedroom

for his swim trunks.

"Oh...and I'm having a hard time getting past the lock on that phone you found. I tried for a while this morning but couldn't get past it. I messaged a guy I know; he will be able to help us get in."

"Oh awesome! I hope he can!" Anna said excitedly. "I'm going to go get my swimsuit on." Anna walked back to the guest bedroom.

"Damn!" she said to herself, realizing that she had forgotten to get a swimsuit from her place again. She looked through the underwear that she had brought. She felt like her best option would be a silky black pair with a matching bra.

She put them on and looked in the mirror. The black silk panties were very cheeky but not too overly revealing. The matching black silk bra pushed her perky breasts up, making them look more full and perfectly round. The black silk made her exposed skin look radiant. The dark color contrasted against her white skin beautifully, like a black-and-white film. She was sexy.

Anna looked at the gun, still on the side table next to the bed. She walked over and picked it up. It was the same jet-black color as the sexy lingerie she was wearing. Anna turned back to the mirror.

"I am sexy!" she said to herself in the reflection. She was that woman now. Anna was free.

Maybe the gun is a little too much, she thought with a laugh. She put the gun back down and walked out of the bedroom.

Bern nearly choked on a mouthful of orange juice when he saw Anna walking up in the seductive-looking lingerie.

"You forgot a swimsuit, I take it?" Bern said, admiring Anna's luscious body.

"Yep! You're okay with this, right?" Anna asked with a grin.

"Of course! You look amazing! I'm not complaining!" Bern said, thinking of all the things he wanted to do to her.

He watched her walk out through the sliding glass doors. The black silk hugged the curves of her perfectly round ass.

Bern walked out behind Anna and watched her bare skin slowly go under the water as she descended the steps. She floated around seductively, dressed like a lingerie model. Her hair got wet and became alluringly messy.

"Come get in!"

"I will. I'm going to smoke first." Bern set the ashtray down on the table, grabbed a cigarette from the pack, and lit it.

Anna slowly walked up the steps and out of the pool. Drops of water beaded and rolled down her almost naked body. Her soaked bra caressed her breasts perfectly. The cool morning breeze made her nipples hard under the cool, wet, revealing silk.

Anna's black underwear clung seductively to her skin. Bern could see every curve as he stared lustfully. Every tiny detail underneath the smooth, black fabric was visible.

Bern was aroused. This was the sexiest-looking that he had ever seen his best friend. She was intoxicating.

Anna grabbed the cigarette. She looked at Bern sensually, her eyes appearing to burn with lust. She put the cigarette to her lips slowly. Her lips looked soft and inviting.

The end of the cigarette glowed orange. Anna playfully blew the smoke into Bern's face and handed him the cigarette back.

She turned and walked back toward the pool. Bern could tell Anna was trying to get him to watch—the way she moved her hips, the way she swung her arms. She was trying to be seductive, and Bern thought she was doing one hell of a good job of it. Shy, awkward Anna, it appeared, was gone today. She'd checked out.

She slowly slid back into the water and looked over at Bern. She knew he had been watching. "I want you...to get in the pool," she said, as she splashed water on her breasts with her hands. Her nipples were still poking through the cold black silk bra.

Bern finished up his smoke. "I'm coming!"

"Wait, whose keys are these?" Bern asked, lifting a set from the table.

"Those are David's. I must have set them there yesterday when I was out here," Anna replied. "Now get in the pool!"

"Wait, what is this key for?" Bern asked, pointing out a small, dark one.

"I don't know; they're not mine...now come get in!" Anna was becoming impatient.

"I will, just give me one second." Bern walked inside with the keys, leaving the sliding doors open behind him.

"Anna!" Bern yelled from inside.

"Oh my God, Bern, what?! If it's not about getting in the pool, I don't want to hear it!" she replied loudly.

"Anna, it fits!" Bern yelled.

"What are you talking about?" Anna asked, puzzled.

Bern ran outside. "This key! It fits the lock on the box!" Bern said excitedly.

"Are you kidding me?!" Anna screamed. "I'm so

excited! I always wanted to know what was in there!"

"I didn't open the box; that's for you to do. But I made sure the lock would open." Bern held the keys out.

"Sometimes what you are looking for is right in front of you the whole time," Anna said, looking at the small key that she hadn't paid any attention to before. "Of course David hid it in plain sight. I should have known."

"I don't know how we didn't notice that key on there. That should have been the first place we looked! Are you ready to go see what's inside?" Bern asked.

"Yes! I'm soooooo excited! I'm so glad you noticed the key and remembered the box." Anna grabbed a towel from the chair and dried off her body and what little clothing she had on.

Wrapping the towel around her, she walked inside with Bern.

There, the box sat on the coffee table, beautifully handcrafted, antique metal, wrapping around the sides of it. It looked magnificent. Anna ran her hand along the box that she had always been in love with.

She took the lock in one hand and held the key in the other.

The old lock clicked open with a firm turn of the key. Anna opened the box and saw a bundle of brown paper wrapped with twine. The bundle had a white envelope on top.

'To: Anna,' the envelope read in bold black ink. It was a beautifully artistic, loose handwritten script.

Anna looked over at Bern.

"It's...to me?" She looked shocked.

Here comes the emotional downswing, Bern thought.

Anna slid her finger under the flap and ripped the envelope open.

"Fuck!" she screamed.

The yell startled Bern, causing him to jump. Anna grabbed her finger with her other hand.

"That hurt so damn bad!" she said, sucking the blood off her finger.

"Ouch," Bern said squinting his eyes. "Paper cuts suck."

Anna slowly pulled a letter out of the envelope. Some of her crimson blood had now soaked into the top right corner of the page.

'Dear Anna,' the letter started in the same beautiful, handwritten black ink, which matched the envelope.

'I hope this letter finds you well. If you are reading this, then, unfortunately, it means something has happened to me.'

Anna continued to read aloud in confused wonder.

'Years ago, I promised your father I would keep a secret from you. A promise that I have kept until my death. I decided to provide you with this information to let you decide for yourself. I thought this was only fair, with my obligation to your father now complete. If you want to know the truth, that choice is now yours.

Anna, this is a big decision. I want you to think about it carefully. The things in this box will change your life forever. Nothing will ever be as it was. I know you are very smart and will make the right decision. I trust you. I have faith in you.

"What the hell?" Anna said, looking over at Bern with wide eyes.

"I have no idea," Bern shook his head. "This is crazy!"

Anna stared intently at the way the black liquid had stained the white paper, making up the words that she had just read.

Anna continued to silently contemplate whether she wanted to know the mysterious truth that the letter spoke about. The words were so foreboding. The truth sounded scary.

"What does this all mean?" she said out loud.

"Do you want me to look at it for you?" Bern offered.

"No. David intended it this way. I really need to make

this decision for myself and then accept the results either way," Anna said, explaining the way she felt.

Things already aren't the same. Things are completely different, she thought.

Anna felt that if she had read this a few weeks ago, then the warning would have meant more. But, what if it did change things from the way they were now? She searched for any logic that would help with such an important decision.

Anna had just finally started to feel like she was finding herself. The newly discovered love of painting, her shift in priorities, her focus on truly living and enjoying life, her whole perception of the world around her...everything had changed, mostly for the better. Anna didn't want her world to change again; she was just starting to fall in love with this marvelous new one.

Anna hadn't noticed that her towel had fallen down, and she was still only wearing the damp, black, silk bra.

Without a sound, she ripped open the brown paper that made up the bundle. On top was another white envelope, this time unsealed.

Under the envelope was what appeared to be a journal. It was an aged-looking, leather-bound book. The dark brown leather was soft and slightly weathered. Lying on top of the beautiful journal was a silver plastic card.

The silver card had red writing on it: 'Na#8rn!' The bright red letters seemed to jump off the plastic. Anna flipped the card over—nothing.

She opened the envelope and removed another handwritten letter. The style and ink were the same as the previous one. She unfolded the letter and started to read.

'You have decided to learn the truth and I'm proud of you. I do feel I need to give you one more chance. This will change your life completely. If you do not stop reading now, things will never be the same.'

Anna trembled and paused. "I don't know," she said, shaking her head. "I thought about everything and was pretty confident a minute ago...what do you think?" Anna turned to Bern.

He just shrugged his shoulders and shook his head. He had no idea what to tell her—not without knowing what 'the truth' was.

Without another word, Anna slowly turned to the second page; she had decided to continue reading.

'Anna, I have kept a secret from you. I have felt bad about this until the day I died. The choice is now yours to pursue the truth.

In this box are pieces that will paint a large picture of the truth about who you are. These items will paint a picture of who Anna really is.

Please take your time as you go through the contents.

Remember, above everything else, to always live your life. It's too short to waste.

Love always,

David

Anna bit her nails and looked at Bern. "I'm not sure I want to do this anymore."

"Honestly, there isn't much more that could change in your life right now. You seem to be a completely different person than you were just a couple of weeks ago. Think about that," Bern said reassuringly.

"I know; I have already thought about that. I really don't have anything to lose. If things change, at least I'm completely free to change with them," Anna said, explaining her conclusion to Bern.

Looking down in the box, she saw a patient record file sticking out from under the brown leather journal. She slid the paper out from under the book.

'David Oxford' the patient name on the file read. 'Patient #583484'

"Are you fucking kidding me? That is one of our stacks. He is the patient with the implant! Look! This is the procedure report!" Anna screamed excitedly.

Anna set the brown journal aside, picking up more of

the reports that were underneath it.

Anna and Bern read through the files. They saw the wireless memory device explained. They learned how it uploaded data directly from David's brain to a computer and stored it, recording every memory in real time.

"David had this?!" Bern said. "How old is this report? 2009. What if David still had this device? What if it was still working? If he was still uploading his memories the day he died, then maybe we can see who shot him!"

"Oh my God! You're right!" Anna said, as she realized what this meant.

They noticed a small section on the report that had a web address, username, and password.

"Bern, grab your laptop," Anna said, as Bern had already started walking to go get his laptop, one step ahead of the bewildered scientist. He quickly returned to the living room, turned on his laptop, and entered the address in the browser. A window opened and a prompt for a username and password appeared.

Anna typed in the information from the sheet and hit 'enter.' The window was replaced with another one— 'Key phrase.' Anna and Bern searched but could only find a username and password.

Anna tried the red text from the silver card, now lying

out of the box on the coffee table.

'Na#8rn!'

'Invalid,' the computer screen responded.

"Oh well. I guess that didn't work." Anna sighed. "But hand me David's stack, patient number six, from over there." Anna pointed to the living room floor.

"So, if the person who shot him knew about all this, then maybe it was one of these other patients. If we can figure all this out, we can find out who shot him. I'm sure of it! We just need to be able to piece all this together," Bern reiterated.

Anna flipped through what now seemed like a near-complete file for David.

"It's too bad that some info is still missing." Anna pointed to the doctor's name on the front of David's reports.

The name was blacked out with a dark marker.

"Maybe it was your father. Maybe that was the secret. Think about it. All these files show that the project failed. People lost their memories; some even showed signs of brain damage," Bern suggested.

"I'm sure as a highly respected scientist, revered as one of the best in the world, he would have had a hard time with this kind of failure. I'm sure he was devastated. It sounds like you really looked up to him your entire life. I can see how he would want to keep this a secret from you," Bern said, explaining his early conclusion. "I don't mean it with any disrespect; it's just a theory."

Bern grabbed his ashtray and the glass pipe. He smoked the pipe and flipped through more reports that were in the box. He handed the pipe to Anna.

She smoked the green buds from the thick glass pipe as she read through as many of the pages of the reports as she could.

Bern and Anna found themselves at another dead end. The papers were just more reports about David, the implant, and the memory uploads.

"We really need to figure out how to get to David's uploaded memories. If that implant was still functional, we could see who shot him," Bern said as a reminder.

"This weed made me really sleepy," Anna said with a yawn.

Her eyes were now heavy and only half-open.

Bern watched as Anna started to fall asleep, sitting up on the couch with pages of reports still on her lap.

Still in her damp, sexy, black lingerie, she finally slumped over on the couch and mumbled, "Can we just take a nap? My brain is tired. I can't even comprehend trying to put all this together right now.

This stupid puzzle."

Sleeping had turned into part of Anna's escape...well that and painting and sometimes smoking.

"Of course, and you are staying with me tonight," Bern said. "I will go grab some comfortable clothes for you."

"Okay," Anna said without opening her eyes. Bern looked at her curled-up body, almost completely naked on his couch.

He started putting the papers back into the box, along with the envelopes and card. He kept a few papers in his hand that he wanted to take a closer look at. He somehow thought they looked more important than some of the others.

Bern went to the closet in the guest bedroom and grabbed a pair of plaid boxers and a white tee shirt from the drawer in which he kept the older clothes he hardly wore anymore. He brought the clothes to a very sleepy Anna and helped her get into them.

"I'm sorry for everything you've been through. I couldn't even imagine," Bern said, as he watched Anna doze off. "Just remember that I will always be right here."

Anna felt Bern's hand brush down her face, moving the hair away from it and back behind her ear. She was content because, although she was in the middle of another one of life's torrential rainstorms, she knew that she was protected. Bern would always be right there, just like he promised.

Anna fell asleep within minutes. Her restless body twitched occasionally. Bern hoped that she wasn't having nightmares.

Watching Anna made him wonder, *when your reality has become a nightmare, what are your nightmares like? Could she really be dreaming of something worse than what she's living through?* Bern lit the glass pipe again and inhaled.

What was I doing?

Oh yes! He was looking through the reports from inside the box, without really knowing what he was looking for. Out of the corner of his eye, he saw an odd glow coming from the guest bedroom. Through the open door, he could see into that bedroom from where he sat. The glow appeared to be coming from something lying on the bed.

He rubbed his eyes and looked again. He wasn't that high; he didn't *think* he was anyway.

"I am *not* seeing things," Bern said aloud, as he got up and walked into the guest bedroom. He saw a few reports, which had been in the metal box, lying on the bed. He must have set the papers down there when he'd gotten the clothes for Anna. The white papers appeared to glow, in the dark room because of the purple fluorescence of the black heat light over the exotic lizard tank.

Bern picked up the papers and looked more closely. On the top report, it almost looked as if there were other words written on it—handwritten words that seemed to glow faintly.

He walked, with the papers in hand, closer to the purple-glowing lizard tank. Words that he hadn't seen before suddenly became illuminated. Words that were otherwise invisible now glowed brightly under the black light.

The words were scrawled in a handwritten script, overtop of the printed report.

"What the fuck?!" Bern said out loud, as he read the words.

Chapter 22 – Nap Time Is Over.

Anna woke up from her nap. She rubbed her eyes and saw Bern sitting next to her.

"I just had the worst nightmare!" she said.

"About...what?" Bern asked carefully.

Anna looked at the stack of papers and the open box of secrets in front of Bern. "Damn...it was real; it wasn't a nightmare," she said with disappointment.

Bern nodded.

"I went through everything again and the only other thing that I can find that may be a key phrase is this." Bern held up a scrap of paper no bigger than a sticky note. It had some random characters scribbled on it: 'G5sL9tQ1.'

"Did you try it?"

"No. I was waiting for you."

"Why the hell are we waiting?! Let's try it!" Anna exclaimed.

They got on Bern's laptop and tried to use the scribbled characters as the key phrase.

'Access denied.'

"Damn!" Anna said.

"I did find something else really odd! You are never going to believe this! Come with me!" Bern walked Anna to the guest bedroom and shut the door.

He had the paper with the odd hidden message in his hand. Bern walked Anna closer to the purple glow of the exotic lizard tank. The faint words began to glow more brightly.

"Oh my God!" Anna said.

She read the writing out loud.

'Anna, I need you to clean out one of my rooms for me. Please go to my house and read Alice in Wonderland. *Look to Stan for help.'*

"What do you think that means?" Anna asked, looking over at Bern.

"I have no idea." Bern shrugged his shoulders.

"Who would have thought invisible ultraviolet ink?" Anna looked the paper over, closely examining the glowing words. "Only David. It's kind of funny because David taught me how to make and use UV ink like this when I was a kid. He was always teaching me science any chance he got. He even showed me how to write with lemon juice and then use a flame to make it appear. He must have thought I would have remembered the UV ink. Maybe we missed a clue that was supposed point us to this message. Either way, thank God for your lizard tank!"

"Well, do you want to go to David's and look for *Alice in Wonderland*?"

"Hell yes! I want to get to David's memories that he uploaded. I want to see these memory files that they are talking about. If they were still uploading, I want to see who shot David." Anna stared off into the distance with a vengeful gaze, which was so unlike her.

"But...I actually think I should talk to Stan first," Anna added with near certainty.

"I wonder what Stan knows. Maybe he knows what the key phrase is...or maybe the key phrase is inside the book...*Alice in Wonderland*," Bern said hopefully.

"Maybe." Anna shrugged.

"I'm just going to wear this," Anna said, referring to a pair of jeans that she held up. She shamelessly slid Bern's boxers off and pulled her jeans up over her black, silky underwear.

"You ready?" Bern asked.

"Yep, let's go. I'm not going to call. Let's just go stop by his place," Anna said

They got in Bern's car and drove to Stan's apartment. Anna rang the doorbell and Stan greeted them.

"Hi Stan!" Anna said, giving him a hug.

"How have you been?" she asked, noting that he still looked sad and depressed.

"I'm doing okay. It's hard, you know?"

"Yeah, I know." Anna patted his shoulder.

"So, I want to ask you a few things. David left me this box of reports from some project that was done. We are confused and have hit a dead end trying to figure it out. We were wondering if you could help."

"I don't know what you're talking about. What project? What reports?" Stan asked, puzzled.

"Reports about some memory backups. One report talks about a wireless implant in David's brain," she responded.

"I don't know about anything like that."

"Fuck! David said you would!" Anna was angry that this had led them nowhere.

Stan was a little thrown by Anna's out-of-character language.

"Well, wait a minute...David said that?" Stan's interest seemed to peak.

"He wrote in ultraviolet ink...'*Ask Stan for help,*'" Anna tried to explain.

"Well, I guess David really trusted you then. Okay, I don't know much, but I'll tell you what I do know," Stan said. He grabbed a box of old pictures from a bookcase next to the couch and sat down.

"I was friends with your father before you were born," Stan said, as he laid a picture of himself, holding a little girl, down on the coffee table. Anna picked up the picture and examined it. The girl looked like her at around age one.

Anna recognized the room in the picture as the kitchen in the house she grew up in. There was a cake on the counter that read, 'Happy Birthday Anna!'

"But...I remember the day I met you at the office. I was about six. This doesn't make any sense," Anna said with a stunned look on her face.

"Well, now that David and your father are both gone, I can talk about it..." Stan started.

"You know that your dad was the absolute top scientist in the field of neurology and, more specifically, memories. Many times, he had priceless, confidential government data with him. I was David and your father's security escort. That is how we all became friends," Stan continued.

"You think that you didn't meet me until those

operations were suspended and David and your father were brought into the lab to start a new project, and I was brought in for security. I was there the day you were born and have been around ever since."

"I remember meeting you for the first time though. It's one of my most detailed, vivid memories," Anna said, as she started to cry in disbelief.

"You're a fucking liar!" is what she wanted to scream, but she didn't feel like she was certain of anything anymore.

"Anna, your father reengineered your memories of me to protect you. He made sure that I was removed from any early memories you had. He knew that I knew too much about the project and that you would be better off not knowing our past. He knew you would be safer that way...but times have changed, and I think you should finally know the truth."

Anna continued to stare at Stan in disbelief. She was shocked.

"Look," Stan said, as he laid the stack of pictures down in the spot where the first one had been. Anna slowly put down the picture she was still holding, gently laying it face down on her lap. As she leaned forward and grabbed the stack, she felt her heart begin to race. She focused on the top picture as she brought her hand closer to her face.

The picture on top was of Anna's father, mother, and

Stan at the park, with some other friends, for the Fourth of July. Anna, then just a toddler around age three, was waving and saying, "cheeeeeese!" in the foreground while the adults were behind her, laughing.

"I don't understand any of this," Anna said, as her eyes started to water once again.

"I know that something went wrong with the project and your father and David were trying to engineer replacement memories. They had a room at David's house, where they would spend hours making these things. I was the only other person that knew anything at all, and what I do know isn't that much," Stan said.

"I never saw any of what they made. I can tell you, though, that you were different before the failure. You were more outgoing and more laid-back. Whatever happened to your memory, whatever they reengineered, changed you," Stan explained carefully.

"What?! I was part of that project?!" Anna asked, as she burst into tears. "Do you know how much of a mind-fuck my life is right now, Stan?!"

"Anna, I'm so sorry dear," Stan said, hugging her.

Bern stood speechless, trying to process everything. He stared at Stan as he hugged Anna. Bern hadn't seen Stan since the funeral. He thought about how tired and worn-out Stan looked.

Anna sat on the couch and stared off into space. Her tears had slowed to small trickles down her cheeks. She seemed near catatonic.

"What the fuck?!" Bern mumbled softly, running his fingers through his hair. He sat down next to Anna and rubbed her back. She began to cry heavily once again.

"Anna, let me take you home," Bern said.

"Okay," the distraught, overwhelmed woman agreed.

She quietly walked out of the apartment without another word.

"Thanks for the help," Bern quietly said to Stan as he walked out behind Anna.

Bern and Anna drove home. Anna never made a sound. She never looked at Bern. She was completely unresponsive.

Bern parked the car and walked her into his house. He led her to the couch and had her lie down. Bern got a couple of pills from his bathroom cabinet. Valium—it was what he used to get to sleep sometimes. He gave them to Anna with a cold glass of water.

Without looking at Bern, the pills, or the glass, and without a single question, Anna swallowed the pills with a big mouthful of water.

If she couldn't trust her own memories, then what could she trust? What if some of her memories weren't real? Could she even trust herself? These were Anna's thoughts as she stared off into space. Her mind raced with a flurry of thoughts, each one unique like a snowflake. She felt fucking crazy.

Deep in thought, Anna continued to stare up at the ceiling for about fifteen more minutes without making a sound.

Then suddenly, within almost an instant, Anna fell into a deep, diazepam-induced sleep—a temporary escape and a chance to let her overwhelmed mind rest.

Chapter 23 – A More Curious Half.

Bern was right next to Anna the moment he heard her stirring.

"My head hurts!" Anna said, keeping her eyes closed as she rubbed her forehead.

"Bern?"

"Yeah."

"What did I do to deserve all this, Bern? I'm a good fucking person! Why?!"

"I don't know," Bern said, rubbing her back.

"Fuck the man," Anna said. "The only thing that I haven't lost is you! I have even lost some of my own memories. How are they not real? It has fucked up my head so much, Bern. Everything is so surreal."

"I'm not going anywhere," Bern assured her.

"Half of me wants to just start my life over and forget about all of this. The other, more curious, half wants me to find out everything I can... I want to paint. Then I can leave all this behind. I can forget about everything.

Can we paint, Bern?"

Anna asked woefully, showing that she was still the broken Anna who had fallen asleep earlier. Sleep didn't help her cope anymore; her mind had been pushed well beyond that point.

Bern got everything set up. He turned on some soft acoustic music, adding a background track to the usual mellow ambience.

Other than the quiet music, they painted in near silence. Bern just didn't know what to say, and it was killing him.

Anna painted vigorously with mostly dark colors. Her brushstrokes had become heavy and intense. The paint met the canvas with a fury of distressed emotions. Anna's heart and mind unfolded in oil-based paint, creating a dark picture in front of her.

"This one is done. Seven more to go," Anna said, stepping back from the easel after about an hour.

Bern looked at the painting. It was abstract and very dark. It appeared only half-finished. Bern saw Anna in the painting. Anger, sorrow, rage, pain, sadness, regret…everything she had been through, in such a short amount of time, was all right there, unhidden.

"It's really good!" Bern said, staring at Anna's unique, fluid painting style. "I love it!"

"It looks like it's only half-finished, but I'm done with

it," Anna said, as she stared intently at the painting. "I thought about how people would look at it and see it as unfinished. I almost kept going because of that. Then, I thought about how art should be what the artist wants it to be, not what they think people want to see. The way it is right now...it's finished. I'm going to leave it true to that."

Anna took the painting down and swapped it for a new, blank canvas.

"That's really cool. I'm glad you get it," Bern said proudly.

"Thanks. Will you take me to go get a few things from my place today?" Anna asked.

"Yeah, when do you want to go?"

"I was thinking about going before I start this next painting." Anna looked at Bern. Her brown eyes still looked so sad.

"Yeah, let's go now then." Bern set his brush down.

As they drove to Anna's house, she stared out the window. Neither of them spoke.

When they got to Anna's apartment, it was still tidy, but Anna pictured how it had looked. She pictured what some fucking assholes had done to her former safe haven. Anna didn't think it would ever feel the same. It would never truly feel safe. It would never again feel like home to her.

She went through her clothes, picking out a couple more outfits to take with her to Bern's. She finished up and walked out of her bedroom with the clothes.

"Let me just grab a bag to put these in," Anna said, as she walked to the kitchen.

"I'm not in any hurry," Bern reminded her.

"Bern! Fucking come here now!" Anna screamed from the kitchen. "He is in here!"

Bern ran and found Anna, standing in the kitchen, staring at the far wall. He didn't see anything out of place at first.

"He is in here!" she said again.

Looking past Anna, and down at the floor, Bern saw small brown chunks all over the kitchen tile, a torn-open bag of cat food lay by the wall.

"Ruff! Ruffles!" Anna called out. "Come out, Ruffles!"

The pair started looking everywhere—under furniture, in the pantry, behind anything bigger than a cat...but they found nothing.

"Fuck!" Anna yelled.

"I still think he's in here," Bern said reassuringly.

"What if it was just mice or something?" Anna asked despairingly.

"No, I don't think it was," Bern said, not really sure what he believed; but he was trying to stay positive.

"I know!" Anna burst out, running to the small laundry room.

"He *is* in here somewhere!" Anna yelled excitedly. "He has been using the litter box! Where the hell is he hiding?"

She walked out of the kitchen and sat down on the couch. "Do you have anything to smoke?" she asked. "I need to calm down. Maybe we can just relax, watch a movie, and look one more time before we go."

"That sounds good," Bern said, throwing Anna his pack of cigarettes.

"I didn't mean tobacco," Anna said, setting the pack down.

"Open it," Bern said with a laugh.

Anna opened the pack and found two joints and a small lighter mixed in with the regular cigarettes.

"Oh," she said, feeling a little stupid.

The newfound hope that Ruff probably wasn't gone forever had seemed to change Anna completely.

She pulled a joint out and lit it. She turned on the TV and played the first documentary that came up—a documentary about happiness. Perfect.

"Do you want me to get you a drink?" Bern asked, as he grabbed a soda out of the fridge.

"Can I just have a sip of whatever you get?" Anna yelled back toward the kitchen.

Bern didn't respond. As he shut the door, he was startled by a lightning-fast ball of fur running out from behind the refrigerator.

Straight to Anna's lap it went. Ruff flopped over and purred loudly.

"Oh my God! Mr. Ruffles! You're okay!" Anna squealed with excitement. "You must have been so scared."

Ruff rolled over on his back, letting Anna rub his belly; this was one of his most favorite things ever.

Together, the three of them watched a documentary about happiness. This was the happiest Anna had been in a while.

It wasn't exactly heaven but, for today, it was close enough.

Chapter 24 – Broken.

"Thank you for letting me bring Ruff," Anna said, while they drove back to Bern's house. She had the furry cat on her lap, therapeutically stroking his long fur as he purred loudly.

"I'm sure Nickels will be fine with him. It will be like a live chew toy," Bern said with a laugh.

"Hey! Mr. Ruffles is not going to be a chew toy!" Anna protested. "Are you, huh?" she asked, grabbing the tolerant cat's face so she could look him in the eyes. "I'm so glad you're back!" she whispered to the feline, touching her nose against his.

They got home and introduced Nickels and Ruff to each other. Over the past couple of years, they had both smelled each other on their owner's clothes and belongings. The two animals seemed to have a hint of recognition. Nickels quickly lost interest in the creature that was supposed to be his natural enemy. He lay down in his usual spot on the floor by the couch. Ruff curled up on the cushion right above him, just like they were old friends.

"Awwwwwwww, they're cute together!" Anna said

with a laugh.

"Bern, do you want to go to David's and look around? Maybe read *Alice in Wonderland*?"

Bern hadn't pushed digging any deeper into all this mess that was starting to unfold, but he was glad to see Anna wanted to on her own.

"Sure, if you're up for it," Bern said, smiling.

Finding Ruff had sent Anna on an emotional upswing. It was good to see her smile again.

All the stuff from the antique box was now back in it. The lock sat next to it, still open.

"'All the knowledge within'...no fucking joke!" Anna said, looking at the lock's faint Latin words.

Anna and Bern relaxed for a little while, and then they headed over to David's house.

Walking into David's apartment, Anna went straight to the bookshelf that was built into the wall.

"*Alice in Wonderland*," Anna said out loud, as she pored over the words on the spines of the books.

Bern also started scanning the titles as he stood right next to her.

"Speaking of *Alice in Wonderland*...you still haven't heard anything from 'Alice in Cokeland'?" Anna said with a giggle, thinking that her comment was pretty clever.

"Nope!" Bern said. "Maybe she disappeared because she knew how bad she fucked up my house." Bern laughed.

Anna smiled at the thought of Alice's mysterious disappearance. She would never admit it openly, but she was jealous of that elusive woman.

"Found it!" Bern said, pointing to the middle shelf on the left end. The books on either side of *Alice in Wonderland* did not have titles.

"What do you think is going to be in it? The key phrase?" Anna asked excitedly.

"Well, find out...go!" Bern pushed Anna gently in the direction of the book.

Anna reached up and grabbed the edge of the book's spine. "Alice," she said under her breath.

"It's stuck to the other books," Anna said, puzzled.

"Curiouser and curiouser..." Bern said, seeing if Anna would notice what he thought was a well-played reference.

"Hang on. I can tip it backwards, but the books on either side move too. I think they really are stuck together...and...oooohhhhh..." Anna's exclamation trailed off.

"What is it?" Bern asked, trying to look around her to see what caused her odd reaction.

Anna moved over, and he saw the three stuck-together books, flipped completely up and off the bookcase. Now parallel to the shelf, they appeared to defy gravity by use of a hidden hinge on the back of them. In the spot where they had been, was a small LCD panel.

"It looks like a thermostat," Anna said. "It's not turned on," she said to Bern, as she touched the screen with her finger.

The LCD lit up with a bright white light. 'Scan card,' the black words on the glowing screen read.

"Bern! That silver card!" Anna said, as she pointed to the antique box, which Bern had set down on the coffee table.

Bern got the silver card with the red letters and handed it to Anna.

She put the card up to the glowing screen. 'Enter password,' the text on the screen now said. Anna carefully entered the red characters as seen on the card.

'Na#8rn!'

With the last character entered, there was a loud, low clicking sound. The right end of the bookcase moved forward a few inches.

Anna, startled, backed up a few steps. "Are you kidding me?!" she exclaimed.

"Wow!" Bern said quietly.

Anna pulled the end of the bookcase toward them. It swung smoothly on a hidden hinge at the right end.

As the door slowly opened, it revealed a small, brightly lit room, a little bigger than a walk in closet. Motion sensors had detected the pair and switched the lights on as the door opened. It looked like a small lab with computers, test equipment, and files full of papers.

"Holy shit!" Bern said, looking with amazement at the construction of the bookcase, which had been turned into a heavily secured door. "It's built like a bank vault!"

"This is crazy!" Anna said, looking around at everything in the tiny room. "My dad and David used to spend hours in here together, apparently."

Bern looked at one of the computers and turned on its monitor.

The screen lit up with brightly colored graphs, charts, and memory maps.

"Hey, let's see if we can log in here!" Bern said, as he got out the report with the web address on it. He typed it in and it prompted for the username and password, just like on his laptop. Bern entered them exactly as they were on the report.

'Login successful,' the computer screen displayed.

'David Oxford: Patient # 583484.'

The screen showed more charts and graphs of David's brain, along with a section that listed a series of files.

"Look at that file! It was last updated the day he died! Click on that!" Anna pointed excitedly.

A window on the computer screen popped up: 'Playback the selected memory file as a decompressed flat video file?'

The only buttons in the window were 'Cancel' and 'OK,' so, of course, Bern clicked the latter.

The screen opened and said, 'Transmission failed.' The recorded memory was stopped at the very end — the exact time that David's brain had shut down and stopped uploading data.

"Are you sure you want to watch this?" Bern asked, grabbing Anna's hand.

"Yes. I want to know who it is," Anna said with a vindictive gaze.

Bern slid the timeline back thirty minutes.

They watched in suspense as the memory played back like a movie. They watched the video play, as recorded through David's own eyes.

David was sitting, reading the newspaper. Startled by

what sounded like the front door unlocking, he quickly stood and turned around, all in one motion. Two armed figures, dressed in all black, were standing by the front door, frozen like deer in headlights. The two intruders appeared startled and already had their guns drawn on David. He put his hands up in front of him, attempting to show no resistance.

"Where are the documents?" one of the men asked.

"What documents?" David asked, in an unsure, trembling voice.

"Any of the documents about the mind testing and memory engineering! The truth about what the tests were for...the government documents. Just, give us those and we will leave. We don't want to hurt you."

"I don't have much; all that was confidential. We didn't really keep anything from that, but I'll give you everything I have." David walked to his desk, where, over the years, he had spent hours writing, reading, and working. He loved that desk.

Still keeping his hands up as he walked, David slowly reached down and opened the drawer. After cautiously reaching in, he swiftly pulled his hand out, holding a semi-automatic handgun—a gun Anna recognized.

David's reaction was quick like a snake striking. In one swift motion, he raised the gun toward the intruders; it was a split second that felt like an eternity. Time slowed and then...

Click! Click!

BANG!

Anna gasped and covered her mouth in horror at the sight of the gunpowder-fueled flash.

David stumbled backwards, tripping over his office chair.

The memory played back the exact way his mind had recorded it, the way he had experienced it. The view from his eyes showed the room spin and the ceiling come into view.

David's gun fell to the floor as he grabbed his chest and gasped. His lungs gurgled and burned, as if they were on fire. He hit the floor as he was staring at the unrecognized man, dressed in all black, holding the now-smoking gun. David quickly started to lose consciousness as he watched his own blood begin to pool on the wooden floorboards surrounding him.

The voice of a person saying, "We're lucky his gun didn't fire...he would have killed us both," was the last sound David heard. In the foreground, for a split second, as his vision faded in and out, David saw his gun. The clip had become dislodged and, from the position in which he now lay motionless, David could see that the clip had been empty.

'Transmission failed,' the computer screen read. This

was where David's memory ended. Bern and Anna stared at the screen, both speechless.

Anna started to cry heavily. Bern tried to comfort her.

They had just relived the last moments of David's life. This was something neither of them had been mentally prepared for.

They hadn't thought about what those last moments would look like, or what they would feel like. They hadn't thought through the fact that they were going to relive the death of a friend from his own first-person perspective—a bullet to the chest.

"I want to find them! There were two of them! I'm going to find them! Fuck those bastards!" Anna said angrily. Her eyes were soaked with hot tears that burned with rage.

"Bern, the hell if I'm going to let those fucking murderers get away with this! I will find them! If the police won't...I will. There has to be something in all this stuff or that phone we found, to lead us to them," Anna said positively.

"An eye for an eye..." she added softly.

She took a deep breath and continued looking for answers.

Anna double-clicked the computer mouse, opening a folder that contained more memories and projects. She randomly chose a project and clicked to open it.

Elaborate software opened on the screen with a timeline layout like in video editing software that splices video clips together to make a film. The difference was that, instead of editing movies, it edited memories and kept them four dimensional. Smells and sensations, like temperature and emotions, could be easily added to the memories.

"Dimensional memories...this is how they built them. Oh my God!" Anna said.

The pair looked at the different parts of the software. There were soundtracks with special controls, allowing you to choose where it would sound like a noise was coming from, placing it on a three-dimensional soundstage in the project.

"This is so immersive... You can make anything!" Anna said in awe.

They watched as the 'Project Loading...' bar on the screen changed from '99%' to '100%.'

The empty areas of the memory software were now filled in with data and images.

Anna looked at the sequences, recognizing most of them as different times in her life. She saw the picture of the pink horse costume from that Halloween as a little girl. She saw a scene of her father standing in a doorway and another scene of her mother sick in bed.

"My dad made all of this," Anna said, as she began to

cry again.

Anna played an attached memory file. "It looks like this software was actually monitoring and recording his brain while he worked on this part of the project.

The recording of her father's memory started. It played back like a video that was recorded while he was working on this memory.

"This is it!" John, her father, could be heard saying to himself.

This was the image he had been looking for. It was the memory of the view of outside, in the autumn, through the bedroom window.

It was buried in some old memories around Halloween. The memory had Anna, then about age six, playing in front of the large window, but luckily she didn't get in the way of the scene.

Anna's father carefully cut the view, through the window, from the memory. He took the view—just the window—and added it to his sequence timeline so that the views from the windows in the project were playing that autumn scene.

Next, he found a sequence earlier that day, from one of his wife's archived memories. It was of himself, at about age thirty-five, standing in the doorway and smiling back at her.

They had just finished wrestling around and laughing,

and he stood there, looking at his wife lying on the bed, and smiled lovingly. John was gently silhouetted by the sunlight beaming in behind him through the big picture window. It was very bright outside because it had snowed eight inches overnight, and the snow continued to fall gently, blanketing everything outside.

John took this memory of himself and spliced it with the autumn view from the other memory. The end result was a younger John standing in a doorway with golden autumn leaves blowing gently in the breeze outside the window. The reality of the snow had been covered up with a piece from a different memory—the illusion of autumn.

Being one of the world's top memory architects, John knew that the validity of the memory lay in the details. He could not find a memory of the way his wife smelled, but he did find a springtime memory of the blossoms on the fruit trees in the yard. It was the best he could do. The smell would add another level of realism to the memory—the amazing science of the memory of a smell.

John cut the memory of the smell of the blossoms from that sequence and spliced it into his timeline.

He could not believe that all this had happened. He knew that this was one of the last memories that he would ever be creating.

When standard memories were restored in patients, they were two-dimensional. They played more like a movie and didn't have feelings attached. Memory architects could take the two-dimensional memory sequences and splice them with parts of other memories to make them multidimensional, so that they had actual feelings and emotions. Like the memories had been lived through. Experienced.

On the next part of the memory he was building, John watched little Anna come running up to him as she came through the door.

"Hi, Daddy!" Anna shouted. She handed her father a white piece of paper with a colorful picture drawn on it. "I made this for you!"

The picture, drawn in crayon, was of a Halloween costume that she had drawn. Anna wanted to be a horse, so the Van Gogh-esque picture was of an elaborate pink horse costume. She had carefully included all the details she needed, such as a saddle and reins. Anna couldn't escape the excitement of her favorite holiday, and the anticipation of wearing the costume she had drawn. The excitement of a spooky, late night full of candy and fun spilled out of the little girl.

Her father took the picture and looked at it intently. "This is beautiful! We will have to get to work on this so it's ready in time for the big night of trick or treating," he said with returned enthusiasm. "Let's go hang it up in the office."

Anna took his hand, and they walked down the

hallway together.

There it was.

This was the picture John had been looking for. He knew that he would find it somewhere in these memories. He reversed the memory to when he stared at the picture that Anna had handed to him. The memory was blurry and degraded, and the picture was hard to make out.

"Damn it!" he mumbled. He ran the memory forward to the point in time, just a few minutes later, where he and Anna were standing together in the office. They were admiring the new piece of Halloween artwork now hanging on the office wall.

"I love it, Anna!" her father said.

John stopped the memory and examined the colorful piece of paper with the pink horse costume drawn on it. The picture, drawn in crayon, was sharp and crystal clear—a perfect memory object. He carefully cut the picture from the memory and added it as an object on his timeline. He could now add the picture to any part of the memory that he wanted.

John had spent a lot of his career working with Alzheimer's patients, restoring memories that had been lost. For years, he led a team that archived memories of patients that were showing early signs of the disease.

John's small team of memory architects would restore the patients' lost memories and monitor the results.

Scientists had found a way to stop the degeneration of the lobes and frontal cortex and repair them enough to restore normal brain function and reverse dementia.

The problem that it left behind was that, even with a successful reversal of brain deterioration, the memories remained lost, and the parts of the brain affected by the disease remained unstable for holding memories. His team had found a place in the brain, unaffected by the disease, where they could upload the lost memories without the risk of them being lost or damaged again.

Anna recognized all the pieces that she saw in the project. They were all pieces that made up the memory of her mother being sick and in bed. Anna had always loved reliving that memory.

"I can't believe, that...it's not real," Anna said, nearly speechless. "That never really happened...that memory isn't real."

 Dumbfounded, Anna looked for another project sequence to open.

'Anna meeting Stan.'

Anna hesitantly clicked on the file and waited for the project to load. Bern had been standing behind her, with his hands on her shoulders, as he also watched in wonder.

"Hello! It's a pleasure to meet you, my dear. You can call me Stan. I have heard so much about you—all good things, I promise."

They recognized Stan's distinctive voice and unique chuckle. Anna stopped the memory.

"No way! That's exactly what I remember. This is my memory!" Anna argued.

"Look!" Bern pointed to Anna's grandmother's name on the base file.

"I don't understand! That is me…meeting Stan! Why is it from my grandmother's memories?" Anna was visibly confused and struggling to comprehend what was unfolding in front of her. "This is such a vivid memory for me. I think about it and relive it all the time. In a way, I didn't believe what Stan said about knowing my grandmother!"

Anna closed her eyes and relived the memory, this time paying extremely close attention to every minor detail.

She was about six years old. Her father pushed the large glass door, to the lab where he worked and held it open for her.

Anna walked past him, feeling a sudden rush of cold air from inside. An air conditioned chill that steals your breath for a split second.

She turned and waited for him, holding her hand out.

Anna closed her eyes tightly and focused on her hand in the memory. As it was stretching out in front of her, she could see that it was weathered and bony.

Her father let the door close and took Anna's old, arthritic hand in his.

"This is Mr. Row," he said, as he helped Anna over to a man she had never seen before. She walked slowly, taking small steps, leaning on her father for support because her hips hurt today.

The closer they had gotten to Mr. Row, the taller and more intimidating he had appeared to Anna

"Hello, Mr. Row," little Anna said, with a shy smile.

"Hello! It's a pleasure to meet you, my dear. You can call me Stan. I have heard so much about you—all good things, I promise," he replied with a chuckle.

She stared at Stan's face and squinted, trying to see tiny, overlooked details in the false memory. She looked closely over at her faint reflection in a window, and she saw a familiar old lady—her grandmother.

This was her grandmother's memory of herself meeting Stan. Her father had copied it and used it to build a memory of Anna meeting Stan. It wasn't at all real. It wasn't her memory.

Anna started to tremble. All the color rushed from her face, and she turned pale white.

"What is it?" Bern asked. He was visibly worried by the way Anna looked.

"That's not my memory, Bern! It was my grandmother's. My memories aren't real, Bern! My memories aren't real!" Anna said, panicked. Her beautiful brown eyes were now red from all the tears.

"Fuck! I can't do this anymore!" Anna said, as she slammed the computer mouse down on the desk. She began to cry. "Bern, we need to get the fuck out of here!"

They left the small room and shut the secret bookcase behind them. A loud, low clicking sound let them know it was secure again.

They left David's apartment and drove toward Bern's house.

On the drive home, Anna's mind raced as she stared silently out the window. She was reliving every vivid memory that she'd had. She checked the details, looking for any sign of a real, original memory.

Anna continued to cry. In every memory that she replayed in her head, she could find evidence showing that it had been engineered.

"None of them are real..." the devastated Anna said quietly.

"I can't even find a one, Bern. I can't find single one."

Chapter 25 – A Private Pool Party.

"Take these pills and relax," Bern said, handing Anna two white pills and a glass of water.

When they'd gotten to Bern's house, she had sat down on the couch, where she had been nervously tapping her feet ever since.

"Fuck! I wish I could lose the memory of all this. This is definitely a memory I don't want to keep! I wish I could just go back to my ignorance and faith in my memories. I wish I had never opened the box. David was right...everything has changed," Anna said.

"I'm so sorry," Bern said, taking a seat next to Anna.

"What the hell do I do now? What the hell can I do? Start over or rebuild my life...I guess." Anna hated both of her options.

"Maybe I should just wipe my entire memory and start over completely...like what happened to you," Anna said, looking at Bern.

"No way!" Bern said quickly. "You would lose everything. Memories of your parents, David and

Judith, Ruff...me!"

"You're right...but I just don't know what to do," Anna said, teary-eyed.

"I say we paint and forget about all this for as long as we can. If you get those ten done, I can sell them, and you will be free to do whatever you want," Bern reminded Anna.

"Yeah, let's do that. I don't want to go back to my job. I used to love what I did, but I feel different now. I only need to finish seven more paintings," Anna said, wiping a few tears from her cheeks.

"The pills I gave you are for anxiety. Tonight, you are going to forget about everything; I'm going to make sure of it. Besides, you don't need memories when you are living in the moment." Bern knew that Anna didn't need much convincing of that.

He opened a bag of marijuana and some rolling papers that he had gotten from his bedroom. Bern broke apart the green crystal-covered buds and put them in the paper. He rolled the paper and its contents into a neatly formed joint and started on the next one.

Anna watched, always fascinated by how Bern did it. She watched his hands intently as they finished the next joint. She had always thought his hands were attractive—if not the way they looked, then what they did...like painting, driving fast cars, or rolling joints.

Bern put it up to his lips and licked the entire length of the rolled white paper with his tongue.

Anna looked away and started thinking about the box again. That box that she had admired and wanted so badly had now rearranged her entire life. The things that she used to love just weren't the same.

She didn't even want to look at that damn box anymore.

"It smells good," Anna said, as she stared off into the distance. Bern could tell that her head wasn't going to stop fucking with her. Luckily, he had a temporary cure.

Bern continued to roll a total of six joints, placing all of them in the cigar box when they were finished.

"I'll be right back," he said, as he went to his bedroom and shut the door behind him.

On his dresser, he laid a rolling paper out and started making one final joint. This one would be special. Bern was going to make sure this one would definitely give Anna the escape she needed.

He filled the rolling paper with some crystal-covered purple buds that he kept in a separate jar in his dresser. It was something he kept for special occasions.

Bern got out a little box that had brown crumbles in it. He broke the brown crumbles into smaller pieces and sprinkled them across the length of the joint. This was some of the best hash that Bern had ever bought...and not that it mattered, but it was also the most expensive.

To finish the joint off, Bern very lightly dusted the buds with a fine white powder that made most of the purple and brown disappear. Cocaine.

Bern had found a small bag of coke when he was cleaning up the mess left behind from the night with Alice. Bern had kept the dusty drug but hadn't said anything to Anna about it.

He didn't do coke, anymore—at least not that he remembered anyway—but it was nice to have a small amount around for an occasional extra kick, like tonight.

He finished up rolling the joint, ensuring it was nice and tight. It looked perfect.

"This will make her forget her problems for sure," Bern said to himself proudly.

He walked back to the living room. Anna was still staring off into the distance and looked exactly the same as when he had gotten up from the couch a little while ago.

"Here you go," Bern said, handing Anna a lighter and the special joint. "This one has something a little extra."

"Thanks," Anna said. "I'm going to paint once we are done with this."

Anna lit the joint and inhaled. The smoke tasted sweeter and seemed less harsh than normal.

She leaned back on the couch, closing her eyes. Her body was immediately covered in a warm feeling, like curling up on a cold day with a blanket fresh out of the clothes drier.

Anna handed the joint and the lighter to Bern and said, "It's really good," as she exhaled her last puff of thick, white smoke.

"Wow!" Anna said. "I need a drink."

Bern puffed the mixed drugs and watched Anna as she got up and poured a glass of wine in the kitchen.

Anna had already forgotten about the fake memories and the otherwise inescapable mess of a life that her world had become.

She was experiencing a serene happiness that was unknowingly fueled by a cocktail of drugs. Today, her heaven was made out of smoke.

Anna walked back with the glass of wine and sat next to Bern on the couch. He passed her the special joint; she took a couple more puffs and then sipped her wine. Anna was thinking about...nothing.

"Do you want to paint?" Bern asked, puffing the joint that Anna had handed back to him.

"Yes, absolutely!" Anna said, enthusiastically. She got

up and walked to, what was now, *her* easel.

Bern turned some music on and followed her. Together, they painted.

Anna thought about nothing but painting.

Bern thought about nothing but Anna.

He thought about how fucked up everything that she'd had to go through was. He thought about how lucky she was at the same time, now given a chance to start everything over. Bern watched Anna paint and thought about what a beautiful person she was...and a beautiful painter.

After five or six soft, relaxing acoustic songs, Anna took a break from painting and went to pour herself another glass of wine.

"Want a drink?" she asked Bern, as she held up her empty glass.

"No, I'm okay, thanks," he replied.

"Can we put on some music with energy?" Anna asked from the kitchen.

"Sure, what do you want?" Bern inquired.

"I don't know—something I can move to. I want to hear something I can feel, you know... I don't just want to listen." Anna tried to explain with hand gestures.

Bern chose a different station, which was playing soft

electronic dance tracks.

"I like it," Anna said. She could feel the beat as the music went in and out of her body. It pulsed through her veins like blood. The feel of the music made her want to move her body.

She grabbed the ashtray and the half of the joint that was left, bringing it over to the two artists' easels.

Anna lit the joint and puffed it, this time coughing a little. She handed it to Bern and took a sip of her fresh glass of wine.

Anna felt amazing. "I really like whatever we are smoking...I feel sooooo good!" Anna said, as she started to paint again.

Bern said nothing. He would never tell.

Anna and Bern painted for another couple hours, giving Anna enough time for two more glasses of wine and to finish the rest of the laced joint she was sharing with Bern.

"I think I'm going to get a tattoo," Anna said, turning to Bern.

"Really?! Like what?" Bern inquired curiously. He had never heard Anna talk about getting a tattoo...ever. In fact, if Bern had to put money on it, he would have bet that she never would have even discussed getting a tattoo.

"I don't know yet. I was thinking of..."

Anna undid the top button of her jeans and slowly unzipped them. With a hand grasping the denim on each side of the button, she folded them open and pulled them down a few inches, exposing her sexy pink lingerie. Her body continued to move, almost suggestively, to the entrancing music.

"I was thinking something right here," Anna said, rubbing the area just above and below the pink lace waist of the sheer panties. She put her thumb inside the sensuous lace fabric, and then, starting where the sheer fabric hugged her waist, she slid one side of the panties down her thigh a few inches. Using her finger, she made a line that was about four inches long.

Bern imagined how amazing the colorful ink would look on her milky white skin.

"Feel how smooth it is here," Anna said, as she grabbed Bern's hand and rubbed his fingers from her waist down to the pink fabric, which was still being held by her thumb, pinned down on her upper thigh.

"What do you want to get?" Bern asked curiously, as he slowly pulled his hand away.

"I don't know. I have a few things in mind. I saw a beautiful koi fish that I liked a while ago. What do you think?"

"I'm not sure. I never thought of you as a tattoo

person. Maybe we can look up some tattoo pictures online later," Bern said.

"What if I got something here?" Anna turned her back to Bern and looked back over her shoulder. She pulled her jeans halfway down her curvy ass, touching her hip in about the same area as the front. The pink fabric of the thong hugged her round cheeks perfectly. Anna slowly ran her hand down her thigh.

Bern was incredibly high and found Anna about as irresistible as he had ever found her.

"Feel," Anna said again, grabbing and running Bern's hand down her leg, starting above the thong and ending mid-thigh.

"Yep," Bern said, near speechless, as his intoxicated brain attempted to process what was happening.

"Mmmmm, everything feels sooo good! Let's get in the pool!" Anna said, sliding her jeans the rest of the way off and straightening out the sheer pink thong.

She pulled her shirt over her head and threw it down; it landed on top of the freshly discarded jeans.

Bern looked at Anna, standing in front of him in a sheer pink push-up bra. Her breasts were round and full, meeting in the middle to make perfect-looking cleavage. The bra matched the pink thong, with the same color lace and sheer fabric. Bern could see Anna's light, rosy nipples through the fine mesh lingerie.

"I'll go get my suit." Bern said.

"You don't need a suit. I saw you get in at the cocktail party in your boxers. Come on. I'm in my underwear!" Anna said, as if Bern hadn't noticed.

"It's new. Do you like it?" Anna asked flirtatiously.

"It looks...really...good," Bern said cautiously.

Anna walked to the kitchen, her round ass seductively moving. She would have been completely naked if it weren't for the bra and small pink thong.

She poured herself another glass of wine.

"I'm going out to the pool. Come on! Bring another joint of whatever we smoked out there," Anna said.

"I'll go make one quick," Bern replied, as he watched Anna wander out through the sliding glass doors.

Bern walked to his bedroom and got out the ingredients from before; then he stopped abruptly.

He walked into his bathroom and looked at himself in the mirror.

"What the fuck are you doing, Bern?" he asked himself, still flying high from the first laced joint.

"This isn't just another of your one-night stands. This is Anna—your best friend," he said to himself in the mirror.

"You have to think clearly. Think of all she's been through. Bern, you *cannot* break this girl's heart," he firmly reminded himself.

"Okay," he said, as he splashed his face with cold water from the sink.

He went back to the side table and rolled two more large joints, this time with more purple weed, more hash, and more cocaine than the first one.

Bern walked out of his bedroom and over to the two easels. He grabbed the ashtray and then went to the kitchen, where he poured himself a quick whiskey on the rocks.

He joined Anna, who was already in the pool.

"What took you soooo fucking long?" Anna splashed water at Bern.

"I was rolling these," Bern said, holding up the fat joints before laying them down on the table.

Anna smiled like a child who had just unwrapped the one present they'd been hoping for on their birthday.

She walked up the stairs and out of the pool. Now that it was wet, the sheer pink lingerie had almost disappeared. It clung to her body so closely that it didn't take much imagination to picture her completely naked.

Bern took a deep breath.

Anna picked up one of the joints.

Bern pulled out his Zippo lighter and flicked it, igniting the wick. He held the flame to Anna's face as the joint touched her lips. Her face lit up with changing shades of orange as the flame danced.

Anna inhaled deeply.

Bern put the lighter down, and Anna handed him the burning threesome of bundled drugs, still glowing orange at the end.

Bern puffed the joint and closed his eyes, passing it back to Anna, who took another hit and a sip of wine. She set the joint down in the ashtray and walked back to the pool.

Bern opened his eyes and watched as her sexy body, covered by nothing more than the nearly invisible pink lingerie, slowly disappeared underwater.

Anna turned to Bern and, in a playfully commanding tone, said, "Get the hell in here."

Bern got up and brought the ashtray and their drinks with him to the side of the pool. He pulled up his pant legs and sat on the edge, puffing the joint one more time. Anna walked over to the edge and rested her elbows on Bern's knees.

"I think I'm going to start over, Bern. You know...with my life. I lost almost everything; might as well say 'fuck it', right?" Anna took the joint from Bern. The end glowed a bright orange and crackled as she sucked on it.

"I'm sorry," Bern said. He couldn't tell if this was, in fact, a new Anna or just the unusual combination of drugs talking.

For a person who rarely had nothing to say, Bern was at an unusual loss for words.

"I'll be okay. I feel like I'm free now—like I can find myself. It's a good thing; it just came at a really high price. I want to live my life, Bern!"

You are also on three different drugs and alcohol, Bern thought, reminding himself of the inevitable emotional downswing ahead.

"Now just get in the pool with me! Take your pants off and get wet!" Anna said, pulling on Bern's pants. "Tonight we are living life..."

"Okay, okay!" Bern replied with surprise, as Anna grabbed his belt buckle.

Anna smiled victoriously as she watched Bern stand up and take his pants off, letting them fall to the ground.

The sight of his muscles flexing as he pulled his shirt over his head made Anna excited.

"Speaking of getting wet..." she said, quietly enough so that Bern couldn't hear.

Bern walked down the stairs and into the crystal-blue water.

Anna finished her glass of wine, and swam toward Bern. She kept on going right past him and walked up the stairs. Bern watched as the water succulently rolled off her shoulders and down her back. His eyes followed along, past her ass and down her thighs and calves. The glistening droplets glided effortlessly down her silky smooth skin. Every curve was unusually more flirtatious than ever before.

"I'm going to get the bottle of wine," Anna said. "Do you need anything?"

"Nope," Bern answered, as he tried not to stare at her body. The pink bra had all but disappeared as it clung tightly to her breasts.

Anna went in and came back out with the bottle in hand. She poured another glass and walked back down the steps into the water. She stopped and splashed water on her breasts, rewetting the bra and making her nipples hard.

Anna looked down at her chest.

"I didn't realize this would be so see-through!" she said, acting surprised. "Honestly, it's so sheer, why am I even wearing it?" She reached back and unclasped the bra. She sank underwater and slid the straps off her shoulders, letting the bra float to the surface.

Then, with both hands on either side of the pink lace, Anna slid the nearly invisible thong, down her thighs, and guided her long, sexy legs out.

Anna could still feel the music pulsing through her body, still making it move suggestively.

She grabbed the floating bra and, along with the skimpy panties, threw them out of the water and onto the edge of the pool.

Bern stood silently shocked at seeing Anna's completely naked body in the water.

"I feel amazing!" she said, twirling in the water, with nothing between its wetness and her.

"Have you ever been skinny-dipping before?" Anna asked Bern curiously.

"Of course," Bern replied, trying to avoid staring at Anna's body for any significant length of time.

"I haven't...until now."

"Really? Never?" Bern questioned doubtfully.

"Well, the other night, when you weren't here...that was my first time. I got in the pool naked by myself. It feels soooo good!" Anna slowly made her way over to the edge of the pool and sipped her glass of wine. Bern stayed treading water in the deep end.

Anna relit the joint, took a puff, and then held it out in

Bern's direction.

"Come on, you know you want it!" she said enticingly.

Bern swam over and puffed the joint, which was still in Anna's fingers.

"I'm pretty fucked up," Anna said, puffing and inhaling more thick, white smoke. "You should be naked too," she said, admiring Bern's body. "I probably shouldn't say this, but I always thought you were incredibly sexy."

"Thanks," Bern said, wondering why he let himself get into this position. He started looking for a way out.

This was a first for Bern. He had never looked for a way out of a situation like this; he was usually trying to get *into* a situation like this—something he was very good at doing.

"Come on; take these off," Anna said, pulling on Bern's boxers.

"Yeah, I probably shouldn't," Bern said, contemplating the act.

Anna pulled him close to her. Bern's skin touched hers, and his muscles pushed against her inviting bare breasts.

"I want you to fuck me," Anna whispered.

"Whoa!" Bern said as he pulled away.

"What's wrong?" Anna frowned.

"You are far from sober," Bern replied, shaking his head.

"I feel amazing though!" Anna said. "I haven't gotten laid for like over three years! Please! I need this soooo bad!"

"Over three years, seriously?"

"Yes. The last time was with my ex, and it wasn't even very good," Anna said with the usual pouty bottom lip.

"Please. I promise it will be fine tomorrow. No regrets. Don't worry; I'll still respect you in the morning," Anna said with a grin. "Please don't make me beg. Just fuck me like I was a one-night stand. Tomorrow, we can pretend it didn't happen." Anna tried to convince Bern.

"Well..." Bern started to say but was cut short by Anna.

"You don't think I'm sexy...that's it. Fuck, I feel stupid. I'm sorry," Anna said with renewed self-doubt.

"No, trust me, I think you are really sexy, and I do want to do lots of bad things to you; I just don't want anything between us to change. You are my only true friend, and I can't risk losing that," Bern cautiously explained his concerns.

"Okay, well, what is it going to take for me to convince

you that it will be fine?" Anna asked, ready to do almost anything.

"Let me go to the bathroom and get more whiskey. Do you need anything?" Bern said.

"I need to get laid," Anna replied with a smirk.

"I mean from inside..."

"No," Anna said with a sigh. She inhaled another breath of mind-numbing, decision-altering smoke.

Bern walked inside to the bathroom; his mind was cloudy from the drug cocktail and whiskey. He looked at himself in the mirror. He looked fuzzy. He *felt* fuzzy.

Bern's boxers had become tighter because of the aroused stiffness underneath. He adjusted the underwear to hide it as much as possible.

He rubbed his face with his hands.

"What the fuck, Bern? How did you get yourself into this?" he asked his reflection, as he faced one of the biggest and hardest moral dilemmas of his life.

Bern knew that, if it weren't for the drugs, he probably wouldn't even be contemplating this. If this hadn't been Anna, Bern would have already given her what she'd wanted...maybe even twice by now.

The Anna he knew went to bed early, didn't do drugs or go skinny-dipping, and definitely did not have one-night stands.

Bern's mind was torn in half by logic and lust. He thought about the fact that he'd given her drugs that she hadn't even known about. He'd only done it to help her relax more and forget about her world and the horrible things that had happened.

Bern was not going to take advantage of his best friend.

He walked to the kitchen and poured another glass of whiskey on the rocks.

He could see Anna outside—a naked free spirit, floating like an angel in the illuminated blue water. She stood up and walked to the edge, puffing the last bit of the joint. A cloud of thick, white smoke swirled around her nude silhouette.

Seductive.

"Goddamn it," Bern mumbled as he drank a big mouthful of whiskey. He slowly walked back out to the pool.

"Hi, you look really fucking good. I want to..." Anna paused as she thought about her words. "Bern, please? I really need this!" she pleaded.

"I think you should get sobered up a little and then rethink all this. I don't want you to do anything that you will regret," Bern said.

"Okay, I get it; you're worried. Just get in the pool now. I'm not going to ask you anymore," Anna said, sounding sadly defeated.

She was at the edge of the pool, now smoking the second and final laced joint, which she had just lit.

"I have to pee sooo bad!" Anna said, resting the joint in the ashtray.

She ascended the pool stairs naked, her wet, exposed body dripping water from every luscious part that Bern looked at. He gazed at her while she seductively dried off with a fluffy white towel. God damn the things he imagined doing to her!

Bern's mind strayed into a world of pleasurable fantasies. He imagined making Anna scream out with delight.

Anna knew he was watching.

"Do you want anything?" she asked, standing by the glass doors.

Anna's voice snapped Bern out of his arousing daydream.

"What?" Bern asked in a tone that let her know he wasn't paying attention to anything but her body.

"From inside...I'm going to grab another bottle of wine while I'm in there. I spilled the other one," Anna said, as she finished sensually drying her perfect breasts.

Vinal Lang

"Mmmmmm..." she moaned.

The combination of drugs made anything that touched her skin feel amazing.

"No, I'm good," he said, as he tried to look away but continued to stare, mesmerized by the sight of her skin. He followed her body with his eyes as she walked inside. Her ass swayed irresistibly with each step.

She walked into the bathroom that was attached to the guest bedroom. Anna sighed with relief as she let go of all the glasses of wine she had been holding in. She finished up and, on her way out, stopped to look at her reflection in the guest bedroom's full-length mirror.

Anna saw a seductively sexy naked woman staring back...and it was her.

Nothing about her body had changed in the past couple of weeks. The only thing that had changed was Anna's mind and her perception of herself.

Now, she was sexy.

Anna continued to look at herself in the mirror, touching her body where she tried to picture a tattoo. Every small touch felt amazing. She watched her reflection as her hands brushed over her nipples, sending chills across her body. Anna gasped.

She slid her hands down between her legs and experienced an indescribably sensuous rush of pleasure.

Anna lay down face-first on the bed, keeping her hands where they were. She moved her fingers, discovering the most gratifying sensation she had ever felt in her entire life.

Anna looked over in the mirror at her reflection. The curves of her body were enticing. She imagined Bern walking in to find her face down, provocatively naked on the bed, playing with herself. Anna imagined all the naughty things he would do to her.

She moaned and climaxed, breathing heavily from the euphoric, drug-fueled stimulation.

Anna got up; her legs were slightly wobbly and weak. She walked to the kitchen, grabbed a bottle of wine and a corkscrew, and then headed back outside to the pool.

"Why is your face so red? Are you okay?" Bern asked with concern. He was still in the pool, looking up at Anna.

"Yep, I am amazing! I feel the best I've ever felt in my entire life!" Anna replied. The cork popped as she opened the new bottle of wine.

She poured a glass of wine, set it down next to the edge of the pool, and then, without hesitation, she jumped into the deep end. The splash from her naked body hit Bern in his face.

Bern wiped his eyes and saw Anna's exposed, white

body coming toward him underwater. She surfaced right in front of him. As she slowly emerged, her nude body brushed against his.

"I promise that I won't regret this when I'm sober," Anna whispered in Bern's ear just before she bit it.

Anna slid her hands into Bern's boxers. He closed his eyes and took a deep breath.

Anna took his hand and slid it around her waist to her backside, and then pressed her body hard against his. They shared the gratifying feeling of bare skin on skin. Anna kissed down the side of Bern's neck to his chest, his aroused member still throbbing in her hand.

This is happening, Bern thought.

Anna slid her hands up to Bern's shoulders. She could feel his stiffness pushing between her thighs. She lifted her weightless body up and wrapped her sexy legs around him.

Gently, she lowered herself down, sliding Bern inside of her. Anna gasped. Penetration.

Anna moaned sensually as she slowly lifted her weightless body up and down. She rubbed against Bern's bare skin, sliding him in and out her. Pure intoxication.

"Do whatever you want to me," Anna whispered in Bern's ear, between blissful moans.

"Let's go inside," Bern whispered.

Anna slid off of Bern and grabbed his hand, leading him up the stairs and out of the pool. She led him inside to his bedroom where she threw her wet, naked body on his bed, pulling him on top of her.

Bern kissed down the side of Anna's neck and around to her chest. His mouth moved along the full, round curves of her perfect breasts. His lips wrapped around her nipples, one at a time, as his tongue teased them.

Bern's hand slid between Anna's legs, feeling how soft and wet she was.

Anna arched her back and gasped salaciously.

Bern continued down the front of her inviting body, his soft lips kissing across the span of her tight, smooth stomach.

Bern's tongue slowly worked its way to where his hand was—between her thighs. He put his mouth on her warm, wet, soft pink flesh.

Her body was shaved smooth and allowed Bern's mouth to suck on her in a way she had never felt before.

Anna's legs quivered. Bern wrapped his arms around them, restricting their movement. He held them tightly as she tried to move them out of pure, uncontrollable pleasure.

Anna loved the feeling of being restrained...controlled.

Bern continued to lick Anna's soft pink flesh, as he slid one of his hands from around her thigh. He slowly slid a finger inside her, making her squirm with delight. As Anna's moaning became louder, Bern got more excited.

Anna put her hands on the back of Bern's head, pushing him hard into her body. His mind raced at the thoughts of what he was going to do to Anna's amazingly hot body.

Bern slid another finger inside of Anna, making her gasp loudly. Her body stiffened and she screamed as she climaxed from Bern's soft mouth.

"Oh my God!" she said, breathing heavily. "That was fucking amazing! You are fucking amazing!"

"We are just getting started." Bern stopped only long enough to say those five words. He slowly slid his wet fingers out of her body.

Bern's mouth traveled back up Anna's stomach and across her breasts, stopping briefly at each nipple to suck on them, a little less gently than the first time.

Bern's soft lips continued their journey up Anna's neck to her ears, where he sucked and nibbled on them, sending her into an uncontrollable frenzy.

"I need you to fuck me really bad," Anna said longingly. "Please!"

"I'm going to do so many things to you," Bern whispered in her ear.

Anna felt Bern's stiff member slide into her wet opening with ease. Her knuckles turned white as her hands grasped the soft white sheets on each side of her.

Anna moaned with excitement. It had been so long since she had felt anything like this.

Bern began to slide in and out. His body moved back and forth between Anna's legs, making them tremble.

Bern looked at Anna. She was the sexiest woman he had ever been with, he thought.

Anna's mind was racing from the most amazing feeling she had ever had. She was free! This was heaven.

Anna orgasmed, her muscles stiffening with the heart-stopping climax. She screamed out in ecstasy.

Bern amorously rolled Anna over and pulled her up to her hands and knees. She looked back longingly at the seductive artist, ready to beg him to keep going.

As his skin slapped against hers from behind, she looked lustfully at his naked body and his tattoos. He looked fucking amazing. He felt fucking amazing…inside of her.

Bern, now on his knees, reached a hand from behind and grabbed one of Anna's breasts. He took his other hand and reached around to the front of her, stopping between her legs.

Bern intensely rubbed his fingers on her soft pink flesh.

Anna's body shook excitedly. Her mind was experiencing things that she had never felt before. Another orgasm…this time, Bern climaxed along with her. His naked body collapsed next to Anna's.

The couple's waves of carnal pleasure slowly turned into an indescribably sensual calmness.

The sweat made their skin cool and slippery. They both breathed heavily; neither of could remember having experienced anything this amazing before.

Within minutes, they both fell into a peaceful, intertwined slumber.

This was heaven.

Chapter 26 – The Truth.

She was seductively convincing. She didn't seem like she was on drugs, Bern thought, as his fuzzy vision focused on the naked woman that lay in bed next to him.

He was trying to justify what had happened. He wondered what she would be like when she woke up. What if she blamed him?

The room was golden orange from the morning sun coming through the sliding glass doors facing the pool.

Bern looked at Anna.

"Holy shit!" he said, softly rubbing his eyes. The bright light made his head hurt.

"No regrets," Anna said, opening her eyes and grinning. "I have been awake for a while. I was looking at you."

"Oh...well...good morning," Bern said, caught off guard and not exactly sure what to say.

"So...last night happened," he continued, trying to further gauge Anna's reaction.

"It was amazing! What a beautiful escape. Thank you so much. You have no idea how good it was to forget everything and experience that," she said with a big smile. "It just sucks that it doesn't change reality," The smile faded and her expression changed to a somber, defeated look once again. She covered her face with her hands.

"Well, now what?"

"I want to go back to David's and look through more memory files," Anna said, looking over at Bern as she lay illuminated by the sun, her naked body covered only by a thin white sheet.

"Are you sure?"

"Yes, I'm sure. I'll get ready." Anna sat up in bed.

She got out of bed, leaving the thin sheet behind.

Bern stared, one last time, at her beautiful naked body.

"You have a really nice body," Bern said quietly.

"Thank you," Anna replied, blushing as she looked at herself in the mirror. She smiled then quietly walked out of Bern's bedroom.

The pair got ready—Anna in the guest bedroom, Bern in his. Separately, they were both replaying the night from memory, reliving it the way they each remembered it. The same...but different. Each memory unique like a snowflake.

Bern looked at himself in the mirror in his room. He looked rough. He had fresh hickeys on his neck, two bruises on his arms, and one on his leg.

"Damn," he said, as he rubbed his face. He threw on some clothes and sat down on the bed for a minute, thinking about everything that had happened.

Anna looked at herself in the mirror. Her hair was a mess; she looked like a hooker after a big-money night. She spent some time brushing the tangles out. She then washed her exhausted-looking face and got some clothes on.

The two met in the kitchen, both ready to leave. They got into Bern's car and headed to David's apartment. Anna was understandably quiet and melancholy most of the way.

"I still smell like sex," she finally said with a grin, breaking the silence.

Bern grinned and kept driving.

They got to David's apartment and opened the bookcase door, just as they had done the day before, by choosing *Alice in Wonderland* as the key to Anna's rabbit hole.

They sat in the small room, each using a different computer, looking through other people's folders and memories—an oddly satisfying form of voyeurism.

"Look!" Anna said, pointing to a folder on her

computer named 'Patient records.' Bern looked over and saw the contents of the folder on Anna's monitor.

The folders inside all had numerical titles. They matched the numbers of the patient records from David's apartment that they had organized and analyzed.

Anna clicked, on what they now knew was her number—266200.

There it was—Anna's backup file of her memories from the project.

With a nervous, shaky hand, she double-clicked the file.

A screen opened with what looked like a timeline. There were colored spikes along the line. The spikes randomly peaked and valleyed. Along the bottom were marks representing different time intervals, currently marking years. To Anna, it looked like an audio recording, but she soon realized the spikes represented memories.

These were the flat memory files—memories that played like two-dimensional movies

Anna noticed that the last two years of her file were mostly flat, only having a few small spikes here and there. The timeline ended two years ago, making the blank span start about four years in the past.

"It looks like the spikes show memories on a

chronological timeline. See those years that the reports said were corrupt—the last two years? They show almost nothing. I wonder if we can see anything by those tiny spikes. Anna slid the bar to the middle of a small peak on the timeline and pressed play.

'Corrupt content,' the screen read.

"Damn!" Anna said, sliding the bar to another spike.

'Corrupt content,' the screen read again.

"I'm going to look at another file," Bern said, spinning his chair around to the other computer as Anna continued trying to find anything at all from those two missing years.

I'll look at our little buddy with the small file. Maybe we will find something there," Bern said.

Patient number thirteen.

Bern clicked the folder and then opened the memory file.

The memory that opened didn't have many spikes; it was almost completely flat. The only spikes that it did have were within the last two years of the file—about four years ago.

Bern chose the first spike and watched as it started to play back.

"No fucking way!" Bern said, as he watched part of the

memory begin to play.

The memory started with Anna standing in Bern's house, holding a dress exactly like the black-and-white dress that she had refused to try on for the cocktail party...the same dress that she had fallen in love with the other night, once she'd given it a chance...the short dress that reminded her of a giant chessboard. Made up of four black and white squares.

"Thank you for the dress! I love it!" Anna said onscreen, as she leaned in and kissed Bern.

Anna stood up and unzipped her jeans. She slid them off her long legs and threw them on the bed.

Bern's memory continued to play back as Anna pulled her shirt up and over her head, smiling seductively. She stood in Bern's apartment in a pair of sexy lingerie, slid the short black-and-white dress on, and then reached behind her and zipped it up.

"I think this is my favorite dress ever!" she said on screen, as she walked to the closet and put on her favorite pair of high heels. They were white, pink, and black with triangular studs.

"Happy birthday, love," Bern's voice could be heard saying.

'Corrupt content,' the screen suddenly read.

"What...the...fuck?!" Bern said stunned.

"Oh my God! Are you kidding me?!" Anna exclaimed. "That is my dress? I don't remember this at all! The memory file is dated before we even met each other!" She had turned around and started watching when she'd heard Bern's initial reaction.

Bern moved the bar to the next spike which, according to the timeline, was also before they had met. He pressed play.

Bern was standing behind Anna, his arms wrapped around her. She was holding the handle of the cold black steel gun. She braced herself against Bern's body.

BANG!

Anna's body pushed against his with the gun's recoil.

"You're getting better!" Bern said. "It's still gonna take time; don't get frustrated."

He kissed Anna on her cheek.

"Oh, I won't. Thank you for teaching me." The playback froze.

'Corrupt content,' the screen read again.

Bern quickly skipped to the next spike, still dated before they had met and played it back.

Anna stood next to Bern in the memory. He took her hand and brushed it on the canvas.

"Like this. Let your wrist move at the top," he said, guiding her hand through a silky smooth brushstroke. Her hand felt soft in his as he guided his lover's strokes.

"I love you so much," Anna whispered in his ear.

"I love you too," Bern replied warmly.

Anna turned and passionately kissed the handsome artist.

'Corrupt content,' the screen read once again.

"Fuck!" Bern became frustrated as he chose two completely corrupt spikes in a row. He frantically and impatiently continued to click, desperately looking for the next memory—the next piece to the puzzle.

Bern moved the memory ahead on the timeline to the next spike. Anna sat speechless, with her hand covering her mouth.

The next memory fragment started playing.

"David has this antique box that I love," Anna said through the phone, as Bern held it to his head.

"It says 'omnis cognitionis intra' on the lock. I want to look it up, but I always forget. Oh, hey, I got to go. I'll call you back in a little bit. Love you."

Bern hung up the phone and searched for 'omnis cognitionis intra.'

"All the knowledge within...hmmmmm...Latin. I'll have to remember to tell her."

The memory froze.

'Corrupt content,' the screen read once again.

Bern went to the next memory spike and played it. It stuttered into a fluid motion as the two watched in wonder.

Bern walked up behind Anna. She was sitting at his computer desk in just her underwear. A picture of a beautiful, koi fish tattoo was on the screen in front of her.

"What do you think about me getting this right here?" Anna asked, as she used her finger to make a line about four inches long down her thigh.

"Wow! That looks really amazing! Look at the detail. I love it!" Bern said. "I think it would look really sexy on you."

Anna stared at the beautiful koi. "I'm going to do it. I really like the colors and the way the shading is done."

"I'm excited, baby! I think—"

The screen went black.

'Corrupt content,' the screen read once again.

Some of Bern's memories lasted for only a few shocking seconds, while others were a few unpredictable minutes long. All these memories had happened during Anna's two years of missing memories.

Anna only had a couple of the short memories that would play from that missing two-year period. They only lasted for a matter of seconds.

One memory showed Anna picking up a thick, colorful glass pipe and smoking. The pipe was made of blue-and-gray glass. The colors twisted together down the center.

Anna thought about how much she loved this pipe. She coughed a little and then handed the pipe to Bern.

The screen went black.

'Corrupt content,' then flashed on the screen once again.

Anna could slow down or pause the memories, making them last forever if she wanted.

The next memory that played skipped and stuttered, looking more like a series of sequential still photos. It started with Anna lying naked on her back on Bern's bed. She was holding a joint in one hand as she playfully touched herself with the other. As the memory progressed, you could see Bern's hands touching her body. His hands slowly rolled Anna over onto her hands and knees. Anna looked back over her shoulder, her sexy naked body inviting Bern inside.

And then...

The screen went black.

'Corrupt content' then flashed on the screen one final time.

"Wow, we've done all this before! We were together... We have already lived this and now, we're living it all over again!" Anna said in shock. She stared at Bern, looking for his reaction.

"I am number thirteen," Bern said in disbelief. "I was part of the project too..."

Anna and Bern sat together as they watched more broken memories—memories of them laughing, loving, living life together, and discovering themselves and each other during those two missing years. Anna was now the same as, or at least very similar to, the woman they saw in Bern's memories—the same person she had become over the past few weeks.

As they watched the final memory, an older memory of when Anna and Bern had first met, Anna began to cry.

The short memory played.

"...so that's why I was arrested," Bern finished.

"So you were in jail? I will definitely have to keep you a secret from everyone, especially my dad, for a while at least. My parents loved my 'perfect' ex-fiancé too much. Jumping to a convicted criminal next won't go over well. My dad will probably run your record the same day he meets you. He is very protective," Anna said with a laugh.

"That's fine. I'll be your little secret," Bern said with a wink. He then leaned over and kissed her lovingly.

Anna blushed.

'Corrupt content,' the screen read once again.

"Oh my God…" Anna said. Right then, she realized she hadn't changed who she was; she had changed who she wasn't. Bern had helped her come out of her shell once before.

Stan was right; she *had* become different after the project failed. She had rediscovered the person she used to be. She had become herself again. With the help of Bern, Anna had been reborn.

"What do we do now?" Bern asked, shaking his head as he tried to comprehend everything.

"Let's talk to Stan. He has to know more than he's saying," Anna said. "I think I'm still in shock."

Anna grabbed Bern's hand.

"Feel my heartbeat," Anna said, placing Bern's hand on her chest.

Anna felt her heart pounding from the overwhelming

feeling of learning something that her mind could not quite comprehend.

"I'm sorry I didn't see you in there before," Bern whispered, as he looked into Anna's eyes. "You were there the whole time. I just didn't see you. The Anna I thought I knew wasn't the real you. This is the real Anna; this is my Anna," Bern said, as he brushed his other hand down her cheek.

"I missed you!" Anna said.

Bern grabbed Anna and held her tight—the tightest she had ever been held in her life. The couple reveled in their newly rediscovered love.

The connection had been made.

Bern took Anna's head in his hands. Their lips slowly met.

Anna and Bern kissed passionately. Somehow, it now felt like they had always been together. It felt like things had always been this way—exactly as they saw in their former memories. Their old reality, the one of yesterday, started to disappear.

In a ball of frenzied emotions and lust, the couple made their way from the small secret room to the living room couch.

Their clothes quickly came off, and the two unleashed the previously hidden deep, fiery passion that they had for each other.

Bern, now on top of Anna on the couch, kissed down her slender neck. The soft touches from his lips gave her chills.

His tongue glided across her chest, leaving a cool, wet sensation behind. It found its way to one of her soft pink nipples.

Bern's teeth bit down gently around the erect nipple, followed by his warm mouth. The sensation of very mild pain from the incisors, followed immediately by the pleasure his soft lips brought, made Anna have a small orgasm.

She gasped loudly as she arched her back. Anna bit her bottom lip and looked down at Bern. He was on top, with his mouth now at her stomach.

Bern kissed around Anna's navel, sending an uncontrollable tickling sensation across her entire body.

Anna's face was flush, and her heart was pounding.

She grabbed the couch cushions with her hands, as Bern's mouth started down the inside of her thigh.

Anna grabbed his head and brought his soft, heavenly tongue right between her legs.

"Mmmmmmmm..." Anna moaned, as Bern's tongue licked her most sensitive parts.

His mouth was all over her soft, wet skin. Her muscles

locked up. She pulled Bern's head against her body with incredible force.

Anna ended the frenzy with a scream and the release of Bern's head.

Her body trembled from the climax.

Bern wrapped his arms around her thighs and pulled her toward him.

He took Anna's arms and pinned them above her head. He slid deep inside her warm body. Anna's body, now wrapped around his stiff rod, pulsed with pleasure.

She quivered at the feeling of Bern throbbing inside her.

Bern's strong, naked body slapped against Anna's soft skin. The couple climaxed in unison, their bodies coming to rest on the couch, their cool, damp skin still touching as they lay side by side.

"Where have you been my whole life?" Anna whispered. "I love you."

"I love you too." Bern smiled.

Chapter 27 – The End is the Beginning.

Later that day, Bern and Anna arrived at Stan's house uninvited.

Anna knocked, and Stan opened the door.

"Hi, Stan!" Anna said, hugging the towering man. "How have you been?"

"I'm okay. How about you? When are you coming back to work?"

"I don't know. I told them I was taking a few weeks off. Maybe I won't go back. I really want to start painting! I love it so much!" Stan could see how excited Anna was.

"Stan! We found out that we were together! Me and Bern!" she explained. "Do you believe that?"

"Wait, you guys didn't know that when you were here the other day? You seemed like you were together. You had chemistry."

"No! We just found pieces of memories Bern had...today!" Anna answered, shaking her head.

"Oh my God! I thought you had that part figured out already. I did know about that. You guys were never seen together very often back then. You kept your relationship very private. Your father really had no idea."

Stan explained how Anna's father had seen some of the corrupt memories of his daughter with the handsome mystery artist—a secret lover he never knew about.

Her father saw the sparks; he saw the love. He saw everything he missed about his wife, his other half. He wanted Anna to have a chance to get that back. He knew that Bern was why she blossomed.

"When he found out," Stan continued, "he was devastated knowing that you two would lose each other. He assigned Bern as your patient in hopes of you rediscovering each other and maybe falling in love again. But, Anna, you just weren't the same, and it didn't work out. It never clicked again like it had during those two years. I'm sorry, dear."

"Oh, Stan! It's going to be okay. I feel different now; I feel reborn. I can't go back to yesterday, because I was a different person then. I think I'm finally the real Anna again!" she said, as she looked at Bern and smiled.

"Stan, we think the project is why David was murdered. If we can figure the entire project out, I'm sure we can find his killers. The cops aren't looking for the right people, so we will look ourselves. What else can you tell us about the project?"

"Well, the project was part of a government experiment..."

"Government?!" Anna said, cocking her head.

"Oh yeah, the government owns the company. They used it to do testing without raising the alarm that it was actually them doing it. I thought you knew that much, especially because of your father's status at the top of the global neurological scientific community. You and me, we technically work for the government. David and your father also worked for the government."

"Wow, I had no idea..." Anna trailed off.

"Most people don't, but I thought you knew because of your father. Only the top scientists and executives of the company know—no one else. The government runs it as a completely self-sufficient business with almost no visible ties to the government," Stan explained further. Anna was still in disbelief.

"I would put money on the killer being someone who is looking for some kind of link connecting the project to the government. You know, a growing number of people out there are looking for these answers, believing that the government is hiding this kind of testing. I agree that we as a people should be allowed to know," Stan said. "I bet it was one of those crazy, extreme conspiracy theorists! There are rumors that some documents about a similar project at a different lab got leaked. If that's true, the media will hit on it within a few days...and it's going to explode." Stan was very serious and factual when he spoke.

"What the hell! This is all so crazy," Anna said, shocked at everything they had learned. "Well, I was thinking about quitting anyway, so that's good," she said, always trying to look at the bright side.

"Whoever they are, we are going to find them, Stan. Is there anything else you can tell us?"

"No, nothing else," Stan said, shaking his head.

"Thank you so much. We're going to get out of here. We have a lot of things to do." Anna looked over at Bern and smiled.

She gave Stan a big hug, and the couple left.

"I'll drive!" Anna said, grabbing Bern's keys, which were dangling from his hands.

"So now what?" Anna asked, as she slid behind the wheel of the sexy, midnight-black Porsche.

"Well, I guess I have to find a new doctor," Bern said with a laugh.

"Maybe you don't need one," Anna said, blowing Bern a kiss.

"Well, my nightmares *have* stopped since you've been

hanging around constantly..." Bern smiled. "I know a guy in California who's a genius computer hacker. He could definitely get us into that phone we found and, I was thinking, since you are actually a government employee, I wonder if your log-in can be used to get onto restricted government networks. Can you imagine?! We could find all the answers! If anyone can find out, it will be this guy. Trust me, he's brilliant!" Bern looked out the window.

"So, I'm thinking...road trip!" Bern turned and said enthusiastically.

"Yeeees!" Anna exclaimed, as she pictured driving across the country in the sexy black Porsche with her best friend and rediscovered lover by her side.

"We're here!" Anna said, pulling into a parking spot in front of a small downtown shop.

"This is why you drove?" Bern asked, with a laugh.

"Yep!"

They walked in and talked to the local artist, looking at different pieces of work. There was so much amazing art on the walls; Anna loved almost all of it. The artist had a unique style with exaggerated nonstop lines and beautiful shades.

"I like this one," Anna said.

"Are you sure?"

"Yeah, I'm sure."

The hum of the tattoo gun and the sting of the needles set the soundtrack for the thoughts of what lay ahead with her best friend and lover by her side, each thought, unique like a snowflake.

This was Anna's heaven. She had finally found it...in herself, and she was going to make sure that she never lost it again.

Anna got up and looked in the mirror. In the reflection she looked at the small, colorful koi fish that appeared to delicately lay on the inside of her wrist. Drops of blood speckled across the freshly punctured smooth, soft skin. It looked more amazing than she had ever imagined!

"I love it!" Bern said, kissing Anna.

"It's beautiful!" Anna said.

"I missed you and I didn't even know it." Bern said, looking at their reflection. He took Annas hand in his.

She smiled. "I missed you too. I feel complete now."

She turned, wrapped her arms around Bern and laid her head on his chest. She closed her eyes and listened to his heartbeat.

The two lovers held each other for what seemed like an eternity. Standing together in a tattoo shop, surrounded by amazing artwork.

Rediscovered love, a long road trip, and the search for David's killer...that is what lay ahead.

They both knew...this was the beginning of something big.

Keeping Minds

The End is the Beginning…

****

…a word from the author.

Thank you for taking the time to let me tell you this story. I hope you enjoyed experiencing it as much as I enjoyed writing it. Hopefully you experienced something unexpected that made you laugh, cry, gasp, sigh and think…among other things. I have tried not to force this story into a genre because I consider it to span many. It was intended to be a story about memories, life and the human experience of certain events and the way they unfold.

This story is followed by a second book titled **Failing Minds**, whose plot and timeline runs parallel to this one. The two stories intricately intertwine, most of the time unknowingly to the two books, mostly separate, cast of characters. The next book is very dark and gritty, with many surprises. It will allow you to see how certain events and decisions, that are made in life, can impact the lives of others without you ever knowing.

The third and final book in the series is **Losing Minds.** This story takes the worlds from the first two books and collides them together in an unimaginable story, with twists and turns that you will never see coming.

I hope you find this to be a unique reading experience that will make you completely rethink the all the stories in a bigger picture.

~Vinal Lang

Made in the USA
Columbia, SC
26 November 2022

71844933R00213